EBURY PRESS
AMBAPALI

Born in New Delhi, Tanushree Podder worked in the corporate sector for eight long years before she quit the rat race to write.

She is a well-known travel writer and novelist, and climate change and the environment are of special interest to her. She enjoys exploring various subjects, and this has led to her writing across genres, including historical, military, crime and the paranormal.

She wrote several non-fiction books before moving to fiction and has now published sixteen novels. Her books include *Nur Jahan's Daughter*, *Boots Belts Berets*, *On the Double*, *Escape from Harem*, *Solo in Singapore*, *A Closetful of Skeletons*, *Before You Breathe*, *No Margin for Error*, *The Teenage Diary of Rani Laxmibai*, *The Girls in Green*, *Spooky Stories* and *An Invitation to Die*. *Ambapali* is her seventeenth novel.

Her *Decoding the Feronia Files* is the first Indian cli-fi thriller.

Three of her books, *Boots Belts Berets*, *A Closetful of Skeletons* and *The Girls in Green*, are being adapted into web series.

She lives in Pune.

Ambapali

a novel

TANUSHREE PODDER

EBURY
PRESS

An imprint of Penguin Random House

EBURY PRESS

USA | Canada | UK | Ireland | Australia
New Zealand | India | South Africa | China

Ebury Press is part of the Penguin Random House group of companies
whose addresses can be found at global.penguinrandomhouse.com

Published by Penguin Random House India Pvt. Ltd
4th Floor, Capital Tower 1, MG Road,
Gurugram 122 002, Haryana, India

Penguin
Random House
India

First published in Ebury Press by Penguin Random House India 2023

ISBN 9780143459439

Typeset in Bembo Std by Manipal Technologies Limited, Manipal
Printed at Thomson Press India Ltd, New Delhi

www.penguin.co.in

MIX
Paper
FSC FSC® C010615

For my sisters, Jayashree, Sharbari and Sujata

'In the cookies of life,
sisters are the chocolate chips.'

—*Anonymous*

Author's Note

I've always been fascinated by Ambapali's story, and indeed, she is someone who has intrigued generations of Indians. Known as the most beautiful and talented woman in the entire Jambudweepa (Indian subcontinent), Ambapali was said to have been wealthier than most kings. Feted and courted by thousands of men, she renounced everything to become a Buddhist nun.

Ambapali lived at a time when the world was young. Civilization was in its early stages, but the Indian subcontinent prided itself on having a cultured society. There are no elaborate historical accounts of the era in which she lived. It was the period of bards and storytellers, and with the passage of time, verbal accounts have been altered or lost. Thus, the origins of the stunningly beautiful woman remain shrouded in mystery. According to legend, a royal gardener came upon a baby girl in a mango grove. Hence, she was named Ambapali or Amrapali. While her origins may not be known, she was certainly not a figment of some storyteller's imagination. Her life has found mention in many Jain and Buddhist scriptures, folktales, and Jataka tales—it was in a Jataka story that I first stumbled upon her. Indeed, everything we know about

Ambapali has been gleaned from the stories in Buddhist and
Jain scriptures.

Ambapali was born in Vaishali, which was the capital of
the Vajji confederacy. The confederacy comprised eight clans
that ruled over the region of Mithila in northern Bihar. Their
capital, Vaishali, lay north of the Ganga. The members of the
eight clans met every seven years to elect their chief and a
council of ministers, who would administer the republic. The
Vajji republic was the only democracy in the entire region.

According to Buddhist texts, Vaishali was inhabited by
7707 clan rulers, each of whom had large retinues, many
palaces and pleasure parks. It was a prosperous place. Trade
flourished, the granaries were full and the people happy.
The city was famous for all this and was also famous for the
courtesan, Ambapali.

The Ekapanna Jataka describes Vaishali as one of the sixteen
mahajanapadas—great kingdoms—and says it was secured
by three layers of high walls with the distance of a league
between them. According to the Pali canon, just outside the
town, leading uninterruptedly up to the Himalayas, was the
Mahavana, literally the great forest. Wide roads connected the
city with Rajagriha to the south, and Kapilavastu and Shravasti
to the north.

The city of Vaishali saw many eminent men and important
events. The twenty-fourth Jain Tirthankara, Lord Mahavira,
was born here in 599 BC, his mother being a Licchavi princess.
Vaishali was where Buddha gave his last sermon before his
death. It was also the cradle of democracy. Ruins of the
Abhishek Pushkarni, the coronation tank, and Raja Vishal
Ka Garh, the fort of King Vishal, believed to be the ancient
parliament house, can still be seen at Vaishali.

The Vajji capital was one of the most prosperous and cultured places of that era, and it was not surprising that the kings of neighbouring territories, mainly Bimbisara, the ruler of Magadh, wanted to subjugate it. Despite the many battles he fought, his wish to subjugate Vaishali remained unfulfilled, largely due to the unity of the confederacy. Ambapali's beauty and allure threatened to fragment that unity, and that is why she was crowned as the nagarvadhu.

The practice of electing a nagarvadhu was prevalent in some parts of ancient India. The king anointed the most beautiful and talented woman as the nagarvadhu. Essentially a courtesan, she could not marry. Instead, she had to entertain anyone who could pay her price.

Not every courtesan has gone down in the annals of history or attained the status Ambapali enjoyed. Even today, her name conjures up visions of dazzling glamour, daring romance and sacrifice. Not only was Ambapali beautiful, but she was also a highly intelligent woman. Immensely wealthy and powerful, she wielded substantial influence over the nobles in the Vajji republic. Crowned as the 'nagarvadhu janpad kalyani', Ambapali occupied a prime place in society. She is said to have had more power and wealth than the king of Vaishali. Little wonder that she was treated as one of the most precious assets of Vaishali. She interacted with princes on equal terms and was invited as a guest of honour to the important functions that took place in the city.

Generous to a fault, Ambapali became one of the most loved women of her time. She commissioned temples, homes for beggars and ran many charities for the poor. Several struggling musicians, artisans and artists flourished under her patronage. A connoisseur of art, she also commissioned many murals, sculptures and paintings.

The course of Ambapali's life changed when the king of Magadh, Bimbisara, disguised as a merchant, visited the city to meet the famous beauty. The king fell in love with Ambapali and spent a week with her. Their union resulted in the birth of a son.

Theirs was an ill-fated love story, though. Ambapali suffered many tragic events. The Magadh king was later imprisoned by his ambitious son and died in prison. The heartrending experiences had a profound effect on her. She realized the transient nature of love and material things and embraced a spiritual life.

Ambapali lived in the age of Buddha and Mahavira, when spirituality and hedonism coexisted without infringing upon each other. While Buddha embodied spirituality, she represented the hedonistic side of society. Yet, their paths met. Ambapali could have married a king and continued to live a luxurious life, but she chose to walk the path shown by Buddha.

On his last journey, as he passed through Vaishali, Buddha accepted Ambapali's invitation to dine at her home. He did so after turning down an invitation from the royal family. Old Pali texts and Buddhist scriptures mention that the Enlightened One stayed at Ambapali vana, where he preached the famous Ambapalika Sutta. Eventually, Ambapali was accepted into the Buddhist fold and became a Buddhist nun. She went on to write several verses that form a part of the Buddhist text, Therigatha (often translated as Verses of the Elder Nuns).

This is the story of an innocent and unambitious woman who was forced to become a courtesan because of the machinations of powerful men. The book was not an easy one to write; it was like diving into an ocean to search for rare pearls. Unlike medieval Indian history, there is a paucity of information about ancient India. Hampered by scant authentic material, I had to give wings to my imagination to fill in the gaps and embellish the story. A couple of characters do not a book make, so it was essential to conjure a string of supporting characters to flesh out the story. Likewise, I had to depend on various sources to envisage and recreate life as it was during those days. As I wrote this book, I was reminded of something Pulitzer prize-winner Geraldine Brooks said: 'The thing that most attracts me to historical fiction is taking the factual record as far as it is known, using that as scaffolding, and then letting imagination build the structure that fills in those things we can never find out for sure.' Despite the hurdles, I experienced a feeling of satisfaction as I typed the last sentence of the book.

Tanushree Podder

One

The bhikkhuni stroked the older nun's head reverently. Once a famed beauty, the nun now lay frail and ailing on a rough mat on the floor of a tiny cell. Across Jambudweepa, bards had once sung paeans of her beauty; kings and nobles had showered their wealth on this woman, who had spent the last few years begging for alms.

She, who had ruled over the hearts of many men, was now a mere skeleton, her skin brittle like dry leaves in autumn. The eyes that had been compared to glittering jewels were now clouded with cataracts. The lips, the sensual curves of which had made men swoon, were cracked. The supple body that had driven men crazy, was now a wasted and shrunken one.

Her name was Ambapali—the one found under a mango tree.

The vaid had proclaimed she would die within a few hours, but under the gentle massage of the bhikkhuni's hands, the old woman's heart continued to beat stubbornly. The wrinkles on that wizened face whispered many stories. Stories of broken hearts. Stories of the battles men had fought to win her favour. Stories of wealth that had overflowed in her coffers. Disenchantments and fulfilment. Dejection and ecstasy. Oh, there were a thousand stories that would last lifetimes. Some were known to all. Some known only to the woman who lay shivering on the thin mat, her mind wandering in a realm beyond the familiar.

For the past few months, unable to walk or beg, the old woman had taken to bed. She survived on the few morsels of food brought by the young bhikkhuni, who bathed her and looked after her.

As the bhikkhuni kept vigil, those dry lips parted. Understanding that she was thirsty, the bhikkhuni poured a few drops of water into the mouth. It curved into a radiant smile. And then the woman began to sing in a low voice. Tones dulcet and divine.

> *Black as night, like the down of the honeybee,*
> *Curled and flowing was my raven hair—black silk.*
> *Now, with age, it resembles strands of hemp.*
> *What the Buddha has said is true—I have no doubt.*

She stopped singing. Her chest heaved. Then, with great effort, she started on the next verse.

> *Once fragrant as a basketful of blossoms,*
> *Belonging to the gods, my cherished tresses.*
> *Now, with age, they smell like animal fur.*
> *What the Buddha has said is true—I have no doubt.*

The feeble body shook with a racking cough. Drained of strength, she collapsed like a broken doll. The bhikkhuni poured a few more drops of honeyed water into her mouth and the woman gazed at her gratefully. With a trembling finger, she pointed at the young woman, who spoke up, eager to help.

'You want me to bring you something?'

'Do you know the rest of the verses?' wheezed the old nun.

'Yes, I have heard you singing them many times, grandma. They are beautiful.'

'Will you sing them for me?'

The bhikkhuni felt a surge of compassion for the undemanding woman.

In a ringing voice, she sang:

Like a well-planted grove in the forest, thick
And gleaming was my hair, adorned with combs and pins.
But now, with age, my locks are sparse and thin.
What the Buddha has said is true—I have no doubt.
My hair was a glorious shining mantle,
Braided and adorned with golden ornaments.
But now, with age, I am completely bald.
What the Buddha has said is true—I have no doubt.
Like two crescents finely drawn by an artist
My brows were exquisite, alive with youth.
Now, with age, they only wrinkle and descend.
What the Buddha has said is true—I have no doubt.
And my eyes, like royal jewels, they shone
Sparkling and resplendent, long and wide and black.
Now, with age, they fade and dim; they shine no more.
What the Buddha has said is true—I have no doubt.

The young bhikkhuni paused, trying to recall the next verse.

'When I was young . . .' prompted the old woman. ' . . . my nose . . .'

Nodding her head, the companion continued.

When I was young, my nose was delicate, yet firm—
A gentle peak, rising from the softness of my cheeks.
Now, with age, my nose is a shrivelled shape.
What the Buddha has said is true—I have no doubt.
My earlobes were a thing of beauty, like bracelets
Fashioned and finished by a master craftsman.
But now, with age, they hang and droop.
What the Buddha has said is true—I have no doubt.
In the past, my teeth dazzled with their whiteness
Shining like the colour of the plantain bud.
Now, with age, they are chipped and broken and black.
What the Buddha has said is true—I have no doubt.
Once I warbled sweetly, like the cuckoo that lives
In the jungle thicket, in a grove of trees.
Now, with age, my voice is weak and faltering.
What the Buddha has said is true—I have no doubt.
I remember: my throat was like a conch shell,
Well-polished by the sea, delicate and graceful.
Now, with age, my neck is bowed and bent.
What the Buddha has said is true—I have no doubt.
Formerly, both my arms were round like crossbars,
Strong and beautiful. Now, with age, they are weak
As the limbs of the trumpet-flower tree.
What the Buddha has said is true—I have no doubt.
Adorned with golden rings, smooth and soft, these hands
Of mine were fair to look upon when I was young.
Now, with age, they are like the root-vendor's roots.
What the Buddha has said is true—I have no doubt.
Once my breasts were round and full,

They rose up into the air, side by side.
Now, with age, they sag like empty water bags.
What the Buddha has said is true—I have no doubt.
Oh, the beauty of my body, in the past—
Like a sheet of gold, polished to perfection.
Now, with age, fine wrinkles cover it.
What the Buddha has said is true—I have no doubt.
Like the elephant's curving trunk, firm and smooth
Were my two thighs. That was in my youth, I know.
Now, with age, they resemble shafts of bamboo.
What the Buddha has said is true—I have no doubt.

'Smooth and soft, adorned . . .' prompted the old nun when the companion hesitated. Smiling affectionately, the younger woman resumed singing.

Smooth and soft, adorned with golden anklets
Once my calves were firm and full. Now, with age
They are like the twigs of the sesame plant.
What the Buddha has said is true—I have no doubt.
Once my feet were elegant, like sandals filled
And stitched with cotton from the silk-cotton tree.
Now, with age, they are cracked and wrinkled.
What the Buddha has said is true—I have no doubt.
Such was this complex form, I called it mine.
Withered now and old, the abode of aches and pains,
It is the house of age. See the plaster fall.
What the Buddha has said is true—I have no doubt.

Ambapali silently mouthed the lyrics as the bhikkhuni sang. Her mind no longer wandered. She knew each word by heart.

And when the song ended, and the bhikkhuni left, she lay back with a smile. They say that one's entire life runs through the mind when death beckons. Now, a montage of images flashed before her eyes, vivid and intense. Pausing, mulling or skipping over what she wished to forget, she watched her mind rearrange a lifetime's worth of memories. Oh, there were so many memories. Priceless. Indelible. So much love. So much adulation.

She felt no regrets, no attachments. Just compassion and gratitude for those who had transited through her life, enriching it with their presence. It didn't matter if they had wronged her. It didn't matter if they had harmed her. She was grateful for each one of them.

Ambapali felt the moment her spirit broke free of her body, floating beyond it, as if into a dark tunnel. Light as a feather, she moved, hurrying towards the glow at the end of the tunnel. There lay bliss. Unafraid and expectant, she continued to drift.

Two

The melodious chiming of hundreds of temple bells across the city announced the dawn. Vaishali stirred awake. It was the day before the Spring Festival, the much-awaited annual event that was celebrated with pomp and gaiety. Feverish activity overtook the city for many days before the week-long festival of entertainment and pleasure. Set on the banks of River Ganga, the capital of the Vajji republic was pulsating with excitement for the forthcoming festivities, dressed up to welcome spring.

The first rays of the sun kissed the myriad golden spires looming over the skyline—all 7707 of them. Symbols of the affluence of the clan rulers, they reflected the importance of the confederacy of Vaishali.

Flowers bloomed in 7707 gardens across the city, athwart splendorous structures, their fragrance permeating the air. The streets filled with morning ragas as people stepped out of their homes. Musicians who had heralded the dawn with their mellifluous renditions ended their practice with invocations to god and good fortune. Maidens, freshly bathed, giggling, picked flowers to weave garlands for the deity and to adorn themselves. Young men swaggered towards the bathing ghats and kitchens buzzed with activity.

The Licchavis were proud of their capital and justifiably so. Among all the neighbouring states, theirs was the only confederacy; the others were ruled by monarchs. The opulent palaces of the 7707 rajas dotted the beautiful city. The rulers of the Vajji confederacy met every seven years to vote for one of their members as the maharaja, to function as the chief of the confederation, assisted by one *uparaja*, a deputy king, and a parishad of nine. The rulers were just, and the people cultured. There was prosperity, unity and peace in the land.

All roads led to Vaishali on that day, as people from all over the kingdom headed there. Tents sprung up by the wayside as bullock carts trundled along the roads fringed with fluttering flags and ribbons hanging off poles. Vasant Utsav, the celebration of a bountiful harvest, was a time for thanksgiving, an occasion to indulge one's hedonistic side in good food and wine. It was a day to proclaim good fortune without guilt. It was a celebration of the end of winter—of love, life and renewal. Colours were smeared on faces. People sang, danced and congratulated each other, gossiping and bantering.

Garlands of flowers festooned the doors of freshly painted houses.

A carnival was set up in the huge open ground near the city centre. The grand amphitheatre near the royal garden on the banks of the Gandak hosted the crowds who had gathered to enjoy gymnastics and various kinds of competitions: chariot races, bull racing, swimming and boating events. There were wrestling, archery and javelin-throwing competitions for sports enthusiasts. For the artistically inclined, there were poetry competitions, and dance and music recitals.

Fortunes were made and lost at these events, as spectators flouted the law to bet clandestinely.

For weeks before, young men could be found on playgrounds, training for the games, and the river was dotted with swimmers and rowers. Dance and music rehearsals would go on at the Kala Kendra. The prizes were big, and the prestige earned by the winners was even bigger.

The grand finale was held on the last evening when the raj nartaki performed before a gathering of the rajas and the common citizens. It was the one day when aristocrats and plebeians rubbed shoulders to watch the court dancer's performance. Even more exciting than her performance was the competition that followed—it was when the next court dancer was chosen; either the incumbent raj nartaki would dance better than the other competitors and hold on to her position, or be replaced.

The position of court dancer was a coveted one: the rewards and the monthly allowance were generous, but little compared to the privileges that came with the position—a luxurious mansion, a retinue of guards and servants, a chariot drawn by white horses. Not just that, she would mingle with royalty and nobility at all the major events, where her presence would be avidly sought. The richest and most influential men vied for the raj nartaki's attention. To cap it all, several privileges continued to come her way even after her retirement.

No matter what they did during the day, evenings drew people towards the amphitheatre. For two days, drum-bearers had gone around town announcing the date and time of the events in the amphitheatre. Excitement travelled far and wide, through the city and beyond, leaving none untouched.

It was impossible for the two people living in a small house on the fringe of the king's orchards to escape the excitement overtaking the city. Dharma Datta was employed as a royal gardener and lived with his daughter, Ambapali.

Now, sixteen-year-old Ambapali, dressed in her finest clothes, was goading her father to hurry.

'You are taking too long to dress!' she scolded. 'My friends will be here soon. We want to spend some time in the market before going to the rangshala. The amphitheatre must be so crowded already. I am so keen to see Nishigandha's performance.'

'You forget I am not as young as you,' the indulgent father said, laughing. 'In any case, I think you dance much better than Nishigandha. You can easily win the contest.'

Ten years of training under a retired court dancer had honed young Ambapali's innate talents. Imbued with grace and beauty, she was her teacher's favourite student.

'I have no interest in participating in the competition. All I want to do is to watch the contestants pit their skill against the court dancer,' Ambapali said, straightening her father's uttariya. 'You should wear brighter colours. These dull ones make you look older than you are. I wish you paid a little more attention to your clothes.'

'I will leave the brighter colours for you.' Dharma Datta pinched her cheek affectionately. 'Imagine what will happen if the women are attracted and want to flirt with me,' he teased.

'Pali, where are you?' they heard Priyamvada call out.

Ambapali peeped out of the window and saw Priyamvada and Urmimala waiting impatiently near the gate. Her heart leapt with excitement at the sight of the young man who was loitering in the background. Her friends were here. In keeping with the mood of the season, they had worn yellow. The two girls were wearing yellow uttariya, while Satyakirti had put on a yellow turban over his jet-black curls.

'Coming!' she called back. Turning to her father, she said, 'Don't take too long.'

'I will be with you in a couple of minutes,' Dharma Datta reassured his daughter as he fussed with his headgear, and Ambapali skipped out of the house, patting her hair.

'There you are,' said Satyakirti, drawing his breath sharply at the sight of the girl he loved. She looked beautiful.

The four of them had grown up together, playing pranks, ribbing and comforting each other. The orchard was their playground, where they escaped during the summer months to steal fruits, play hide-and-seek and share secrets. The trees were a witness to their sorrows and joys. It was under a mango tree that Satyakirti had confessed his love for Ambapali and stolen his first kiss from the blushing girl.

'I thought we would grow old before Her Majesty obliged us with her presence,' Satyakirti teased. His eyes rested on the radiant face of his beloved Ambapali, who looked ethereal in a red antariya and an embroidered muslin uttariya draped over a yellow kanchuki. Her tiny waist was girdled with an engraved silver belt. She wore no jewels. She needed none. Her eyes were brighter than sparkling diamonds, her lips redder than rubies.

Ambapali stole a look at the young man standing before her. The white uttariya failed to hide his broad shoulders. He was not a handsome man, but an immensely lovable one. She loved his lopsided smile and the way his dark brown eyes twinkled with humour. Those eyes were now gazing at her with hunger.

The spell was broken by his giggling companions, who prodded each other and whispered conspiratorially.

'Let's hurry,' said a flustered Satyakirti.

Dharma Datta emerged from the house, and the five of them headed to the carnival.

The young friends walked excitedly through the stalls set up, especially for the festival: there was jewellery, clothes, perfumes, toys, knives, spears and the most interesting curios they had ever laid eyes upon. The tantalizing aroma of freshly made sweets and other foods drew people to the stalls that lined the periphery of the grounds. Of all these, it was the wine stalls that attracted most revellers, kept supplied with different kinds of suras such as the madhvi, brewed from honey, which was costlier than the medaka, brewed from rice. Then there was the prasanna, brewed from flour, the asava from sugar and the maireya from molasses. The sura makers tried to invent their own versions by blending them with various kinds of salts, fruits, vegetables and condiments to create bitter, hot and sour tastes.

Musicians, clowns, snake charmers, archers, magicians and dancers had set up makeshift stages, and spectators thronged in front of them.

Dharma Datta stopped to chat with a friend at one stall. 'Why don't you go ahead while I catch up with Rudra?' he said to them. Turning to Satyakirti, he said, 'I am relying on you to see the girls home.'

'Don't worry, sir, I will get them home safely,' promised the young man.

'I want to look at some trinkets,' said Priyamvada.

'What's the use of looking at jewellery when we can't afford to buy anything,' Urmimala said, laughing. Pointing at the bolts of cloth piled up at a stall, she said, 'Let's go to that shop. I have saved money to buy some muslin.'

'I would rather spend money on the sweets,' declared Satyakirti, patting his pouch. He knew the exact number of karshapanas in it.

None of them had much money. Priyamvada was an orphan being brought up by her uncle's family and Urmimala's father was a soldier in the army.

Satyakirti's father, Vivaswat, was the village vaid. He could have made more money, but the kind-hearted man often forgot to charge his patients. As a result, he barely made a living. Despite the vaid's efforts, Satyakirti had no interest in learning about herbs and medicines. Instead, he made a living crafting and selling musical instruments. His tiny shop attracted customers because Satyakirti made the finest flutes in town, but he spent more time playing the veena than selling instruments, and that didn't benefit his business.

'Why don't we have apupa? I am feeling rich, so I will pay for everyone.' Satyakirti stopped at the confectionary shop. His love for the fried sweet confection was no secret to his friends.

'No! I don't want apupa.' Urmimala pouted. 'I would rather buy muslin.'

'I am not too fond of apupa either,' said Priyamvada. 'Enjoy the sweets while I accompany Urmi to the muslin shop.' The two girls walked away.

'What about you, Ambe?' Satyakirti turned and looked beseechingly at Ambapali. 'Won't you keep me company?'

Satyakirti was the only one who called her Ambe, and she loved it. 'I don't want anything, really,' she said. 'And I don't want to be late for the dance competition. Let's go get Urmi and Priya.'

They found the two girls in the muslin shop. Urmimala turned to them when they approached. 'I can't decide between the red and yellow. Which one do you think looks better?' she asked, draping the two pieces across her shoulders.

'I think yellow looks better on you,' said Satyakirti.

'What is your opinion, Pali?'

'I think both are nice.'

'You are trying to play safe. I will have to decide for myself.' Urmimala ignored their suggestions and settled for the red muslin.

'What an indecisive girl!' grumbled Priyamvada, as they joined the crowd hurrying towards the amphitheatre. 'You spent so much time deciding between the yellow and red. I couldn't look at the trinkets because of you.'

'We could return tomorrow,' Urmimala pacified her. 'I would like to go to the trinket stall too.'

'Silly girl! The Vasant Utsav ends tonight. The stalls won't be here tomorrow,' Satyakirti chuckled.

The long walk took them to the flower-festooned amphitheatre, lit up with hundreds of lamps. Although they had been attending the festival every year, the stunning structure never failed to impress them.

They lingered for a few moments near the brightly lit entrance, marveling at the beauty of the intricately crafted marble pillars.

Right in the centre of the theatre stood a huge marble platform, with a few rows of seats on either side of the stage earmarked for the artistes. Built to deliver almost perfect acoustics, the amphitheatre was divided into several tiers with aisles running in between. The front rows of marble seats, cushioned and covered in silk, were exclusive to the members of the confederacy. Behind them were the seats reserved for the rich merchants and setthis, who were the pillars of the economy. In the farthest part were the seats meant for commoners.

The four friends stood near the entrance, their eyes scanning the amphitheatre. 'Just as I feared. We're too late to find seats.' Ambapali sighed.

'We could stand right at the back,' suggested Urmimala. It was obvious she was not very interested in the competition. 'Or we could go back to the stalls and then head home.'

'I have been looking forward to the dance competition the entire year,' snapped Ambapali. 'You can leave, but I intend to watch the entire programme.'

'I will stay here with you, Ambe,' Satyakirti declared loyally.

'I don't mind sitting in the aisle.'

'You can't sit in the aisle, Pali. The ushers won't let you,' reasoned Priyamvada. 'I can see two seats right there at the back. You and Satya take those seats. Urmi and I will find seats somewhere else. Once the show is over, we can meet at the last pillar to the left of the amphitheatre and go home together.'

'We should remain together, Priya,' Satyakirti said. 'It's easy to get lost in the crowd. Let's sit in the aisle till someone tells us to go.'

'Good idea!' said Ambapali.

They were making their way to the aisle at the back when an usher approached them. 'Which one of you is Ambapali?' he asked.

'Why are you looking for her?' Urmimala raised her eyebrow.

'Devi Suvarnasena has asked me to lead you to her.'

The four friends followed him towards the rows where the retired raj nartaki sat. Besides, the current court dancer, Nishigandha, had been one of Suvarnasena's students, and it was customary for the pupil to invite the guru.

The lady's face brightened on seeing her favourite student. 'Why were you loitering at the back?' she asked.

'We were looking for a place to sit, devi,' Ambapali said as she bent to touch her teacher's feet.

'It's lucky that I spotted you. Sit down here. The competition is about to begin.'

'Devi, can we accommodate my friends?' Ambapali said, pointing at the vacant seats near the lady.

'Well . . . these seats are meant for my friends.' Suvarnasena hesitated. 'But since they haven't arrived, yes, you may ask your friends to sit here.' Pointing to the seat next to her, she said, 'You sit near me. I want to point out the mistakes made by the dancers so you can improve.'

They had barely settled when an usher announced the arrival of Maharaja Chetak and his entourage. Once they were seated, two huge brass gongs on either side of the stage sounded, announcing the start of the competition.

'She is so beautiful,' whispered Ambapali, as Nishigandha walked on to the stage.

'You are more beautiful, Pali,' Priyamvada whispered back loyally. 'If I were to dress you—'

Ambapali's shocked gasp interrupted her words. Nishigandha had not sought Suvarnasena's blessings before the recital. Tradition required the raj nartaki to do so. Gurus were held in great esteem. No one, not even royalty, dared to dishonour them. Ambapali couldn't believe that the dancer had flouted convention at such an event, attended by thousands of people. It caught everyone's attention. She stole a look at Suvarnasena and noticed the tightening of her facial muscles. *Pride has ruined the greatest of artistes*, she muttered.

After an invocation to Goddess Saraswati, Nishigandha began. Nimble-footed and graceful, she was proficient in all forms of classical dance. Her expressions and mudras were perfect, and she had mastered the different talas. How could anyone surpass her?

'The contestants are wasting their time. She is unbeatable,' said Ambapali.

'No, she is not,' retorted Suvarnasena. 'You are a far better dancer. It's only in confidence and ambition that she scores over you.'

The raj nartaki executed a complicated series of moves, each one more difficult than the other. The recital ended with the most complex Anand Nritya, the joyous dance of eternity. It was a stunning performance that left everyone spellbound. There was a moment's silence, and then a thunderous ovation sounded across the amphitheatre, as she folded her palms in gratitude. Mesmerized, Ambapali stared at the woman who could create magic with her moves.

She had thrown the gauntlet. The competitors had to outperform her to claim the raj nartaki's crown.

One by one, the contestants took up the challenge. Some were good. Some floundered. Some were brimming with confidence, while some appeared defeated even before they had begun.

It was several hours before the competition ended. It was time for the winner to be announced. The judges conferred and spectators debated. At last, the raj guru went on the stage to declare the winner.

'It is with delight that I announce that none of the contestants could meet the high standard set by our raj nartaki. Devi Nishigandha has proved that she is the best dancer in the kingdom, and so—'

'Pardon me, Arya,' Suvarnasena interrupted him. She stood up and, folding her palms, faced the king. The audience may have forgotten Nishigandha's disrespect, but her guru had not. 'My humble apologies to the maharaja and the judges. I beg to differ. I know of a better dancer.'

A ripple of murmurs followed her declaration. 'Who is the dancer? Why hasn't she come forward?' shouted some spectators. 'We want to watch her performance,' they demanded.

'Devi Suvarnasena,' said the king, aware that the dance teacher wanted to avenge her humiliation, 'why hasn't the dancer put forth her name for the competition?'

'Maharaja, the dancer is reluctant to compete,' she said.

A sudden realization hit Satyakirti, and he turned to look at Ambapali. Priyamvada and Urmimala were already staring at the dumbfounded girl.

'Who is this talented dancer? You have claimed her to be a better dancer, so she must perform, failing which you will render a public apology for interrupting the proceedings.' The king's stern voice reached Ambapali's ears, and she shrank in her seat.

Suvarnasena bowed her head. 'I will request her to go up to the stage.' Turning to Ambapali, she said, 'Pali, it is time to prove your talent. I want you to dance as you have never danced before. That is the dakshina, the fees, I demand as your teacher.'

'I can't, devi,' Ambapali said as she shook her head nervously. 'I can't compete with Nishigandha.'

'I will be humiliated publicly if you don't dance.'

'I . . .'

'You have a duty towards your teacher, Pali,' reminded Urmimala.

'Don't be nervous, Pali,' urged Priyamvada. 'You are a better dancer than her.'

Only Satyakirti remained silent.

Seated at the back of the amphitheatre with his friends, Dharma Datta looked anxiously at his daughter.

The crowd was getting restive. It had been a lengthy day for most of them, and the competition had gone on for a long time. They wanted to go home.

The king tapped his fingers irritably.

'What have you decided, devi?' the chief minister asked.

'Pali,' Suvarnasena ordered, her voice quivering with emotion, 'I want you to redeem my honour by defeating Nishigandha.'

I can't let down my teacher, Ambapali thought. She owed her so much.

The process of grieving for her mother had been long and emotionally draining. It was Suvarnasena who had held her hand, wiped her tears, counselled her about the myriad little things a mother would normally handle. She had taken the role of her mother and guided her through the tough years. This was her chance to show her gratitude. She couldn't let her teacher down. Ambapali stood up and faced the audience. She bowed to the king and touched Suvarnasena's feet to seek her blessings.

'My friend, Satyakirti, will play the veena,' she said. Aghast, Satya stared at her.

'I can't do this without you,' she appealed. His presence on the stage would boost her confidence. 'Please, Satya.'

After a brief moment of hesitation, he followed her to the stage, where one of the musicians handed him a veena.

Three

Ambapali muttered a silent prayer. This was her first public performance, and the stakes felt sky-high. Not in her wildest dreams had she imagined dancing before such a grand audience. Her pulse raced and beads of perspiration dotted her forehead. She felt her mouth go dry. Distressed, she looked at Satyakirti for comfort. He nodded imperceptibly. It was as if a silent message had passed between them, and the air crackled with chemistry. She smiled and squared her shoulders.

All eyes were on the girl on the stage. Unlike the other contestants, she was plainly dressed. Her eyes sparkled like twin stars on a dark night. Raven hair framed a pale face with high, delicate cheekbones and a perfectly shaped nose. Her bow-shaped lips were like a pair of trembling rosebuds. She had a regal bearing, but her slender figure and tiny waist gave her an air of vulnerability. The audience felt an instinctive sympathy for her. She had the innocence and the sensuousness of a woman on the cusp of adulthood. They had not seen a woman as beautiful. She seemed the very incarnation of the celestial dancer Menaka.

Satyakirti closed his eyes and began playing the veena. The percussionists struck up a rhythm. The melodious notes animated her frozen limbs. She folded her hands and bowed towards the king, her guru, and the audience.

Ambapali began dancing. Her feet followed the dictates of the veena and the mridanga. She pirouetted and swayed. She twirled and floated. She lost herself in Satyakirti's music. The instructions of her teacher rang in her brain: *Dance is a seamless amalgamation of taal, nritya and natya. Use your eyes, face, feet and hands to breathe life into your movements. Let them take you to another realm and unleash your soul.* Suvarnasena's heart swelled with pride as she watched her pupil execute the most complex moves with ease. As Dharma Datta watched his daughter, inexplicably, a fist of fear squeezed his heart. For some reason, he felt the consequences of her victory would be tragic. No parent in the world would want his child to fail, but he prayed for her failure.

Nishigandha had performed the Anand Nritya, the cosmic dance of a joyous Shiva. Ambapali chose to reply with the Lasya, which was the dance of femininity that portrayed grace, beauty and happiness—the dance of Goddess Parvati. Ambapali's movements were soft, fluid, merging in a graceful blur with nary a sharp edge. Captivated, the audience watched the girl, who appeared as ethereal as the Goddess herself.

When the dance ended, the spectators remained in an entranced silence for a few moments. Then there was tumultuous applause. The audience had decided in Ambapali's favour, but it was for the judges to decide the winner. The audience's hoots and shouts could be heard as the judges conferred.

It was a unanimous decision. Ambapali was the winner.

'Devi Ambapali has surpassed our expectations by winning the contest. She deserves the crown of raj nartaki!'

Stunned by the dizzying blur of actions that unfolded following the announcement, Ambapali's eyes searched for Satyakirti. She felt overwhelmed by the sudden attention on her. Weighed down with the garlands and the crowds, she sought the reassuring warmth of friends, but they were nowhere to be seen.

Suvarnasena pushed the bashful girl towards Maharaja Chetak and said, 'She is my student, Maharaj.'

'Your student deserves the crown, devi,' said he. The kindly king was a man of few words. His face creased in a gentle smile. 'I am glad you brought her to our notice.'

'She is the royal gardener's daughter,' the raj guru informed him.

'Ah! The child who was found in the royal orchard?' asked the king.

'Yes, Maharaj. She is Dharma Datta's daughter.'

'Where is your father? Didn't he come with you?' The king turned to the girl.

'Baa . . . baba . . .' Ambapali stammered, her eyes searching the crowd.

'It's all right,' the king hastened to comfort the nervous girl. 'Tell him to present himself at the court tomorrow.'

She nodded mutely and the king smiled before walking away.

The world seemed to spin around her, and she felt faint. Ambapali clung to her teacher's hand and mumbled, 'Devi, I want to go home.'

'Don't worry, my child. I will take you,' said a beaming Suvarnasena. Ambapali had redeemed her honour. The child had taught a lesson to the ungrateful and arrogant Nishigandha. The jubilant woman led her protégé towards her chariot.

'But my friends . . . Satyakirti . . .'

'They'll find their way home. You are now the raj nartaki. Forget about your past and get used to a new life, Pali. Satyakirti is a part of your past.'

Stung by her teacher's words, Ambapali interjected, 'No, devi! He's my present and future.'

Wisely, Suvarnasena decided to remain silent. It was something she could handle later.

It felt like the longest journey of Ambapali's life, as the intricately crafted chariot wound its way through the throng of people leaving the amphitheatre and emerged on the road that led to Ambapali's home.

'It's been an exciting evening for you,' said Suvarnasena, as they alighted from the chariot. 'Soon it will be morning. Try to sleep for a while. Tomorrow will be a hectic day.'

'Thank you, devi,' said Ambapali, folding her hands together.

'Don't worry, Pali. I am here to guide you.'

The house was quiet. Her father was nowhere to be found. Where was he? She had been held up by all the ceremony, but he should have returned a long time back. Anxiety flooded Ambapali's mind. She wanted to speak to him. She needed his reassuring presence. Her world had been turned upside down. She felt cold, lonely and abandoned.

All she knew was that she didn't want to be a raj nartaki. What would she do now? A host of thoughts sped through her mind, refusing to slow down. Her breath was laboured, and the room began spinning.

Disquiet clutching at her heart, she sat near the door, waiting for her father to return.

It was an intoxicated Dharma Datta who entered the house as it dawned. Shaken after the evening's events, he had gone to a tavern and drunk himself to oblivion. And then, shame kept him from returning home. He didn't want to face his daughter.

He found Ambapali dozing by the door. Her tear-stained face told him that the girl had cried herself to sleep. All intoxication evaporated in an instant, as he was seized with guilt.

Poor child! Bleary-eyed, Dharma Datta gazed upon her for a minute. And then he crouched near her. He stroked his daughter's hair, just as he had done since he had found her under the mango tree. 'I can't bear to let you go,' he mumbled.

She woke up and rubbed her swollen eyes. 'Where were you, Baba? I was so frightened!' Her slender body racked by sobs, she clung to him. 'I don't want to be a raj nartaki!' she cried.

All she had wanted was to get married to Satya and raise many children together. A small house filled with love, laughter and music. Those were the essential threads of her happy dreams. Wealth, glory and status had no place in them.

'Nor do I.' Sadness filled his heart. 'I can't afford to lose you, my child. I have no one else in the world.'

'When was the last time you ate?' he asked, suddenly concerned. The pallor on her face troubled him.

'I am not hungry.'

'But I am hungry.' He smiled. 'You know I don't eat without you.'

'What are we going to do, Baba? Will the king be angry if we tell him I don't want to be the raj nartaki?'

'Let's not think about all that. A hungry stomach knows no sense.' He pulled her up and led her towards the kitchen. 'Let's eat first.'

'What are we going to do?' she repeated as soon as they had eaten their frugal meal.

'I will think of something,' said Dharma Datta, placatingly, though he had scant idea what he could do to handle the situation.

'The king wants to meet you today. He told me so,' said Ambapali.

'In that case, let me not keep him waiting.'

'Please tell him to reinstate Nishigandha. She can be the raj nartaki till the next Vasant Utsav competition.' Ambapali brightened at the idea. 'The king will surely agree to that.'

'Do you want me hanged?' joked Dharma Datta uneasily. 'It's not for us to tell the king what he should be doing.'

'In that case, take me with you. The king is a kind man. I will beg and plead for mercy.'

'No, my child, you will do nothing of the sort. Let me meet the maharaj and hear what he has to say.'

Dharma Datta left for the palace. He was at a loss as to what he could do to stop his daughter from becoming a part of palace property. All he knew was that he couldn't live without her.

Suvarnasena landed at their doorstep minutes after he had left the house. She had not slept a wink after returning from her scene of triumph at the amphitheatre. The lady had spent the hours planning and plotting the next course of action. Ever since her retirement, she had lived a quiet life. She'd had no idea that the wheels would turn in her favour when she started the dance school to eke out a living.

She missed the attention, the expensive gifts of fawning nobles and the luxurious life she once led. Her reign as a court dancer had lasted for three years until she was replaced by a younger girl. It was difficult for a raj nartaki to last for more than a couple of years in a court full of nobles who were constantly in search of nubile girls to entertain their jaded senses.

She was in her mid-thirties now, and the retired raj nartaki had not yet found a man she wanted to marry. Suvarnasena wasn't a hypocrite. She had no scruples in admitting her weakness for men and wine. Nor did she harbour any illusions about the longevity of her beauty. She knew she had to make contingency plans to live comfortably in retirement.

Not in her wildest dreams had Suvarnasena imagined that things would take such a thrilling turn. She had hoped to taste the fruits of success when Nishigandha had been chosen as the raj nartaki, but that woman had been ungrateful. The arrogant pupil had not bothered to acknowledge or reward her for the long years of training.

She had waited four full years to get even with the thankless wretch. Ironic that it was Nishigandha's disrespect that set in motion the string of fortunate events. Ambapali was everything Nishigandha was not. Obedient, gentle and unselfish, the girl was a total contrast to her former pupil.

The lady found Ambapali sitting dejectedly in a corner of the house.

'You don't look well, Pali.' Squatting near her student, she touched her forehead. The girl's body was burning with fever. 'You are ill,' she exclaimed.

'I am scared,' Ambapali said in a miserable voice. 'I don't want to go to the palace.'

'Hush!' said Suvarnasena, leading the girl to the bed. 'Stop worrying, my child,' she said soothingly, covering her with a thick blanket.

Fetching cold water, she dampened a cloth and sponged the girl's forehead to bring down her temperature. 'Where is your father?' she asked. 'We have to call the vaid.'

'I am cold,' mumbled Ambapali.

Suvarnasena hurried out and instructed her charioteer to fetch the vaid. He arrived quickly and examined Ambapali.

'She needs rest,' he declared. 'The girl seems to be in shock.'

Although the vaid had not attended the event, it hadn't taken long for him to be apprised of Ambapali's appointment as the raj nartaki. Satyakirti had returned home from the amphitheatre at dawn.

'We expected you to return in a cheerful mood,' remarked his mother. 'Why are you looking so gloomy, son? Didn't you enjoy yourself?'

'She has been snatched away from me,' he had replied emotionally. 'I have lost Ambapali.'

Aghast, the couple listened to the happenings of the previous night. They were fond of the girl and had been looking forward to welcoming her as their son's bride.

The sight of Ambapali in this state broke the kindly vaid's heart. The girl's fate had been decided by her guru and the king. There was not much he could do.

'She has to be presented at the court. When will she recover?' asked Suvarnasena, following the vaid out of the house.

'Ambapali is suffering from severe anxiety. She needs rest. I forbid her to go anywhere for at least a week,' the vaid said in a stern voice. 'The poor girl has suffered immense mental pressure, and that has brought on the fever. She needs her loved ones around.'

'But—'

'Devi, you asked for my opinion, and I have given it to you,' he said coldly. The vaid was a good judge of human nature. Suvarnasena's pushy behaviour didn't escape his notice. 'Let her rest till she recovers. Please ask someone to collect the medicines from my house.'

The servant was dispatched with the vaid, and Suvarnasena paced the room in great agitation. *Ambapali has to be restored to good health. I will ensure that she gets the best of nutrition and medicine so that she recovers soon. Pali has to be presented at the court as soon as possible.*

Soon, Ambapali had been given the medicines, and the charioteer had been sent to the market to fetch fresh fruits. But Dharma Datta was yet to return. *Where is he?* Suvarnasena was restless. She needed to go to the palace and inform the parishad about Ambapali's indisposition. *I can't leave until he gets back. The girl's meals have to be arranged.*

It was a long time before Dharma Datta returned. He was not surprised to find his daughter ill. Anxiety had always made her sick.

'I am grateful for all that you have done, devi,' Dharma Datta said as he folded his palms.

'That's all right,' Suvarnasena snapped impatiently. 'Are you aware that Ambapali is expected to present herself at court today?'

'I . . .'

'They must be informed about your daughter's indisposition.'

'But . . .'

'I don't think you are aware of the protocol, so I shall go to them and explain the situation.'

'You are very kind, devi,' the gardener said, his head bowed.

Suvarnasena nodded. 'I have made arrangements for a woman to take care of your cooking. The kitchen has been stocked with provisions. All you have to do is to ensure that your daughter recovers. I will visit her every morning to check her progress,' Suvarnasena said peremptorily, as she hurried to her chariot.

Dharma Datta entered the house slowly and sat by his daughter. He mulled over the audience he'd had with the king. On his way to the palace, he had gone over what he would say and the reasons he would present for his daughter's inability to become the raj nartaki. All those reasons flew out of his mind the moment he prostrated himself before the king.

'Your daughter is a very talented girl,' the king had said, smiling kindly at him. 'You are a lucky man.'

The gardener remained at the king's feet. *How could he tell the king of Ambapali's reluctance to be the raj nartaki?* he wondered.

'I will request the parishad to give you a monthly allowance. We will promote you to the post of head gardener, so you can take things easy,' the king said.

He had returned home from the palace without saying the things his daughter had wanted him to say, aware that he had failed her.

Seated by his daughter's bed, the unhappy man recalled the day he had found Ambapali. Despite the worry in his heart, a smile came to his face when he thought of that day. A day that had brought him so much joy.

Four

It had been the month of Asadha. Ominous clouds loomed in the sky and the sun had just gone down. A bolt of lightning streaked the charcoal sky, chased by a roll of thunder. Heaven's drumroll announced the revival of a monsoon that had seen a lull of a few days. A caterwauling wind carried a warning of heavy showers.

Dharma Datta glanced up at the clouds and shook his head. A downpour was imminent. He would have to get home before the rain began lashing the ground. After a late start to the season, the mango trees had delivered their bounty, and his harvest that day was plentiful.

The royal orchards were famous for the superior quality of mangoes yielded by their trees. Not merely for royal consumption, the mangoes also served as gifts to neighbouring rulers.

The royal garden was located right on the banks of the Gandak. There, Dharma Datta's family had served as gardeners for several generations. He was ten when he began working in the orchard with his father, learning all there was to know about plants. Upon his father's death, the laborious job fell on him, and he tended to the hundreds of trees under his charge.

At forty-four, he was an unambitious man. The one dark cloud marring his life was the absence of a child. He and his wife, Kanaklata, had a great love for each other but still felt an emptiness in their lives. The couple had visited every temple, vaid and astrologer in the city, but to no avail.

As the days went by, he had to accept that there would be no more sons to serve the royal orchard.

The sky grew darker still as he gathered his implements and packed up for the day. Then he paused. His ears had caught the sound of a shrill wail. He listened intently. It came again. The cry was primal. It was high-pitched and desperate, loud enough to drown the whistling of the wind. It seemed to be born of discomfort and hunger.

What was it? Was it an animal in pain?

No. He shook his head. *It sounded like a baby crying.*

He began to walk towards the source of the wails, the cries growing louder as he walked.

It was a baby; he was sure. But why would there be a baby in the orchard? Had the mother halted to steal a few mangoes from the trees? Wouldn't the woman have quietened the baby if she were stealing?

Soon, Dharma Datta was at the far end of the orchard. His eyes fell on a wicker basket lying under a mango tree. In the basket, wrapped in a piece of red velvet, a baby lay, bawling. *Strange! Where has this baby come from?* he wondered. An hour back, when he had passed through the area, it hadn't been there. He looked around. Perhaps the person who had placed the little one there was around. But not a soul could be seen anywhere.

Dharma Datta hesitated. This wasn't the time for thought. It would start raining any minute. It wasn't wise to linger.

No, he couldn't get involved in this. He turned to go, but the pitiful cries halted his steps. It would be inhuman to leave the baby behind. Besides the rain, there were deadly snakes and other wild animals that occupied the orchard by night.

He picked up the baby from the basket and held it close to his body. Soothed by human touch and his body heat, the baby stopped crying. It was a baby girl. He gazed down at her.

How could anyone be so heartless to abandon such a beautiful baby?

'We're going home,' he cooed.

The gardener's mind was in turmoil as he hurried home. For so long, he had craved a child who would fill his little home with laughter and sunshine. Had God finally granted his wish? An overwhelming feeling of warmth poured through him. He would not part with the baby. It was his baby now.

His wife was waiting anxiously by the door of their modest mud-plastered house.

She spotted him approaching with a bundle in his arms. The sheepish grin on his face alerted the woman.

'Whose baby are you carrying?' she demanded.

He beamed. 'Look at her, Kanak,' he said and handed the baby to her. 'She is so beautiful. Take her inside, quickly.'

Has he stolen the child? Kanaklata scanned his face suspiciously.

'She must be hungry,' her husband said. 'God knows when she had some milk. I will milk the cow and bring fresh milk for her.'

She looked down at the baby in her arms. It was swaddled in expensive material and had a thick gold chain around the neck. Clearly, she wasn't born to a humble peasant.

'I won't take her in until you tell me the details,' warned Kanaklata, her jaw set.

'I found her lying under a mango tree in the orchard.'

'I don't believe you. Tell me the truth. I know you have been longing for a child, but I won't bring up one that was stolen from her mother.'

'I haven't stolen the baby. Don't you trust your husband, woman?'

'Well . . .' Kanaklata looked searchingly at her husband. He stared unflinchingly into her eyes. The long years of marriage had taught her to recognize his expressions. She knew he was not lying.

Lightning flashed in the sky and rain began pelting the ground. 'Don't stand gaping,' Dharma Datta shouted. 'Do you want the baby to catch a chill? Go inside while I fetch milk for her.'

Kanaklata went into the house, but was torn. His explanation had not convinced her. And the longer she held the little body, the more likely she was to get attached. No. She couldn't let that happen. But as she lay her on the bed, the baby began to cry. Maternal instinct surged in her heart and she picked up the little one, holding her close to her heart. She paced the room, singing a lullaby.

Outside, the rain fell steadily. Dharma Datta returned with a pot of fresh milk, his clothes drenched.

'Here, feed her the milk,' he said, handing the vessel to his wife. 'Imagine what would have happened if I hadn't brought her home. The poor soul would not have survived the night.'

'You are right. She would not have survived.' Kanaklata shuddered at the thought of a wild beast attacking the baby. 'She is our child now. I will bring her up with all the love and care she deserves,' she said, as she spooned milk into the baby's eager mouth.

Happy that she had come around, the gardener smiled. 'We have to give her a name,' he said, watching tenderly as the tiny mouth sucked greedily on the spoon. 'What shall we call her?'

'How about Nayantara?'

'It's nice, but our child should have an uncommon name, as beautiful and unique as her.'

'Madhumalti?'

'No. Let's try to think of a better name.'

'What about Kumudini? It is a unique and beautiful name.'

Dharma Datta rolled the name on his tongue. A sudden thought struck him. 'Wouldn't it be wiser to consult the astrologer before naming her? He will prepare a horoscope and then suggest a suitable name for her.'

'You are right. Let's take her to the temple tomorrow.' A strange warmth filled her chest as Kanaklata glanced at the sleeping infant.

It was a long night for the couple, as the excitement of the event kept them up, grappling with a host of thoughts. Frequently, they checked on the baby to make sure she was comfortable.

The next morning, as the bright sun greeted them, the pair set out for the village shrine. After they had offered prayers for the baby's well-being, the couple requested the priest to bless the child.

'Where did you find the baby?' the priest wanted to know. He knew of their fervent prayers for a child.

'She's a gift from the heavens.' Dharma Datta's face was lit up with joy. He narrated how he had found the baby under a mango tree in the royal orchard.

'God has answered your prayers,' said the priest. 'It is now your responsibility to bring her up. Don't forget to inform the king about the child.'

Nodding, they left and headed to the old astrologer.

'How can I cast her horoscope without the date, time and place of birth?' said the old man.

'She came to us yesterday evening, so please consider that to be her date of birth,' Dharma Datta said with folded hands.

'It will give us peace of mind,' Kanaklata added.

The astrologer nodded. 'All right, but the horoscope won't be accurate.' He regarded the gurgling baby. 'She looks angelic,' he said, his face softening.

Dharma Datta and Kanaklata waited anxiously as the old astrologer worked on the child's chart.

'As per this kundali, she has raj yoga, a royal fortune. She will have a brilliant career and financial prosperity. Your daughter will have kings at her feet. Wealth, fame, name—the girl will have it all. But . . .' the old man paused.

'But?'

'But it will all come at a price. She will be snatched away from her loved ones and thrown to the wolves. Heartbreak will hound her at every step.'

'Will she be happy?' Kanaklata asked anxiously. She glanced at the baby sleeping in her lap.

'Happiness doesn't come with wealth or fame. It comes from finding love and security,' said the wise man. 'This child may find those elements elusive.'

Seeing the couple exchanging a worried glance, the astrologer hastened to set their mind at ease. 'These predictions are based on an inaccurate kundali, so they may very well be wrong. Just ignore the predictions and bring her up well. One thing I can foretell, even without looking into her horoscope, is that the child will bring sunshine and happiness in your lives.'

'We will heed all the good omens and ignore the bad ones,' promised Dharma Datta, reassured by the astrologer's words.

'We have not named her yet, Guruji,' said Kanaklata, stroking the baby's head tenderly. 'Please suggest a name for her.'

'Since you found her in the royal orchard, it's the king who should give her a name. I suggest you take her to Maharaj,' the astrologer advised.

Agreeing with his suggestion, the couple left the temple and went to the palace. It wasn't easy to meet the king, but the two of them waited patiently outside the sabhagrih. When the maharaja finally stepped out, Dharma Datta fell to his knees and placed the baby at the king's feet.

'What are you doing? Don't you know you must not place a baby at anyone's feet?' chided the king. He picked the baby up and handed her to the gardener. 'I am glad to see you have been blessed with a child,' he continued, anger ebbing at the sight of the baby's innocent face.

'She is not born to us, Maharaj,' the gardener said. 'I found her in the royal orchard.'

'You found her in the orchard?' The king raised his eyebrows in disbelief.

'Yes, Maharaj.' Dharma Datta recounted the events of the previous evening, his mind unsettled with the worry that the king would order them to find the parents and hand her back. 'I looked all around the orchard, but there was no one. Maharaj, we seek your consent to bring up the baby,' he pleaded.

'She is God's gift to you. No one can take that away,' said the king. 'From today, you will be her parents.' Removing a pearl necklace from his neck, he put it around the baby's tiny one.

'Thank you, Maharaj,' said the grateful gardener. His eyes brimming with tears of joy, he folded his hands in supplication. 'Please be kind enough to name our baby girl.'

The king seemed amused at the request. 'The baby was found under a mango tree, was she not?' he asked.

Dharma Datta nodded in affirmation.

'I think she should be called Ambapali.'

'That's a beautiful name, Maharaj.' The royal gardener bowed reverently and touched the king's feet. 'We will name her Ambapali.'

Dharma Datta continued to chant the name as the couple walked home.

'It is perfect,' Kanaklata whispered approvingly. 'We couldn't have found a better name.'

'Ambapali,' they chorused happily.

The couple returned in a joyous mood, cooing at the baby, who was now awake. The neighbours were surprised to see Kanaklata carrying a baby in her arms. When questioned, she smiled mysteriously and said, 'She is Ambapali, my daughter.'

It wasn't long before the story spread through the neighbourhood, and soon there was a rush of people to their house. They arrived with gifts for the little one, wanting to hear Dharma Datta's story about how he found the infant.

'She is God's gift to us!' claimed the couple.

Visitors blessed the baby, fussed over her and went away talking about the miracle that had come the childless couple's way.

The story was retold many times by the couple and travelled from villager to villager until it grew into a legend.

Five

Dharma Datta's reverie was broken by Ambapali's soft moaning. 'How are you feeling, my child?' he asked, staring anxiously at her flushed face.

She opened her eyes and smiled weakly before going back to sleep.

By evening, the potions sent by the vaid began working their effect, and Ambapali's fever subsided. Priyamvada and Urmimala were delighted to find her in a better condition when they visited.

Ambapali perked up at the sight of her friends. 'So, you finally found time to visit?' She pulled a face. 'I have been lying here waiting for some company.'

'I wonder what caused the sickness,' said Urmimala, picking up a guava from the pile of fruits near the patient's bedside and taking a big bite. 'It must have been exhaustion,' she diagnosed. 'You had been on your feet the entire day, and then there was the competition.'

'Don't be silly, dancing doesn't exhaust Pali. It was the emotional pressure that did it.' Priyamvada cut a guava, sprinkled salt on the pieces and extended the plate towards her friend. 'I want you to finish this.'

'I don't feel like eating anything.' Ambapali pushed away the plate. 'Where is Satya?' she asked.

'He will come later. Only after you finish the fruit.'

'The guavas are delicious,' Urmimala declared. 'So juicy and sweet. I am sure these have come from the royal orchard.'

'You're right. The king has sent the baskets of fruits,' said Suvarnasena, as she entered the room. She fussed around the sick girl for a couple of minutes and added, 'Your friend is an important person now.'

'Devi, we heard you had gone to the palace.' Priyamvada was curious about the dancer's life. 'Has it changed since your days as a raj nartaki?'

'A palace doesn't change. Only the kings do,' Suvarnasena retorted. Peeping into the kitchen, she asked, 'Where's the cook?'

'She's left,' replied Ambapali.

'Did she prepare the barley gruel?'

'Yes, Devi, she prepared everything as per your instructions.'

'Did you have the karambha?' Priyamvada asked her friend.

'Priya, please ask Satya to come,' Ambapali sidetracked the question. 'I need to talk to him about something important.'

'Satya is moping around the village,' Urmimala said in her usual tactless manner. She picked up another guava. Rubbing it on her dress, she took a bite and nodded appreciatively. 'I could eat the entire basket.' She took another bite before continuing. 'He isn't speaking to anyone.'

'Is he upset?'

'Urmi is exaggerating, as usual.' Priyamvada darted a warning look at the girl, whose attention was now on the bunch of grapes in the basket. Turning to Ambapali, she promised, 'I will make sure he comes.'

'Tell him—'

'Enough!' Suvarnasena shook a finger. 'No more talking. You must rest now.' She directed a stern look at the girls and said, 'I think it's time the two of you left her alone.'

'We . . .' Urmimala began, ready to protest the teacher's high-handed behaviour. The girls were taken aback by her rudeness.

'We are leaving, Devi.' Priyamvada prodded Urmimala.

'Wait!' Ambapali got up from the bed.

'Devi is right, Pali. You must rest. We will see you in the evening.' Priyamvada comforted her friend.

'Don't forget to send Satya,' begged Ambapali.

'I won't,' promised Priyamvada.

'You must not encourage your friends to linger,' commented Suvarnasena, as soon as the girls left. 'They expect you at the palace in a few days, and a busy time awaits you. We have to go shopping before that.'

The teacher's authoritative tone rankled the girl.

'Devi, I don't want to be the raj nartaki,' she declared, defiant.

Stunned, Suvarnasena exploded. 'Don't be stupid. You are not in a position to reject the parishad's decision.'

'I will beg the parishad to release me from the obligation. I will tell them the truth.'

'What, pray, is the truth?'

'That I had gone to the rangshala as a mere spectator and not as a contestant. I had no intention of participating in the competition. You asked me to redeem your honour, and I obeyed you. I have no obligations beyond that.' Ambapali's face took on an air of quiet determination.

'You can't say that,' said Suvarnasena.

'Why not? I am not a slave.'

'You don't understand, Pali. We are not in a position to dispute the king's decision. He is the ultimate authority.'

'I don't intend to dispute his decision. I just want to state the facts of the matter, and ask for his understanding.'

'I will not allow you to do anything stupid,' Suvarnasena thundered. She wouldn't allow this chit of a girl to foil her ambitions.

Ambapali was surprised at the sudden change in her dance teacher's behaviour. She resolved, in her mind, to discuss the matter with Satyakirti. He was the calm one. He was the right person to advise her. But where was he? Why hadn't he come to her?

'Devi, we are discussing my life,' she said stiffly. 'The discussion is exhausting me, and my head is aching.'

The dancer teacher continued, relentless, 'Don't you realize the consequences of your foolish act? They could imprison you. I don't think they will spare your father, either.'

'Why would the king imprison me or my father? We have done no wrong.'

'You are too innocent. I have seen much during my days at the court. A king can take offence at anything and punish anyone.'

'I thought the king was a just man.'

'Insolence and disobedience are good cause for punishment . . .' Suvarnasena began, but then realized it wouldn't do her any good to upset the girl. Softening her voice, she continued, 'Let us discuss this when I return in the evening. Now, stop fretting and get some rest. Don't forget to take the arishta for your fever and the fruits. You must remember, I am your ally, not an enemy.'

Ambapali tossed on the bed for a long time till sleep overtook her. It was evening when she awoke.

Throwing the covers aside, she walked to her veena and brushed away the thin layer of dust with a corner of her uttariya. The veena had been a gift from Satyakirti. She tuned the strings, closed her eyes and began playing. The mellifluous notes of Raag Kalyani filled the room. So lost was she in music that she didn't hear her friend entering the room.

Satyakirti quietly walked into the house, rapt as he heard the music. 'That was very good,' he said. 'You play so well now.'

'Praises won't exonerate you. Didn't you know I was ill?' Putting down the instrument she retorted, miffed.

'Yes Ambe, how could I not know when my father is the vaid?'

'So, what's your justification for not coming?'

'I was upset.' He lowered his head.

'Why were *you* upset? It is I who should be upset. My life has turned on its head, Satya. I can't sleep or relax. It's all so overwhelming and confusing. I want to get away from everything—especially Suvarnasena.'

'Things are no longer in our control, Ambe.'

'I feel stifled in the house. Will you take me to the lakeside?' she said.

The lakeside was one of their favourite places. The two of them had been stealing out to the lake since they were children. Feet immersed in the cool water, they had spent many an hour talking about their dreams, joys and sorrows.

Their other refuge was the mango orchard. Drawn by the sweet scent of the ripe fruit, they would climb the branches to pluck the juiciest ones. Ambapali remembered the scraped shins, the butterflies they had chased, the songs of the cuckoo, and she sighed at the memories.

'It wouldn't be right for you to go out. You are not well,' Satyakirti's voice interrupted her thoughts.

'Please Satya, Suvarnasena could be here any minute and I don't want to see her,' she said.

'You want to walk all that distance just because you don't want to see Suvarnasena?' Satyakirti said, smiling, though his eyes were sad. 'Since when have you started avoiding your teacher? I thought you revered her.'

'You don't understand. I don't know what her intentions are.'

'What has she done to make you feel this way?'

'I get the sense that, for some strange reason, she is trying to keep me away from my friends. Her behaviour towards Priya and Urmi was inexplicable. She literally ordered them to leave!' Ambapali tugged at his hand. 'She won't be happy to see you with me. Let's go before she gets here.'

Satyakirti shook his head. 'Be reasonable. You are unwell and the lake is far. Why don't we sit in the kitchen garden?' The kitchen garden, with its profusion of vegetables and herbs, was a pleasant place at the back of the house. It was Ambapali's hideaway where she often escaped to daydream or play the veena.

'What is it you want to discuss with me?' asked Satyakirti after he sat her down on a roughly hewn stone bench.

'The events that took place at rangshala.' She stared into the distance. 'I didn't want to take part in the competition, but Suvarnasena made it a matter of prestige and her honour.'

'Didn't you know you would win?'

'No! How could I? Nishigandha is the best dancer in the kingdom. I didn't think it was possible to defeat her.' She plucked off the petals from a flower, her fingers moving involuntarily.

'Well, you did. You are the raj nartaki now,' he said, his tone hollow.

'That's the problem. I don't want to be a court dancer. Baba is distraught and so am I.' She shredded the flower into tiny bits and picked up another one. 'But Suvarnasena has warned me that the king will be displeased if I suggest that Nishigandha remains as raj nartaki, and Baba and I will be punished for insolence. What should I do, Satya?' Ambapali sniffled.

'I have no answers, Ambe. My mind has been reeling with a dozen thoughts since that night.'

'I don't want to go to the palace,' she repeated. 'All I want is to be with you.'

'Do you think I don't want that? Unfortunately, our wishes don't matter anymore. We can't change the course of things.'

There was silence for a few moments.

'I have an idea,' Ambapali said suddenly. Her eyes brightened as she spoke. 'We could get married, Satya. No one wants a married raj nartaki. That could be our way out of the problem.'

Satyakirti had expected her to come up with that idea. For the past two days, he had lain in bed pondering over the possibilities, only to grapple with the realization that he was not ready for such a responsibility. Rushing into a marriage was likely to prove the undoing of their love for each other.

His heart ached at the outcome of his decision, but he felt strongly it was the right one.

'I can't marry you, Ambe. Not now. Not when I have no money. I want to give you all the things you deserve. I want to give you a beautiful house with a large garden, just like the one you dreamt about.' He lowered his head, refusing to meet her eyes.

'I don't want a beautiful house, Satya,' Ambapali said softly. 'All I want is you.'

'Marriage is not child's play. It comes with many duties. Neither of us is ready for them.'

'Don't you want to marry me, Satya?'

'Of course, I want to marry you. But . . . it has to wait till I can provide for a wife and family.' He clutched her hands and said, 'Guilt will swamp me if I deprive you of a good life. What about our children? Wouldn't you want to give them the best?'

'You don't understand.' She shook her head. 'Time is running out. I have to report at the court as soon as possible.'

The sun dipped toward the horizon. Ambapali shivered and wrapped her arms around herself. She had pinned many hopes on Satyakirti, and all those hopes were turning into ashes in her mouth.

'You're cold,' he said. 'Let's go in.'

'I am not going in till we have solved our problem.'

'Don't be stubborn, Ambe. You can't afford to be ill. The king and his ministers may assume that you are feigning sickness to avoid obligations. We will find a way. Don't worry.'

He pulled her up and held her close.

They clung to each other in desperation. 'I will always be there for you,' he mumbled into her hair.

Hand in hand, the two of them walked into the house.

'There you are. Where have you been?' Suvarnasena confronted them the moment they entered.

'She needed fresh air,' said Satyakirti, leading the girl toward the bed.

'Where did you take her?' Suvarnasena demanded. 'Don't you know that she is ill?'

He refused to rise to her bait and tucked Ambapali into bed.

'What kind of friend are you, young man?'

'She wanted to be out in the open.'

'You should know better than to take her out of bed,' she snorted. 'I will take care of Pali. You may leave now.'

'I—'

Suvarnasena held up her hand. 'I don't want you to visit till she is well.'

He paused at the threshold, fumbling for words. Finding none, he turned on his heels and stomped out of the house.

'Pali, don't you realize the harm you are causing to yourself?' Suvarnasena pounced on Ambapali.

'Devi, I . . .'

'I don't want to hear anything. You will not leave the house as long as you are unwell. If it is fresh air you want, we can go for a ride in my carriage.'

She's so maddening, Ambapali thought, wishing she would go away and leave her alone.

'Devi, I am exhausted. I would like to sleep,' she said.

'You are exhausted because you left your bed and sat outside in the open. Your friends are immature and uncaring. It was absolutely irresponsible of that young man to take you walking when you are unwell.'

Irked by the teacher's remarks, Ambapali retorted, 'My friends are not uncaring and immature, devi. We have grown up together. They love me, and I love them too.'

Suvarnasena shrugged. 'Well, I don't want them to return and do something foolish again. So I will wait here till your father returns.'

Helpless tears streaking down her cheeks, Ambapali turned on her side and closed her eyes.

Six

A full week had passed since the dance competition. Ambapali could delay her departure no further. Although she had recovered physically, her spirits remained low. Despite long discussions, the father and daughter could not find a way out of their predicament.

Like frogs in monsoon and mice at harvest-time, persistent and unwanted, Suvarnasena had taken to frequenting their house. Her disdain for Dharma Datta did not escape the man. She thought of him as a fool who failed to realize the benefits of his daughter's position. He exasperated her.

'Why are you moping? You should celebrate your good fortune,' she lambasted the gardener. 'You will be a rich man. A luxurious residence, servants, wealth, you can have everything.'

'Pali is my life, devi,' he said, avoiding her eyes. The woman's callousness knew no bounds. 'Mansions, servants and treasures are of no interest to me. I have been content without them.'

'Well, I don't think you have a choice in the matter. It's time you accepted the inevitable. Most people would rejoice. You should embrace this opportunity to change your life, and hers.'

'You won't understand my feelings, devi. I can't live without my daughter.'

The time of reckoning was upon them. Suvarnasena had sent word that the young woman would attend the induction rites, and the parishad had prepared all that was necessary for the function. The carriage waited at the gate, yet Ambapali was reluctant to leave.

'I don't want to go, Baba,' she sobbed. Dharma Datta struggled to comfort her. Mere words could not express his grief. He allowed his tears to speak for him. Seven seasons ago, he had said goodbye to his wife with much sorrow. Separating from Pali was like giving away another piece of his heart.

He watched silently as Pali wandered from room to room, touching each object, reminiscing about the joyful days of her childhood. So many memories were locked within those walls that had been her home for sixteen long years. Within its walls, she had had love and happiness. She ran her hands over the rugged clay floor, the ancient wooden door which was cracked and peeling, and the windows that opened to welcome the dawn. She sobbed over the broken toys and trinkets in the crumbling wooden chest.

'I will come and see you every day,' she promised.

It was a false promise; her father knew that. Once gone, no one returned. Time continues to pass, never once turning back. The past is forgotten, and soon the present retreats into the past. As for the future, no guarantee could be made.

Tears were aplenty that morning. Priyamvada and Urmimala wrestled with their emotions, failing to control their tears. From a distance, a forlorn Satyakirti stared at the girl he had loved since the age of ten. She had reached out to him and he had let her down. Her accusing look that morning conveyed her feelings more strongly than words. He would never get over his guilt.

Neighbours arrived to bid goodbye to the young woman they had seen grow up. They came with soothing words and tears. Suvarnasena was the only cheerful person around.

Once again, she tried to propel her protégé towards the carriage. She had been doing so for the past hour. 'It's getting late, Pali,' she warned in a low voice. 'There are a host of things that need to be done before the initiation rites begin.'

'Give her a little more time,' said Priyamvada acidly, as she embraced her friend again.

'You will visit me, Priya. Won't you?' cried Pali.

One by one, her friends hugged the girl. Not once did she look at Satyakirti. She couldn't forgive him for rejecting her suggestion.

Finally, her body weighed down by grief, Ambapali allowed her teacher to lead her to the carriage.

Tears flowed as she watched the house and people disappearing in the distance.

A well-furnished chamber near the sabhagrih had been assigned to Ambapali for the evening. Shoulders hunched, she sat in a corner while Suvarnasena inspected the arrangements. A bath with warm water, rose petals floating in it, awaited the raj nartaki. Jewels and clothes had been laid out by two dasis, maid servants, employed for the purpose. Under the watchful eyes of the teacher, they helped the girl get ready for the ceremony. The servants bowed and left the room once the lady was satisfied.

'Stand tall, hold your head high and straighten your shoulders, Pali,' instructed the teacher. 'You are the raj nartaki and have to behave like one. An imperial posture is essential

to the position. This is the start of a new chapter in your life.
I will be with you every step of the way. From this moment,
I am your father, mother, friend and mentor.'

The dasis had done a good job. Ambapali looked magnificent
in a crimson uttariya, and a honey-coloured antariya draped
across the delicate shoulders. A brocade kanchuki covered her
breasts, and her hair was styled in an elaborate coiffure. Deft
strokes of kajal highlighted the brightness of her eyes, and her
lips were made redder with the clever use of crushed rose-
petal unguent. Suvarnasena added a few finishing touches to
the hairstyle and nodded her approval.

Nervous, Ambapali followed her teacher past stony-
faced guards standing at regular intervals along a long passage
adorned with striking frescoes. She gazed, awestruck, at the
polished brass urns with lighted incense and floating flowers
placed all along the passageway. Carved arches led into the
court where the parishad met for discussions on State matters.
The guards at the entrance uncrossed their spears and the
heavy brass-studded wooden doors swung open as they
approached the hall.

The Vajji republic's assembly hall was an impressive place.

One hundred and eight intricately carved wooden pillars,
adorned with sculpted flowers, vines and peacocks, lined the
hall and supported the gilded ceiling. The walls were covered
with delicate murals, and a series of enormous windows
overlooked the luxuriant gardens. Scores of ivory inlaid seats
had been placed for the assembly members, hailing from the
ruling clans. At the far end, on an elevated platform, under an
ornate canopy, stood a superbly crafted gilded throne.

The centre of the hall was where the court dancer
performed, and the musicians were seated in two rows to the

sides. Daunted by the grandeur, Ambapali remained frozen at the entrance. The initiation was very serious business, she realized.

'The first rule is not to allow others to see your anxiety,' whispered her mentor, nudging her in the back. 'Pretend to be confident. Smile. I am with you.'

Suvarnasena guided the girl towards the far end of the room. Soon, the rajas and nobles began filtering into the hall. Conversation and laughter filled the room as they took their seats. Ambapali felt herself cringing as a few directed curious looks in their direction.

Maharaja Chetak strode into the hall, followed by his retinue of ministers, and everyone stood up and folded their palms in greeting. The king raised his hands in greeting and took his seat. The others followed suit.

'Don't fidget,' Suvarnasena whispered. 'Focus on the dance and take deep breaths.'

There was a terse silence as the king talked to the mahamatya, who functioned as an adviser. The chief minister knew that Maharaja Chetak had a soft corner for Ambapali and was protective of her. Ever since he heard that the baby had been discovered in the royal orchard, he had shown an unusual concern for the young woman.

'Mahamatya, please provide the new raj nartaki with a suitable residence and security,' the king was saying.

The aged mahamatya nodded imperceptibly. He was aware of the troubles the girl was likely to face from the ardent nobles eyeing her.

A gong announced the start of the ceremony and a hush descended on the assembly.

'We gather here today to bid farewell to Devi Nishigandha, who performed her duties as a raj nartaki for four years. She's been an asset to Vaishali and we wish her well. We are also here to welcome Devi Ambapali, the new court dancer of Vaishali,' the mahamatya declared in a resounding voice. Thunderous applause followed the announcement.

The retiring raj nartaki looked ethereal in a gold-edged white muslin antariya, red silk kanchuki and yellow brocade uttariya. Her hair was a complex series of spiral curls interwoven with pearl strings. Ambapali observed that she was loaded with jewellery.

Nishigandha bowed before the king and the gathering, before stepping toward a large eight-tiered diya stand. Her movements graceful and unhurried, she started lighting the diyas.

'She's so beautiful and poised,' said Ambapali in a hushed tone.

'Don't idolize her, Pali,' said Suvarnasena. 'Try to imitate her poise. She was as nervous as you when she attended her initiation ceremony. That woman has learnt a lot in four years, and so will you. Besides, you will have my help.'

The ceremony would begin with one last performance by the outgoing raj nartaki, after which she would hand over the title to the successor.

As Ambapali watched her light the diyas, she noticed Nishigandha throwing her a quick, resentful look. The woman did not know Ambapali had tried her best to give up the post. She'd had no wish to take the title from her.

Invoking Goddess Saraswati, Nishigandha started dancing. The impassive expression on her face conveyed her disinterest in the performance. It was obvious that she had no intention of entertaining the court, now that they had chosen a replacement.

The dance ended with lukewarm applause from the audience. The lacklustre performance had made no impact on the discerning audience. Instead, it allowed them to justify their decision to appoint a successor.

Suvarnasena nudged her protégé towards the centre of the hall, where Nishigandha waited. Ambapali's mouth was dry, her palms sweaty and heart pounding, as she made her way to the previous raj nartaki. She wished the knots in her stomach would ease. Notwithstanding her mentor's encouraging words, she couldn't control the tremor in her hands.

Nishigandha cast a scathing look at the nervous girl and curled her lips in a patronizing smile. 'You must be feeling victorious, but it won't last long,' she hissed under her breath. 'Soon, a younger and prettier girl will snatch away your position just as you have snatched mine. These men don't like old and jaded dolls.'

Ambapali searched for a suitable reply to the vicious statement. Finally, she said mildly, 'You are wrong, devi. I don't feel victorious . . . I feel sorry for you . . .'

Nishigandha's lip curled slightly, to show that she didn't believe the girl. Then, conscious of the king's eyes on them, the smirk turned into a smile. In a symbolic gesture, Nishigandha removed the gold anklets from her feet and handed them over to Ambapali. That one gesture conveyed the handing over of her post to her successor.

There was loud applause as Ambapali bowed to the king and the audience. She was now the raj nartaki. She touched the anklets reverently before strapping them to her ankles. Aware that Nishigandha's arrogance had led to her downfall, she walked over to her teacher for her blessings. Then, drawing a deep breath, she began her performance.

Her eyes narrowed, Nishigandha studied her rival's movements, trying to find fault. There was none to be found. Ambapali's movements were fluid and graceful. The rhythm and expression were flawless. Light on her feet, she swayed to the music like she was born to dance.

Ambapali loved dancing. It freed her soul and spirited her away to a dream world, a world that had neither shackles nor tears. She pirouetted and whirled, spinning on her feet, light as a feather, her movements transitioning seamlessly with the tempo of the music. She forgot the obligations and duties that awaited her. The many assemblies she would have to entertain. The dignitaries she would have to please. The important men she would have to fend off. For the moment, the magic of music and rhythm captivated her mind and body.

Wonderstruck, the august audience watched till the music hit a crescendo and the dancer appeared to be floating in the air. The dance ended with a crash of cymbals, and the spell broke. Her head bowed, a breathless Ambapali stood waiting for the reactions.

Maharaja Chetak was the first one to clap. Soon, the hall resounded with applause.

'We welcome raj nartaki, Devi Ambapali, to the court,' said the mahamatya. It was a lofty title, one that would be a challenge to live up to.

'Your pupil has done you proud, Devi Suvarnasena,' remarked the king.

Palms folded, Ambapali stood rooted at the spot, smiling as the congratulatory remarks rained down on her. A few setthis, the town's rich merchants, lingered around her, trying to seek a rendezvous.

The chattering men finally left the hall, and the two women were left alone. They made to step out of the hall when a guard walked up to them.

'Devi, the mahamatya wishes you to approve the residence arranged for you,' he said. 'We can make an alternate arrangement if it doesn't meet your requirements.'

The sprawling, two-storey mansion was within striking distance from the main palace. Tall trees surrounded the structure of polished teak, and a meticulously laid-out garden fronted the house, abloom with myriad flowers.

It took less than a moment for Ambapali to fall in love with the house. The guard departed after introducing them to a matronly woman with a kind face. She welcomed them with folded hands, introducing herself as Lilavati, and ordered a servant to serve fruit juice before taking them on a tour of the house.

The entrance opened onto a very large, rectangular hall that could easily seat fifty people, designed to entertain the aristocracy. Its marble floors were covered with thick silk carpets, and the walls were dotted with recesses for ornate lamps as well as tall windows lined with drapes that billowed in the breeze.

Doors on either side of the hall opened into passages leading to several smaller rooms that formed a part of a quadrangle around an inner courtyard of the house.

'There are eleven rooms in the main wing, six on the ground and five on the upper floor. These do not include the kitchen and the stores and dining rooms. There is a smaller hall on the upper floor,' Lilavati informed them. 'The larger hall on the ground is for entertaining guests, and the rooms flanking it function as guest rooms. You are at liberty to change things according to your liking, of course.'

They went up the wooden staircase with carved balustrades into the smaller hall, which Lilavati mentioned had been used as a practice room by the previous raj nartaki.

'Did Devi Nishigandha live in this house?' asked Ambapali.

'No devi, it was the raj nartaki before her who lived here. Devi Nishigandha, I have been told, didn't find this house to her liking. She requested for one closer to the palace complex.'

Ambapali was surprised that Nishigandha hadn't liked this mansion. More surprising was the information that she'd had the courage to demand another house.

They went through the rooms on the upper floor, Suvarnasena's eagle eyes noting all the features.

'I would like to take this room,' she declared as they entered the largest room next to the practice hall right in front of the staircase.

A room at the other end of the passage caught Ambapali's fancy. She had no wish to stay in a room near Suvarnasena. Although smaller, it was a cozy corner room that opened onto a huge wrap-around terrace with an enchanting view of the garden.

'What about the servants?' asked Suvarnasena.

'The mansion has a staff of twelve. There are three dasis for cleaning and taking care of the house, a cook and his helper, two guards for security, a coachman and a groom who maintain the carriage and stable. There's a gardener and an accountant.' The amiable woman smiled. 'The guards, cook and two servants live in the houses within the complex. The rest of the staff comes in daily. You can fix their timings according to your convenience. There are also three musicians who live in the other wing.'

'You are the supervisor?'

Lilavati nodded. 'Yes, devi, I have been working in this house for close to ten years. Most of the staff has been here for a long time.'

She led them back to the ground floor.

'I think the gardens are the best part of this house. Hariprasad, the gardener, is a very hardworking man,' said Lilavati. 'Devi Ambapali, would you like to see the gardens?' She had noticed the yearning look on the girl's face.

'I would like that very much,' Ambapali said. Ignoring Suvarnasena's stern look, she continued to prattle. 'My father is an excellent gardener. He can perhaps come here someday and meet Hariprasad. They can—'

'I'm sure Lilavati is not interested in knowing the details of your family,' Suvarnasena interrupted her mid-sentence. The harshness in her voice reflected her displeasure. 'I will be inside,' she said. 'Join me after you have finished with your inspection of the garden.'

'I can see the garden some other time,' said Ambapali.

Over the past week, Ambapali had noticed a transformation in her teacher. Ever since the Vasant Utsav competition, the lady had turned completely authoritative. Her voice and body language were uncomfortably overbearing.

'It's all right. You might as well satisfy yourself,' said Suvarnasena, striding into the house. She had observed the surprise in her student's eyes.

The scowl on the teacher's face hadn't escaped Lilavati's sharp eyes and the unreasonable behaviour took her aback.

The young woman just wanted to walk around the garden. There was no reason to rebuke her.

They walked through a series of arches laden with flowering creepers, and Ambapali exclaimed with delight. The place was bursting with colour. Pink, yellow and white bougainvillea jostled for space with bleeding heart vines, ivy and golden shower trees. The marble pavilion, curtained by flowering creepers, was a perfect place to spend a peaceful evening. It stood by the lotus pond at the far end of the garden. The ceiling was ornamented with frescoes of amorous couples, and a carved marble bench occupied the centre.

'What a beautiful place!' said Ambapali. She sat on the marble seat and closed her eyes to enjoy the scent of jasmine and madhumalti. 'I could spend the entire day in the garden playing the veena. Satyakirti could join me. I will invite all my friends and my father as soon as I am settled.'

Lilavati looked tenderly at the excited girl, so close in age to her daughter. 'I am sure your father will be happy to see you living in this beautiful house.'

Ambapali felt herself warming up to the woman. Lilavati's words were a soothing balm after Suvarnasena's harshness.

'We should return to the house,' Lilavati said. 'You must have a hundred things to do before you move into this place.'

They entered the hall and found Suvarnasena interrogating the staff.

Seven

Things worked differently in the mansion, Ambapali realized on waking up the next morning. While she slept, her things had been brought from her village house and arranged meticulously. She didn't own much. Right from childhood, she had been satisfied with the few clothes her father gave her. As for jewellery, she had just one or two precious pieces. A day before the ceremony, Suvarnasena had pointed out that she needed to replenish her wardrobe.

'Devi, I can't afford to pay for expensive clothes,' Dharma Datta objected after the lady brought over chests full of new ones.

'They are gifts,' said the teacher. She did not confess that the expenditure was just a small part of the generous purse sanctioned by the king for the raj nartaki's expenses. The rest of the gold coins were feathering her nest.

'In that case, we can't accept them.'

'You are a fool,' Suvarnasena snapped. 'Your daughter can't wear those faded clothes to the court. You can't afford to buy expensive silks, but your ego doesn't allow you to accept my gifts.'

Her words were aimed at hurting Dharma Datta.

'Devi, the money you have spent on the clothes will be returned to you. Consider it a loan,' he replied doggedly. He would return the money if it was the last thing he did. Suvarnasena couldn't be allowed to get away with demeaning him. 'I may be a poor man, but I am also a proud one.'

'Pride has ruined better men than you,' snorted Suvarnasena.

Lying awake now, Ambapali recalled the derision in the teacher's eyes. She flung away the soft silk cover and stretched. Used to sleeping on the floor, she had tossed and turned on the soft and unfamiliar bed, and in the end taken to the cool marble floor with just one flimsy cover, waking at dawn to creep back into the bed.

Everything was unfamiliar. The very air she breathed seemed different. She missed the small house and the simple life they had led. She missed her father.

Just then, a young maid walked in with a bunch of fresh flowers and started arranging them in brass containers around the room.

'Who are you?' Ambapali asked the girl, who couldn't have been more than fifteen years old.

'I am Indumati,' replied the girl shyly. 'I will take care of all you need.'

The thought of someone waiting on her seemed preposterous. 'Well, Indumati, you may tell Lilavati that I can take care of my own needs,' she said.

The girl seemed taken aback by her words. 'Devi, please don't tell them you don't need my services,' she begged. 'Lilavati will throw me out. My family is very poor. I need this job.'

Ambapali immediately felt guilty. 'I will not say a word, don't worry. You can stay and look after me,' she hastened to comfort.

Indumati's face brightened at the assurance, and she promised, 'I won't give you any reason to be unhappy. Would devi like to begin the day with some fruit juice?' She recounted the varieties of drinks available that morning. 'We have buttermilk, bel and amla, and . . .'

Ambapali smiled. 'I am not very fussy. I will be happy with whatever you bring.'

'My recommendation would be the bel juice, devi. It's my favourite. I will bring a glass of it.'

The juice was as good as promised. Ambapali sat on the terrace sipping it, watching the sunrise. It was a glorious sight that wiped away all traces of gloom preying on her mind. She had barely finished the juice when Indumati informed her that her bath was ready. The cheerful girl had been handed a roster of duties and she was working through her list, one by one. Her enthusiasm amused Ambapali.

'This way, devi.' The girl led her to the bath, where a huge copper pot of water with rose petals awaited. Fresh towels, soaps, unguents and a change of dress were arranged on one side. Indumati looked anxiously at Ambapali.

Realizing that the girl was seeking approval, Ambapali patted her on the back, saying, 'You have done a good job.' An older maid walked in just as Indumati started rubbing the oil in her hair.

'I am Kaushalya, your chief maid and masseur,' she said with a bow, and Ambapali learnt she had not one but two maids to look after her needs.

Submitting herself to their ministrations did not come easy. She would have to discuss the matter with Lilavati.

It was the longest and most elaborate bath Ambapali had ever had. Using a scrub made from walnuts, dried petals, herbs, turmeric and sandalwood, the masseur continued to rub till her nerves tingled delightfully.

A sandalwood oil massage followed the scrub. Kaushalya's expert hands kneaded and pressed her bunched muscles until they turned pliant. She used a wooden roller between the shoulder blades to ease stiffness in the muscles. The bath that followed was refreshing, aided as it was with a paste of soap nuts, sandalwood, lotus petals and tulsi.

Once the bath was over, the maid dabbed her body with the towel and seated her in front of an enormous mirror. Her hair was dressed in the latest style, herbal unguents and salves were applied to her face. Fresh clothes and jewellery worn, she stood up.

'You look like a queen,' Indumati said, the wonder in her eyes endorsing her statement.

'What next?' asked an amused Ambapali.

'The cook expects you to do justice to the spread he's prepared,' giggled Indumati, leading her towards a large room adjoining the kitchen.

The girl had not been lying. Wanting to make a good impression, the cook had prepared an incredible array of dishes. Ambapali was used to simple food. Most of the time, she had been satisfied with karambha, ghee and a piece of fish or meat.

'I can't eat so much,' she protested.

Hurt, the cook emerged from the kitchen. He selected a few dishes and laid them before her, saying, 'Devi, you must sample these.'

There was much warmth in his voice, and a contrite Ambapali forced herself to eat till she couldn't move.

Lilavati arrived soon after. 'Would you like to meet the gardener?' she asked.

'I would like that very much,' replied Ambapali, following the woman out of the room.

They had barely gone a few steps when Suvarnasena made an appearance.

'Surprabhat, devi.' Lilavati wished the teacher good morning.

Suvarnasena ignored the greeting. 'Where are you going, Pali?' she asked.

'Lilavati is taking me to meet Hariprasad.'

'That can wait. We have other things to do.' She walked away, clearly expecting Ambapali to follow.

'Where are we going?' asked Ambapali, hurrying to keep pace with the teacher.

'I want you to keep the staff at a distance,' said Suvarnasena. 'I don't approve of how friendly you are with your maids and Lilavati.'

'She's a very warm and caring person, devi.'

'Lilavati is a housekeeper. You must treat her as one.'

Ambapali bristled at Suvarnasena's patronizing words, but suppressed the urge to retort. Everything was so sudden and intimidating. The luxurious mansion, the retinue of servants and Survarnasena's behavior. She felt inadequate.

Eight

Eight weeks passed in a flurry of activity. They felt like a century to Ambapali—she felt like her universe had completely transformed. Her day began with music and dance rehearsals at the crack of dawn and ended only after the exit of her suitors. Sessions with jewellers, clothiers and perfumiers filled the intervening hours. Her requests to visit her father and friends were rejected by the teacher.

As the days flew by, Ambapali could see changes in herself. The mirror confirmed that change. She was poised and graceful. The confusion was slowly evaporating. She was finding her feet; she was less awkward and more confident. She missed her father, though, and wished he could live in the mansion with her. It was wishful thinking, Ambapali knew. Her father was a gentle and humble man. He would not be comfortable in this house. She wished, also, that her friends could spend time with her. Above all, she wished to speak to Satyakirti.

With time, too, she was growing more wary of Suvarnasena. Many of the teacher's actions confounded her, including the shake-up of staff in the house. Just a week after their arrival at the mansion, the lady had gone on a sacking spree. Lilavati had been the first one to go, and one by one, all the other servants had been replaced. No reasons were given, no explanations were offered. Tears shed by the old cook, the pleas of the others; nothing had worked on the ruthless lady.

At the end of two weeks, the gardener and the two men who worked in the stables were the only ones to keep their jobs.

Horrified, Ambapali watched them go. She couldn't understand her mentor's motives. She had liked Lilavati. She had also liked the cook and Kaushalya. Suvarnasena replaced the previous staff with impassive women who served as spies for her. It was only when Indumati was asked to leave that she challenged Suvarnasena.

'I am happy with her services and see no reason for her to leave,' she said defiantly. The bright and bubbly girl was her only ally in the huge house. 'I don't want Indumati to go.'

The stubbornness in her voice made the lady back off. It was a small victory, but Ambapali felt a tinge of satisfaction.

The past four weeks had unmasked some of Suvarnasena's ambitions. Gone was the genial façade, and reality emerged. She was a slave driver, who sought perfection in everything.

Apart from the endless dance and music lessons, Ambapali had to undergo instructions in makeup and the preparation of herbal cosmetics. From hairdressing, poetry and painting, to preparing and presenting a betel leaf, everything was an art. There were so many things to learn.

A raj nartaki was expected to master the chatushasht kalas, the sixty-four forms of art, she was told by Suvarnasena. Geet, vadya, nritya and natya vidya, the science of song, instrument, footwork and dance, were just a few of the things she was expected to learn.

These, Ambapali didn't mind. What she hated was that she was apparently required to master the art of coquetry, and flirt with the setthis and princes who came wooing with expensive gifts and artful words. They flocked around her each evening after her dance performance at the court, wanting her attention. In those weeks, she had danced every evening at the court until she was ready to drop, and smiled till her face muscles began aching. The aftermath tired her more than the dancing. The lewd looks from the drooling and fawning nobles, some of them older than her father, stripped away her dignity. The constant warding off of preying hands wearied her more than anything.

Her mind full of Satyakirti, the compliments paid by the nobles failed to evoke feelings in her. At first, the poetic praises embarrassed her, and then she learnt to take them in her stride. But Ambapali's indifference only whetted their interest. They swarmed around her like bees, attracted by her dimpled smile, graceful figure and seductive eyes.

It was left to Suvarnasena to handle these suitors. She efficiently barred the ardent men from barging into the dancer's bedroom. Sometimes gently, sometimes tactfully, she saved Ambapali from the pressing attentions of her most persistent admirers. Yet, sometimes things took an ugly turn. Twice in the past few weeks, inebriated nobles had to be persuaded to leave the house.

One evening, Ambapali, unable to ward off the roving hands of a rich setthi, fled to her bedroom. The inebriated and determined suitor followed her into the room, insisting on being served wine there. Scared out of her wits, she screamed for help. It had taken much persuasion by the housekeeper and the servants to get the setthi out of the bedroom. He stormed out of the palace, warning Ambapali of dire consequences. The unpleasant episode left her shaken.

Suvarnasena had been busy settling accounts with the jeweler. 'Our palace runs on the generosity of the patrons. You can't displease the setthis,' she had scolded Ambapali, on hearing of the incident. 'You need to handle these situations more diplomatically. They are bound to happen in our line of work.'

The unpleasant episode made Ambapali pine for her friends. She felt trapped in the mansion. She wanted to get away, even if it was for a few hours. She wanted to breathe freely and mull over the complexities of her situation.

The next day, Suvarnasena refused again her request to visit her father. 'There's no time for that. You have so much to do and learn.'

'I will return in a few hours, devi,' pleaded Ambapali. 'I have not seen him for so long. I don't know how he's doing.' The truth was that she had never been away from her father. This was the first time.

Suvarnasena shrugged. 'If he's not well, the local vaid can handle it better than you.'

How can she be so insensitive? Ambapali fumed. She walked to the pavilion to put some distance between herself and her mentor.

The gardener, Hariprasad, was surprised to see her sitting there. 'You look unhappy,' he said, handing her a white lotus. It was her favourite flower.

'I feel lonely and miserable,' she cried out. 'I have not seen my father for so long.'

'I have no right to advise you, but I can offer a suggestion,' he said. His kindly eyes twinkled merrily. 'Sometimes, it helps to take charge of one's own affairs.'

His words made her smile. 'Thank you, Hariprasad,' she said. 'You have given me the right advice.'

Calling for the carriage, she jumped into it.

'Isn't Devi Suvarnasena coming with you?' asked the carriage driver, aware that Ambapali never went out without the teacher.

'She's not coming and neither are you. I will drive the carriage myself.'

'Devi, I cannot—'

'Get down, Krishna,' she commanded, snatching the reins from his hands.

She was off before anyone could stop her.

The horses responded to her prodding, and she rode quickly away from the mansion. It was thrilling to be free from Suvarnasena's clutches.

Her spirit on an upswing, exhilarated and buoyed by the adventure, she rode. Her mood improved as she neared her house.

Dharma Datta was surprised and dismayed as he saw his daughter draw up at his doorstep. 'Where is the carriage driver?' he asked.

'I left him behind,' she chuckled.

'You shouldn't have done that,' chided Dharma Datta, stern but fond. 'It will upset Devi Suvarnasena.'

'Forget her, Baba. I have been wanting to come here for so long, but Suvarnasena has kept me so busy with practice and tutors.'

'I am so happy to see you.'

'Why didn't you come to visit me? I was waiting for you.'

He did not tell her that he had indeed gone to meet her, but Suvarnasena had turned him away, saying his daughter was busy. It was not sensible to complain to Pali. She would demand an explanation from her teacher, and that could lead to unpleasantness. Instead, Dharma Datta related to her all the amusing incidents that had taken place in the village. He wanted her to laugh and relax. He would do anything to keep her happy.

Ambapali's thoughts ran along similar lines. She did not tell him about her unhappiness or the ugly incidents that took place in the mansion. Time was too short to spend ruing things. She didn't want her father to be sad or worried. An hour passed and then two, and she showed no sign of leaving.

'You must meet your friends,' Dharma Datta said. 'I will inform them of your arrival.'

Not long after, the two girls rushed into the house. There was much excitement as they hugged each other. They had much to share and would not stop chattering.

'What a grand carriage!' exclaimed Urmimala. She ran a hand over Ambapali's silk uttariya and said, 'This is gorgeous. I heard you live in a palatial house with lots of servants. I wish we could stay there for a couple of days.'

'Who told you I live in a palatial house?' Ambapali laughed. 'You are more than welcome to stay with me. I may live in a big house and wear good clothes, but I am lonely.'

Priyamvada noticed her friend's eyes straying to the door. 'Satya didn't come,' she said.

'Why not? Didn't you tell him of my arrival?'

'We did, and we asked him to come with us, but he refused,' said Urmimala tactlessly.

'Why?' Ambapali was shocked. She had expected him to rush over.

'He didn't give any reason.'

'Where's he?' asked Ambapali. 'I want to meet him.'

'He's in the mango grove, as usual. That fellow has been behaving strangely since you left,' Urmimala whispered in a conspiratorial tone.

'Stop it, Urmi!' Priyamvada said. 'Why are you upsetting her?'

'Hide nothing from me, please,' begged Ambapali. 'What has he been doing? Tell me everything.'

'He's done nothing but mope and tinker with his music instruments,' said Urmimala, ignoring the warning look Priyamvada shot at her. 'He has no interest in food or sleep. Just yesterday, his mother told me that the family is anxious about his health.'

It shocked Ambapali to hear about Satyakirti's condition. The two of them could have defeated the course of destiny if they had married, but it was he who had decided against it. 'I will speak to him,' she said, getting up.

'I will come with you, Pali,' Priyamvada said and followed her friend out. Ambapali demurred.

'Let me handle this on my own, please.' Bidding them farewell, Ambapali hurried to the orchard.

The mellifluous notes of the flute greeted her as she neared the orchard. She saw him sitting under their favourite mango tree. Satyakirti was lost in the music, eyes closed. His curly black locks were ruffled, and sweat dotted his forehead. Her eyes lingered on his careworn face and his muscled frame, clad in a soft white antariya. Her heart ached. This man with cracked lips and hollow eyes was a far cry from the Satya she knew.

He was playing her favourite raga, his fingers moving frenziedly over the instrument. She leaned against a nearby tree, listening. As the tempo quickened, he played like one possessed until the music reached a crescendo and he ran out of breath.

Satyakirti opened his eyes, jarred out of his reverie, and stared at the flute, too distressed to continue. Grief filled his eyes as he contemplated it, struggling to control the emotions that had surged with the quickening of tempo.

'Satya . . .' Ambapali's eyes overflowed.

His head snapped up. 'What are you doing here?' he asked sharply.

She rushed to him and kneeled next to him. 'Our love drew me here.'

'Our love was doomed the day they crowned you as the raj nartaki. I wish we had not gone for the Vasant Utsav.'

'You have been in my thoughts every moment of the day. You don't know how much I loathe that place. I would do anything to return home and be with my father, be with you.' Tears flowed down her cheeks. 'How long do you want me to wallow in the filth? I feel suffocated, Satya.'

Her sobs softened Satyakirti's attitude. He had wanted her to have a better life. Not for a minute did he dream she would be unhappy. *What have I done? Why didn't I agree to her request to get married? I have caused such misery for both of us. And now, it's too late.*

'Don't cry, Ambe.' He reached out to stroke her hair lovingly. 'Have faith. We will find a way out of this.'

'How?' Ambapali asked, crying.

'I have no answers,' he admitted and hung his head. He felt like kicking himself. Yet, he had neither the courage nor the willpower to defy the king. He was a coward. 'Nothing is forever. We will find a way.'

It was a hollow promise, but she took heart and began to cajole him to come home with her. It was past noon when he finally relented.

'Where did you disappear to, Pali?' Dharma Datta asked when she got home. He had prepared her favourite dishes.

Ambapali pushed the sulking young man forward by way of answer. 'I had gone to the orchard to meet him.'

'You will share a meal, I hope.' Dharma Datta looked affectionately at Satyakirti, whom he loved like his own son.

Satyakirti shook his head, 'I have to leave, it's—'

'You are not leaving,' Ambapali forestalled him.

Her father had outdone himself. It was the most satisfying meal Ambapali had eaten in a long while, but Dharma Datta noticed that the young man was picking at his food.

He asked Satyakirti why he wasn't eating. 'Pali cooks much better, of course,' he ribbed gently.

Satyakirti was quick to disclaim it. 'No, it's not that. The food is delicious, but I am not hungry.'

'What a pity! A young man like you must eat well.'

The trio had just finished eating when a carriage arrived and a fuming Suvarnasena stormed into the house.

'Oh, no,' murmured Ambapali.

'How dare you?' Suvarnasena said to Dharma Datta. 'How dare you encourage her to come here without informing me?'

Ambapali rose to his defence. 'Don't blame my father, devi. It is you who turned down all my requests, so I finally came here without your consent.'

'She is not to be blamed, devi,' Satyakirti said. 'She should have been allowed to visit her father.'

'Keep out of this, young man,' Suvarnasena snarled. 'You have no right to interfere. Pali doesn't need the likes of you as her friend.'

'Don't insult him, devi,' Ambapali said angrily. 'I won't tolerate this disrespect. This man is a special friend.'

Dharma Datta was surprised at his daughter's audacity. When did the timid girl become so bold? Where did she find the courage to defy her teacher? This was not the Pali he knew.

There was silence for a couple of minutes as the two women glared at each other. Suvarnasena was the first to blink. Realizing this was a line her pupil would not allow her to cross, she resumed in a honeyed voice, 'I am not your enemy, Pali. I am only doing what is good for you.'

'You mistake things, devi. I am grown enough to know what is good for me. My father and friends are what I need. A lavish mansion, servants and jewellery are poor compensation.'

'I am doing it all for *your* welfare, Ambapali. Do you realize how much work it takes? There is so much for you to learn and time is short. That's why I discouraged you from coming here,' reasoned Suvarnasena.

'Am I not entitled to some leisure? A day off?' complained Ambapali.

'Enough, Pali,' Dharma Datta said. It would do no good for Pali to offend her teacher. He joined his palms and continued sombrely, 'I am sorry for her disrespectful behavior, devi. You may take her back now.'

Suvarnasena smiled triumphantly. 'You will accompany me in my carriage,' she instructed Ambapali. 'The carriage driver can take the other one back.'

Misty-eyed and helpless, Dharma Datta watched them leave. He hadn't wanted this to happen, but how could a poor gardener flout the king's command? 'Suvarnasena is to blame for everything. That greedy and ambitious woman has ruined my daughter's life,' he mumbled.

Satyakirti placed a comforting hand on the troubled man's shoulder, at a loss for how to console him.

Nine

No two days in Ambapali's life were alike. Each day brought a fresh challenge. Her circumstances changed, and so did her attitude. Her diffidence was the first casualty. She grew more resolute with each passing day and pushed back against Suvarnasena's intimidating ways.

'Although a raj nartaki is not a ganika, a prostitute, she is expected to please the king and the ministers,' Suvarnasena enjoined her pupil. 'She has to be an artful flirt and a skilled raconteur.'

Ambapali understood the veiled hint behind her mentor's words and scrunched her nose in disgust. King or no king, she would draw the limit. No one would have access to her bed.

The mansion teemed with admirers vying for her attention. Each evening brought more gifts and wooers. The princes and setthis arrived bearing jewels, hoping to outbid each other. Their lust-filled eyes, lascivious smiles and roving hands made her recoil. The veneer of decency slipped as soon as they were denied their desire. Lips mouthing sweet nothings one minute would begin to spout curses. There were many ugly scenes. Often, swords drawn, rivals duelled each other.

Ambapali dreaded evenings. Within a few months, she had tired of the drama that awaited her after a dance performance. Dancing, which had been a pleasure, lost all charm. Her spirits were low, and she felt exhausted all the time. One day melded into the next as she was driven by her ruthless teacher.

It was only a couple of months later that she was able to visit her father and friends again. After three months of continuous rain, the monsoon had started waning. Waterfalls gushed, lakes overflowed and the rivers flowed rapidly. Earth changed its garb. The ground turned a dazzling emerald and wildflowers nodded cheerfully. The paddy and millet fields were green once again, and farmers were happy with the promise of an abundant harvest. Sighing with pleasure, Ambapali rode home.

She loved the rains. The smell and sounds enlivened her spirit. A joyful song stirring within, she goaded the horses to go faster. Once again, she had left the chariot driver behind. She'd also sent a messenger with gifts and a missive to her father the previous day.

Dharma Datta was waiting for her. He rushed to wrap her in his arms. 'You are soaking wet,' he said, handing her a towel. 'You should have waited till the sky cleared.'

'I couldn't wait any longer. It's been so many days since I saw you.' She turned her rain-soaked face towards her father.

'Silly girl!' he admonished gently. 'Change your clothes before you catch a chill.'

Dharma Datta bustled around the house, fetching juices and snacks, while she changed into dry clothes. He watched over her as she ate the simple fare placed before her. Everything was just the way she liked.

Suddenly, it was like old times. They chatted about their lives and gossiped about the happenings in the village. He did not, however, tell her the bits he knew would upset her, like the growing intimacy between Satyakirti and Urmimala. It made him sad to watch the two of them spending so much time together. Dharma Datta had wanted Satyakirti as his son-in-law, but that dream seemed far-fetched now.

'Let me inform your friends,' he said. 'I am sure you would like to meet them.'

'You are so good at reading my mind, Baba. I'd love to meet them before I go back.' She smiled happily. 'Have you noticed the tiny bitter gourds on the vine? You are going to have a good crop this season.'

'There will be crisply fried bitter gourd with your gruel on your next visit.'

They laughed happily. Still smiling, he left the house to inform her friends.

She wandered through the little garden at the back of their house. Several buds had sprouted on the jasmine bushes, and the tiny patch of vegetables was showing promise.

She was weeding the garden when her friends arrived.

Priyamvada burst into the house and hugged her friend. 'It's so good to see you.' Holding her friend at an arm's length, she studied her face. 'You look beautiful.'

'I am so envious, Pali,' Urmimala exclaimed after hugging her friend. 'What do they feed you at the palace? You are glowing more than ever.' She looked around the room and asked, 'Haven't you brought anything for us?'

'Silly girl!' laughed Priyamvada. 'You are always looking for gifts. What did you expect her to bring?'

'She could have brought us some delicacies. It's selfish to hog without sharing,' pouted Urmimala. 'I have a sudden craving for sweets. Not the usual ones, but the ones with lots of nuts in them.'

'I will remember to bring you some the next time. In fact, I will send you some the moment I am back at the mansion,' promised Ambapali. 'Just don't ask me to leave right away,' she teased.

After a few minutes, Ambapali asked, 'Where's Satya?'

'Your lovelorn friend is sitting by the lakeside, staring into space,' Urmimala said, mimicking Satyakirti.

'Can't you hold your tongue, Urmi?' said Priyamvada. 'He said he would be here shortly.'

'I might need to leave by the time he comes,' Ambapali fretted. 'What is wrong with him?'

'The gentleman is lovesick,' Urmimala replied.

'In that case, he should have come and met me.'

'Did I say that he's lovesick for you? He could be pining for another woman,' Urmimala teased.

'Shut up, Urmi!' Priyamvada scolded the flippant girl. She, too, had noticed the growing friendship between Satyakirti and the girl. The poor fellow needed a shoulder to cry on. He wouldn't fall in love with Urmi so soon after Pali's departure. It had to be a rebound relationship, she comforted herself, there was no need to worry. 'Don't worry, Pali, he'll be here soon.'

'I miss you. Why don't you come to meet me?' asked Ambapali.

'You have no time for us,' retorted Urmimala.

'Who said I don't have time for my friends? I wish you would come and stay with me for a few days.'

'I asked, but my parents didn't allow me,' said Urmimala. 'The raj nartaki's house is a den of vice, they say.'

'Urmi!' Priyamvada warned. 'Stop talking nonsense. You talk too much.'

'It's the truth, isn't it?' said Urmimala. 'I am repeating what everyone says.'

'Don't you ever stop to think?' cried Priyamvada, striking her forehead with her palm. The stricken look on Ambapali's face hadn't escaped her eyes. 'You are so insensitive, Urmi.'

Suddenly contrite, Urmimala hurried to make amends. 'I was thinking, Pali . . .' she said.

'You and thinking?' Priyamvada laughed. 'Please don't pressurize your pea-sized brain.'

'Will you listen? I have a brilliant idea.' Ignoring her friends' eye-rolls, she continued, 'Priya can live with you. You know her relatives—they won't mind if she leaves. And you can get Satya to be with you if you appoint him as one of your musicians!'

Eyes shining, Ambapali turned to Priyamvada. 'That's a wonderful idea! Will you come to the mansion? It will help me a great deal.'

'I could ask my uncle,' said Priyamvada, her forehead furrowed and her head tilted to one side. It was a large family and there were many mouths to feed. Getting rid of one extra mouth would be a relief for everyone. 'I will live with you if they agree to let me go,' she said.

'You are nothing more than a maidservant in that house,' snorted Urmimala. 'They will resent losing an unpaid servant, but considering the cost of housing a person, they will be happy to let you go.'

'So that's settled,' said Ambapali. 'In fact, I will send some money and gifts to your house as a bribe. All you have to do is to discuss the matter with them. If they agree, send word through the messenger and I will send a carriage.'

She turned to Urmimala and gave her a hug. 'Thank you, Urmi! You have come up with a brilliant idea. Now I must speak to Satya.'

'I will come with you,' offered Urmimala. 'He will need a lot of coaxing.'

'No, Urmi!' Priyamvada stopped the girl. 'This needs to be sorted out between the two of them.'

Ambapali hurried towards the lake, her eyes searching for Satyakirti. She heard the soulful notes of the flute as she advanced. The music conveyed his emotions more efficiently than words. Her feet hurried towards him. Ambapali hugged him from the back.

'I have come, Satya! I couldn't stay away from you.' Her voice was a breathless whisper.

He turned around. 'Ambe!' he said. 'I miss you every moment of the day.' He did not want to add to her unhappiness by telling her how the guard at her mansion had thwarted his attempts to meet her. They had been instructed to not allow Pali's friends into the mansion.

'Then come with me,' she exhorted. 'Urmi has found a solution to our problems.'

'Urmi!' he laughed. 'That silly girl! She has found a solution?' There was an unmistakable fondness in his voice as he spoke about their friend.

'Yes, Satya! She has come up with an excellent idea. All I want is your consent, and everything will be all right.'

'My consent?' He frowned. 'What has my consent to do with it?'

'Don't be sarcastic, Satya,' said Ambapali. 'My rights were wrested away the day they appointed me as the raj nartaki. I am but a puppet. My movements are decided by Suvarnasena, the master puppeteer.'

'In that case, how can my consent solve your problem?'

'You could seek an appointment as a musician at the mansion.' Excitement danced in her eyes. 'All you have to do is to agree and I will take care of all the formalities.'

'You want me to be the raj nartaki's musician?' He was horrified at her suggestion. 'You may be happy dancing to the demands of the men who visit your mansion, but you can't expect me to play along!'

'Why not? I see no harm. Think of the opportunities that await you. Wealth, position and luxuries are just a few of the benefits. We can be together, and that's the biggest reward.'

'No!' He gritted his teeth. 'Music is my passion, and I have no intention of becoming the raj nartaki's musician. It's a deplorable idea. Only Urmi could have come up with such a ridiculous idea.'

Stung by his words, she retorted, 'You don't seem to care about our future. After all, I am your Ambapali, not just a raj nartaki.'

'I have no place in your future. It's as simple as that. By becoming your musician, we may be together. But we will never be able to marry.'

'Don't be a pessimist, Satya. A raj nartaki's tenure is not forever. A better dancer may replace me next year. I am just waiting for the Vasant Utsav competition.' Her eyes shone with hope. 'It's just a matter of a few months and then we can marry.'

'You are so innocent,' he said. 'Haven't you heard of the rumours? The Vajji republic is thinking of appointing you as the nagarvadhu.'

Ambapali was stunned. 'Nagarvadhu?' As the city's bride, she knew a nagarvadhu belonged to anyone who could pay her price. 'Why would they appoint me nagarvadhu?' Ambapali wailed.

'They appoint the most beautiful woman in Vaishali as the nagarvadhu, and you are exquisite, Ambe.'

'No!' Ambapali cried out. 'I will commit suicide before that happens.'

An uneasy silence set in as they each avoided the other's gaze. The lake was hushed and still. But there was a tumult in her heart. 'Don't be upset by thoughts of the future. Let's live each day as it comes. I don't want to think about tomorrow,' Satyakirti said finally, holding her shoulders in a reassuring gesture.

'I can't!' she protested. 'I can't go on like this. Let's give ourselves a chance, Satya. Promise me you will think about my idea.'

She put her head on his shoulder and closed her eyes, willing him to reply.

'I promise to think about it,' he said at last.

She smiled up at him, happy. 'I have to leave before my puppeteer comes looking for me,' she said, giving him a final hug.

She rode back to the mansion a little while later, and despite Satyakirti's pessimism, she could not help feeling hopeful.

Early the next morning, a messenger sped towards the village carrying gifts for Ambapali's father and friends. There were basketfuls of fruits and sweets, new clothes for Dharma

Datta and trinkets for her friends. There was also a missive for
Priyamvada's family.

In the meantime, Priyamvada had taken matters into her
hands. Urmimala had been correct in saying that she was
nothing more than an unpaid servant in her uncle's house.
The past twelve years had not been kind to her. Orphaned
at six, she craved for a word of kindness, but no one spared a
thought for her. Her unscrupulous relatives had usurped her
mother's jewellery and father's wealth. She toiled all day for
two meagre meals. She was the vestigial organ, a burden that
could be discarded. She owed them nothing.

The reactions from the members of the large family when
she proposed living with Ambapali were unexpected. They
gathered in the courtyard to discuss the matter. Never had she
seen them together. Not even during festivals. She stood like
a culprit, facing their volley of questions.

'Is she planning on turning you into a ganika?' asked her
vitriolic aunt.

'It's a house of ill repute.'

'You will bring disrepute to our family.'

'Will she pay you for your services?'

'How long does she want you to live with her?'

'What happens when she's no longer a raj nartaki?'

There were as many questions and doubts as the members
in the family. Patiently, Priyamvada answered them all.

No, she was not expected to be a ganika. Ambapali was
not a ganika either.

The raj nartaki's mansion was not a house of ill repute. It
was a temple of art.

She was not willing to accept any payment for her services,
though Ambapali would pay. She would live there as a friend.

At any rate, she had never been paid for her labours by anyone in the past twelve years, she couldn't resist pointing out; but they were too thick-skinned for remorse.

'I will live there as long as she wants. I don't know what the future holds for me, neither does Ambapali. Does anyone know what will happen tomorrow? I am not thinking of my future. My future was doomed the day I lost my parents.'

Several voices rose in protest. They had never heard her speak so much. In fact, they had forgotten she could speak.

She was asked to wait as her relatives considered the matter. Heaving a sigh of relief, Priyamvada walked out of the house. She had put all her cards on the table and it was up to them now. They would either allow her to leave, or her mistreatment would worsen. She would have to take the chance.

A hubbub erupted in the courtyard after she left. The women were outraged at the thought of losing a tireless servant. The men wondered if there was a way to cash in on the opportunity. Priyamvada's closeness to Ambapali could open closed doors. They toted up the profit and loss, balancing mental ledgers.

In the end, they agreed to let her go.

Ten

Ambapali paced the garden, waiting for her friend's arrival. A carriage had been dispatched as soon as the messenger returned with Priyamvada's reply. Happiness coursed through her, vital as warm sunrays on a winter morning. The sun was brighter, flowers lovelier and birdsong sweeter than ever. Everything was going to be all right now. With Priya by her side, she could overcome all hurdles.

That morning, she had gone around announcing her friend's arrival. Right from the cook to the stable boy, everybody was prepared to meet the woman called Priyamvada.

'Will she be staying for long?' Suvarnasena said, attempting to look unperturbed but disturbed by the news. Priyamvada's arrival would upset her plans. The prospect of losing her stranglehold on her protégé wasn't a pleasant one.

'She will be here for as long as she wants,' Ambapali said as she flounced out of the room.

For the umpteenth time that morning, she inspected the room readied for her friend. It was next to hers.

'Did you fill up the salvers with fruits and nuts?' she asked Indumati for the third time. 'See that the bath is ready, and the clothes are laid out. She loves buttermilk, so bring her some as soon as she comes. And ask the cook to prepare venison roast and fish fry. They are her favourite dishes.'

'Everything is being done as per your instructions,' confirmed the girl. Devoted to Ambapali, she was happy to see her mistress in a cheerful mood. 'You must be very fond of your friend, devi.'

'Priya is more than a friend. She is my soul sister.'

The clip-clop of horses' hoofs announced the carriage, and Ambapali rushed to greet her friend. She rained dozens of questions on the girl as she led her inside. 'Did you face any trouble with your relatives? Did you meet my father? Was the carriage comfortable? What—'

'So many questions,' Priya interrupted as they went up the stairs to her room. 'The answer to all of them is—everything and everyone is fine.'

'Indu, where's the buttermilk?'

'Stop pampering me, Pali,' Priyamvada said, laughing. She stopped at the threshold of the sunny room.

'I hope you like it,' Ambapali said, noticing the surprised look on her friend's face. 'I could arrange another one . . .'

'It is gorgeous.' Priyamvada ran her hands on the silk bedcover, her wondering eyes running over the trappings. 'I . . . I . . . I have no words to express my gratitude.' Her eyes misted with tears. 'I am not used to luxuries.'

'In that case, get used to them soon because I intend to spoil you,' said Ambapali. She wanted to compensate for all the years her friend had suffered in her miserly relative's house. She wanted to give her every comfort and joy possible. 'As for gratitude, please don't utter that word again.' She patted her friend's hand, overcome with emotion. 'I want to show you around the house, but first, you must eat.' She pointed at the fruits, juices and sweets laid out by Indumati.

'Are you crazy? I can't eat so much. I—' Priyamvada's sentence remained incomplete as Ambapali pushed an apupa into her mouth. It was just as it had always been.

Hours flew as the two of them went around the house and the garden. Their eyes bright, they giggled and teased each other. They chatted animatedly, discussing everything under the sun and finally fell asleep, only to continue in the same vein upon waking. Ambapali had no interest in getting back to routine. She basked in the warmth of her friend's love, happier and chirpier than ever. Suvarnasena watched from the wings for a couple of days before reminding them of the demands of the schedule.

Things soon returned to normal. With Priyamvada hovering in the background, Ambapali cheerfully yielded to her teacher's wishes. She rehearsed diligently, entertained the setthis and carried out her tasks without complaining. Even the teacher found no reason to reproach her.

Knowing that her friend didn't enjoy idling, Ambapali gave her a free hand in running the kitchen and maintaining accounts. She also gave her charge of her wardrobe and jewellery.

Priyamvada was a tireless worker. Her compassion drew the servants, who were fed up with Suvarnasena's tyrannical treatment. They switched loyalties as the days passed. None of this pleased the teacher, who itched to get rid of the young woman.

The two friends spent all their spare time together. After a hectic day, they liked to unwind by sipping fresh juices and discussing various things with each other. They had no secrets between them. Priyamvada knew her friend better than anyone else. She was Ambapali's alter ego and an efficient counsellor. Ambapali poured all her troubles into her friend's willing ears. She told her about the princes and their rivalry over her, and her distrust of Suvarnasena.

'I am planning to buy a house for Baba,' Ambapali confided one night.

The two of them were lying on the cool marble floor of the terrace, their senses lulled by the scent of night-blooming flowers. Stars winked conspiratorially at them, and a cool breeze blew away their exhaustion.

'That's a wonderful idea, Pali.' Priyamvada rolled onto her side and faced her friend, her head propped on one elbow. 'Your father has worked so hard all his life. He should retire now. I am sure he would be happy to hear of your plan.'

'I have been asking him to stay with me, but he refuses. He could keep himself busy by supervising the gardens. I am sure it would delight Hariprasad too.'

'He's too proud to accept, Pali.'

'Is it because I am the raj nartaki? Like others, does he think I am immoral? Has he lost his faith in me?'

'So many questions?' Priyamvada countered. 'I have no answers to those questions, but knowing him, I don't think it's any of those things,' she said. 'I think it's his self-respect. He wants to be independent. Besides, I don't think Suvarnasena would let him live in this house peacefully, Pali. She will do everything to make him miserable.'

'You're right,' agreed Ambapali. 'She's a malicious woman. Frankly, I am sick of her vitriolic tongue.'

'It takes all kinds to make a world. Forget that woman. She's not worth discussing. Let's talk about the home you are planning to buy for Baba.'

'I wanted to buy a house with a big garden, which will make Baba happy. Also, soon, I will have to give up my position here and live in a house of my own. Someday, Satya and I will marry and have children. All these factors were on my mind while looking for a place.'

'Sounds like a good plan.' Priyamvada nodded her head approvingly. She reached for an apple from the fruit basket and took a bite. 'Have you found such a house?'

Ambapali sat up with excitement. 'Yes! All I have to do is to seal the deal, furnish it, and employ some servants. The hardest part will be to convince my father to move in.'

'It will take a lot of time to do everything. Will you be able to handle everything on your own?'

'Who says I will handle it alone? I will need your help.'

'Do you have any doubts about that? I will be with you all the way.'

'Things have to move fast before the house gets sold to someone else. We will have to do everything in secrecy. Not a word of this should reach our dear friend Suvarnasena.'

'Of course. That woman will only create hurdles in our path.'

'The only problem is money.'

'That should be the least of your worries, Pali. You have enough gold and money to pay for everything. Let's not forget it's *your* money, even though Suvarnasena controls it all.'

'That's exactly the problem. How am I to explain why I need such a sizeable amount? The lady maintains an account of everything that comes as a gift.'

'Why should you explain anything? Just demand the money.' Priyamvada was indignant.

'You don't understand. The curmudgeon won't part with money without a reason, and I don't want to tell her about the house.' There was silence as the two women decided on their course of action. Her eyes shining with excitement, Priyamvada snapped her fingers. 'We will sell some of your jewellery. Less than half of your sets will fetch you the money required for the house.'

'Suvarnasena is sure to smell a rat. She is too smart to be fooled.'

'Most of your jewellery is in my care. We will sell them in small lots, so no one will suspect anything. Besides, those pieces are gifts from your admirers. They belong to you, Pali. Suvarnasena has no right to deny them to you,' she said. 'I fail to understand why you don't get rid of that woman. She is a hurdle in the path of your happiness. Together, we can handle everything.'

'It's not that easy, Priya,' Ambapali sighed. 'We are too young and inexperienced to deal with those devious setthis and temperamental nobles who are at each other's throats for my favours. Suvarnasena has certain skills which we lack. She's shrewd, manipulative, honey-tongued and tactful. Those are essential arsenals required to deal with my patrons. Thanks to her, I have been able to maintain a semblance of dignity and retain my chastity. Besides, she has too many well-wishers in the court. We can't afford to offend them.'

'I guess you are right. We have a lot to learn before we can get rid of her,' Priyamvada agreed.

A few weeks later, an excited pair of women walked into the new house, a double-storey brick affair with extensive grounds. The sale of several sets of jewellery had paid for it, with money left over for the furnishing.

'Just another year, and then we will move here. We will
be free of that wicked woman,' said Ambapali as they walked
around the neglected garden.

Priyamvada parked herself on a stone bench in the garden,
leaned back and began laughing. Her shoulders shaking, she
continued laughing till tears gathered in the corners of her
eyes, threatening to spill over.

'You silly woman,' she said. Her laughter was like a
cascade of rushing water. 'I had forgotten to dream. And now,
you have got me dreaming once again.'

Ambapali had never heard her friend laughing so much.
It was pleasant, like a merrily flowing brook through the
forest. A heavy burden lifted from her heart, and she burst into
laughter too.

Eleven

While things settled for Ambapali, all was not well with the republic. The number of attacks on them had escalated in recent months. The Magadh emperor's ambitions knew no bounds. After vanquishing smaller states, he now cast his covetous eyes on Vaishali.

Although the Vajji army had successfully rebuffed several attacks, the republic's spies had brought disturbing reports about the Magadh army's preparations for a deadlier attack. They were gathering a larger army and equipping their soldiers with better weapons and horses.

That news, coupled with reports of rising disunity among the different clan leaders of the Vajji republic, was causing unease in the assembly. There was disquiet in the sabhagrih as the parishad gathered to discuss the strife between various princes and minor rulers of the confederacy.

'Gentlemen, we are here this evening to discuss the challenges being faced by our republic,' the mahamantri began. 'The Magadh king, Bimbisara, is planning a large-scale attack on Vaishali. Until now, we have been successful in driving back the Magadh forces. The clans have always been united, and our strength lies in the united front we have presented to the enemy. The unity that helped us win is crumbling, and that is a matter of serious concern.'

'The clan chiefs have neglected their armies,' added the senapati. 'Their focus is no longer on the battle. It is our united armies, resources and wealth that made us invulnerable to attack. It is an essential factor if we have to face the mighty Magadh army, which has thousands of foot soldiers, chariots, elephants and horses. I have received reports of Magadh scientists conducting experiments on more efficient weapons made of stronger metals. They are reported to have gathered an arsenal of lethal poisons and trained vishkanyas.'

'All this is very alarming,' exclaimed a minister. 'We can't sit back and wring our hands helplessly.'

'That is precisely the point of this meeting,' said the mahamantri. 'We have to address these concerns and find solutions as urgently as possible.'

'It's a disturbing development,' agreed the king. 'Such a thing has not happened before.'

'I have first-hand reports of discord among the princes. In the recent battle, it was observed that many of them were fighting each other, instead of fighting the enemy,' said the senapati. 'It's a miracle the Magadh soldiers didn't trounce us.'

'My intelligence reports that the Magadh emperor was too confident of victory. That was why he hadn't sent his entire army for the attack.'

'Why was he so sure of victory?' asked the king.

'There can be only one reason. Bimbisara has learned of our disunity.'

His statement caused an uproar in the assembly.

'I think some of us are aware of the reason that has spawned this discord among the princes,' said the koshadhyaksh.

Several eyes swung towards the royal treasurer.

'What do you mean, Amatya?' the king asked.

'The cause is a woman called Ambapali,' Amatya said in self-satisfied tones. He had always been opposed to the appointment of a raj nartaki. Tight-fisted and extremely careful about expenditure, he felt it was a waste of public money. 'She is destroying the peace and stability of our republic.'

There was an uncomfortable silence. Several men shifted in their seats, unwilling to meet the treasurer's piercing gaze. They were guilty of wooing the woman and squandering their money on her. The koshadhyaksh, with his battery of informers, had a list of the names.

'Several princes and setthis have been involved in verbal abuse and scuffles in the raj nartaki's palace,' continued the treasurer.

'It isn't the raj nartaki's fault if they fight over her,' reminded the king. 'My sources tell me that Ambapali tries to keep them away. Also, Suvarnasena is an astute and experienced woman who has enough tact to manage the belligerent ones.'

'Maharaj, the point is not whether she encourages or resists a man. We are discussing the cause of disagreement among the princes,' the treasurer said.

A babel of voices broke out, with a few nodding their heads in agreement.

'I agree with the koshadhyaksh,' said the senapati. 'The main cause of a weak army is dissent and lack of strong leadership. The princes are busy courting the raj nartaki, so they have no time to devote to military matters. An army without a devoted leader is a mob, not an army.'

'A beautiful woman will always attract attention,' said a minister who was one of her wooers. 'The indiscretion of her suitors can't be blamed on her.'

Several voices rose in solidarity with the statement. Arguments broke out and challenges were thrown. Rivals glared at each other, laughed derisively and passed sarcastic comments, trying to embarrass each other.

It was late evening. The members were wearied and tempers were frayed. No amount of sura would get them through the night. The discussion began to derail.

The raj purohit stood up. 'Gentlemen! Let's maintain decorum,' he appealed. 'We are here to address a very serious matter. We are nowhere near finding a solution. The Magadhians have been eyeing our rich mines, and their covetous gaze is fixed upon our territory. There is little doubt that they will defeat us if we continue to fight each other.'

Seeing that he had the attention of the members, the raj purohit continued, 'We should not underestimate the power of our enemies. Don't forget that they are busy fortifying their army while we disintegrate. Does anyone have suggestions on how to deal with the current crisis?'

'We should take the battle into the enemy's territory,' suggested a hot-blooded prince.

'That can be done only after we have sorted out the differences between our members. Together, the 7707 clan members can defeat Bimbisara; divided, we cannot lift a finger.'

'The only way to handle the crisis is by getting rid of the raj nartaki,' suggested a member of the parishad. The Ugra clan ruler was famous for his wild temper and cruel ways.

The parishad members were aghast at his suggestion. Sensing the outrage, he toned down his words. 'We could banish her from the kingdom.'

'That would amount to injustice,' reminded the raj purohit. 'Do we need to carry out such a drastic action against an innocent citizen of the republic? There has to be some other way.'

'Devi Ambapali is a threat to the republic. Getting rid of a single person for the larger good is not injustice. It's statecraft. Wisdom,' contended an aged member.

'Let's have a show of hands,' suggested someone.

A few hesitant hands went up.

'We can't banish our raj nartaki,' protested a young clan leader.

'Why not?' argued the aged member. 'The news of her beauty and talent has spread through the whole of Jambudweepa. The neighbouring kingdoms are envious of our court dancer. They would be happy to appoint her in their court. We all know that Magadh has also been trying to get its dirty hands on Devi Ambapali. All we have to do is banish her from Vaishali. That could buy us peace.'

'Banishing Devi Ambapali will cause public outrage,' opined a grey beard. 'They look upon her as the pride of Vaishali. We can't afford a civil war amid an enemy threat.'

'Well said!' agreed the raj purohit. 'We can't afford to rouse public wrath.'

'We can remove her from the position,' suggested the senapati. 'But we will have to give a valid reason to the public, and I don't think it wise to accept that she is the cause for discord between clan rulers.'

'It would perhaps be simpler to poison her,' suggested a member from the Videha clan. 'We could bribe one of her servants to do the job. That way, no one will get to know. There would be no outcry.'

'That would amount to cowardice. I can't speak for the Videhas, but we Licchavis are no cowards.'

'How dare you call the Videhas cowards?' The enraged clan member unsheathed his sword. 'Take back your words or face my sword.'

'I am not frightened of your sword,' the Licchavi member smirked. 'You proved your cowardice by suggesting that the raj nartaki should be secretly poisoned.'

'Restrain yourselves, gentlemen,' said the king in a stern voice. 'The sabhagrih is not a battlefield. Save your valour for the battlefield. You are here to represent your clans, so I expect you to maintain decorum.'

Mortified, the two members bowed to the king and apologized. An uncomfortable silence hung over the assembly.

Then the raj purohit spoke. 'The Vajji republic has a tradition of appointing the most beautiful woman as nagarvadhu. Although we have not had a nagarvadhu for a few years, there is a precedent. It can't be denied that the tradition was born out of collective wisdom. Beautiful women have caused strife, and this was one way of ensuring that she was available to everyone. Any man who can pay her price has a claim over her.'

There was a moment of deliberation as everyone considered the idea.

'It's an excellent suggestion,' agreed the treasurer finally. 'A nagarvadhu is everyone's property. No single person can wed her and so there can be no rivalry or bloodshed.'

As more heads nodded, it was clear the idea appealed to most members. 'Does the suggestion have the consensus of all the members?' asked the raj purohit.

'Let everyone cast his vote and then we can take a decision,' said the king.

'Should we not have called Devi Ambapali to the court to hear her view on the appointment?' asked a loyal admirer of the raj nartaki. 'It would have been fair to do so.'

'The king is within his rights to take such decisions in the larger interest of the State. There is no need to hear her opinion on this appointment, just as we didn't need to hear her opinion before appointing her as the raj nartaki,' retorted a parishad member.

The raj purohit, who counted the votes, wasn't surprised to find unanimity among the parishad members. They had all voted for a new nagarvadhu.

Twelve

While the parishad was voting on Ambapali's future, the emperor of Magadh was pacing in the council chamber in Rajgrih. His brows were knitted in irritation. Tension radiated from his tall and well-built body. He paused for a few minutes at the window to admire the setting sun and the medley of colour in the sky. He loved that hour of the day, and no matter how busy he was, Bimbisara usually made time to enjoy the sight. But it was not to be that day.

The doors opened and a soldier announced Varshakar, the mahamatya of Magadh. The prime minister was a shrewd man, who had risen to the post by virtue of his intelligence and machinations. His devious manipulations had caused and warded off several wars. Considered a pillar of the Magadh kingdom and a formidable adversary, he was an admired as well as a hated man.

'Pranam, Maharaj.' He bowed reverentially. The king's agitation didn't escape his eyes. He was aware of the reason. The recent attempt at overrunning Vaishali had come to naught once again.

Vaishali was a thorn in Bimbisara's flesh. The ambitious ruler, crowned at fifteen, had proved himself to be an able king. Not only had he avenged the defeat of his father by annexing the kingdom of Anga, but he had also organized a well laid-out plan of expansion that included many other neighbouring kingdoms.

In the initial years of his reign, Bimbisara realized the need to organize a powerful army. Now, the Magadh army was strong enough to strike terror in the breasts of neighbouring regions. It forced the kings of Kosala and Vaishali to buy peace by offering their daughters as wives to him. It was not a poor bargain. Marrying the Kosala princess had brought him Kasi and its substantial revenues. The marriage to the Licchavi princess had resulted in better relations with the republic till things soured.

The king's demand for free passage on the Ganga through the city of Vaishali was rejected by the Vajii confederacy. This had hit their riverine trade. Bimbisara had tried diplomacy and threats, but the Vajjians remained steadfast in their decision.

'What's the progress in our plans to conquer Vaishali?' he asked the mahamatya, coming straight to the point. Anger suffused his golden complexion and his eyes glittered dangerously.

'Despite all warnings, some hot-headed commanders set forth to conquer Vaishali. As expected, the mission resulted in failure. Our soldiers were forced to withdraw.'

The king ignored the barb. 'I am aware of the consequences of that foolhardy mission led by my rash son. What I want to know is why our soldiers could not enter Vaishali.'

'A man of intelligence—'

The king quickly put an end to the mahamatya's sermon.

'Mahamatya, I want to know the precise reason for the Magadh army's inability to enter the city. Was it the lack of courage in our soldiers? Are the weapons inferior, or is it the strategy that failed us?'

'No Maharaj, our soldiers are valiant and loyal. Our weaponry is not inferior, nor is the strategy faulty.'

'What, then, is the reason for their failure?'

'There are several. I would put impatience on top of the list. But, let me give you three other valid reasons. First, the united might of the Vajji confederacy is Vaishali's strongest defence. It is impossible for us to take on the combined army of all the princes. The second factor is the fortification of Vaishali, which makes it formidable. Three of its sides are protected by impenetrable walls that are punctuated by watchtowers at regular intervals. These watchtowers are manned by vigilant guards round the clock. The guards are equipped with arms and brass bugles that can be sounded to warn others as soon as any suspicious activity is noticed. The fourth side of the city has a natural barrier of dense forests and mountains. Also, the river, that—'

'I am aware of these factors,' Bimbisara interrupted impatiently. He wondered why Varshakar was beating around the bush. Clearly, the man liked the sound of his voice. He would have to be brought down a notch or two.

'Allow me to finish, Maharaj. The third reason for our failure was that the attack was untimely. The sudden onset of heavy rains caused the river to swell and reinforcements could not reach in time.'

The emperor spent some time deliberating over his prime minister's words. Was he being too hasty, he wondered. The idea of conquering Vaishali had grown into an obsession.

'So, what do you suggest?' he asked finally.

'We need to be patient,' said Varshakar. 'Victory will be ours the next time around. All we have to do is to plan well and execute that plan efficiently. Besides, the monsoon is not the right time for a battle. Let's use the time to locate the weak spots in the fortification. We can re-equip the soldiers and modernize the weapons too.'

'You're right. Let's discuss this further with the senapati,' Bimbisara said. His mind busy with the points made by the minister, the emperor resumed his pacing of the room.

'There's one more thing, Maharaj. According to my sources, the alliance on which the Vajji republic prided itself is fragmenting. Before long, they will start fighting each other, and that will be our chance to attack.'

'Are you sure about that?' Bimbisara stopped pacing and faced the minister. 'We have tested their unity several times. It's hard to believe that there is infighting. Do you know the reason for it?'

Varshakar smiled slyly. 'It's a woman, as usual. She had caused the minor kings, setthis and princes to come to loggerheads with each other. The rivalry is creating a rift between them.'

'How could a woman cause so much hostility between the princes and minor kings? I find it incredible.' The king pursed his lips in derision.

'It's true, Maharaj. I have it from the most reliable sources. Our spies have sent several reports of the rift. It is said that a smile from her can turn the bravest man into a weak-kneed nincompoop. Her eyes can speak a thousand words and one look brings kings to their knees.'

'Nonsense!'

'It's not nonsense, Maharaj,' the minister said. 'I have received poetic descriptions of the woman. Slender waist, sculpted hips and bust—she has a perfect figure. A complexion like the champa flower and skin as smooth as porcelain . . .'

'Enough!' The emperor put an end to the speech. 'You seem to have taken to poetry now.'

'I am just repeating the words of our spies,' protested the mahamatya. 'Maharaj, I have no time for flippancy or poetry.'

'And who is this woman?' the emperor asked.

'Ambapali. She's the raj nartaki of Vaishali and is said to be the most beautiful woman in Jambudweepa.'

'Impossible!' Bimbisara shook his head. 'She might be the most beautiful woman in Vaishali, but to call her the most beautiful woman in Jambudweepa is surely an exaggeration.'

'I am just repeating what people say, Maharaj.'

'If it's true, she should be in Magadh, dancing in our court.'

'We will have to conquer Vaishali before she agrees to dance in the Magadh court.'

'In that case, I think it's time I go there and meet her.'

The mahamatya was taken aback and silently cursed himself. While describing the raj nartaki, he had not taken the curious nature of the Magadh king into account. While it had resulted in innovations in record-keeping, tax collection, research and weaponry, it had also created complications—such as now.

'You can't go to Vaishali, Maharaj,' he protested, alarmed. 'What if the Vajji soldiers catch you?'

'There's no need to be anxious. I will go in disguise.'

Varshakar remained silent, his mind working furiously. He was convinced it was an unwise decision. 'Give me some time, Maharaj,' he said finally. 'I will present the woman at your court.'

'How do you propose to do that?' Bimbisara narrowed his eyes. His voice tinged with sarcasm, he said, 'Do you think she'll present herself at the Magadh court voluntarily?'

'She won't do that. But I will find a way.' The mahamatya smiled guardedly, aware that he was overstating his abilities. But he had to gain time. 'I beg you not to consider the option of going to Vaishali.'

The emperor remained thoughtful for a few minutes. He wondered what plans were hatching in his minister's mind. It was true that the man had achieved several unimaginable successes, but was he not overreaching in promising something as difficult as presenting the Vaishali raj nartaki at the Magadh court? There was no harm in giving the man a chance, though. In the meantime, he would concentrate on the war plans.

'All right. How long would you require?'

'All I need is three months.' The mahamatya promised rashly.

'I can wait that long,' conceded Bimbisara. 'But not a day more,' he warned. 'After that, either I will visit that city or Vaishali will fall to us.'

Thirteen

'Where are you, Pali?' Priyamvada peeped into yet another room. She had looked all over but couldn't find her friend. *Where could she have gone? It's close to dusk and soon it will be dark.* 'Have you seen Devi Ambapali?' she asked a passing dasi.

'No, devi, I haven't seen her,' replied the dasi. There was concern on her face as she asked, 'Do you want me to ask the others?'

'It's all right!' said Priyamvada quickly. She didn't want the servants to get anxious or to report their concerns to Suvarnasena. 'She must be in the garden. I will find her.'

That morning, the two of them had planned to visit Anand Kanan, where Gautama Buddha and his followers were camped. The enlightened one had a fondness for the city of Vaishali, and made it a point to spend a few days there whenever he passed that way. The sermons he delivered during these visits drew hordes of people to the forest. Ambapali had also heard of the Buddha's arrival and expressed a desire to hear the sermon. However, she had been summoned by the parishad at the same time, so was unable to go. Priyamvada had gone alone to Anand Kanan. Since her village fell on the way, she had made a detour to visit her relatives and that had delayed her return to the mansion. Her relatives had been more hospitable than she expected. They had prepared the choicest of dishes and regaled her with local news. It was late when she returned, and she was in a cheerful mood. She had a lot of gossip to share with her friend.

And now, she couldn't find Ambapali.

Priyamvada walked into the garden at the rear of the mansion. Then she remembered her friend's partiality toward the clutch of mango trees on one end of the garden. There, she found Ambapali under a mango tree, hugging her knees to her chest and sobbing bitterly. The sound of footsteps made her look up. Her dark eyes were vacant and a long strand of hair was stuck to a cheek, wet with tears.

'Priya,' she wailed, and reached for her friend's hand. 'What am I to do?'

'Hush! I am here now.' Priyamvada's comforting arms embraced the distraught girl. 'You are not to cry anymore.'

Ambapali clung to Priyamvada, violent sobs racking her body. 'What am I to do?' she wailed again.

Priyamvada allowed her to cry till she ran out of tears. After a while, her eyes swollen and her throat sore from the sobbing, Ambapali turned to her friend.

'Are you ready now, to share the reason for your sorrow?' Priyamvada asked, still holding her friend.

'I met Satya this afternoon,' Ambapali confessed.

It didn't take any time for Priyamvada to guess the outcome of the meeting. She wished there was a way to wean her friend away from Satya. The fate of their love story had been decided the day Ambapali was made a raj nartaki. A weak man did not make a good lover. Satya was a good man, but not a brave one. Besides, he was sensitive and proud.

The three of them had grown up together, and there were no secrets between them. Priyamvada was aware of the shortcomings of her friends. She knew Satya was not a rash or imprudent man. He was the kind that mulled over matters. Ambapali expected more than he could give. It was true Satya loved Pali, but he would do nothing to endanger her. He, more than anyone else, knew the dangers of defying royal command.

Priyamvada cleared her throat and began speaking, 'Pali . . .'

'Don't, Priya. I know what you will say. We have discussed this many times, but today is different,' Ambapali said. 'The parishad met to discuss an important matter this morning. Can you guess what they debated?' Ambapali stopped and glanced up at Priyamvada, lashes wet. 'They were discussing me; a raj nartaki. Rejoice! Your friend has become such an important person that the parishad discusses her.'

'But . . .'

'Are you surprised?' continued Ambapali. 'So was I. Since when has a mere raj nartaki become important enough to be discussed by the parishad? Well, I have been informed that I am a threat to the unity of the Vajji confederation. The ministers and princes of the confederacy are fighting with each other for my favour. The constant strife has weakened the league. These were their exact words.'

'That's ridiculous!' exclaimed Priyamvada. 'How can you be a cause of the empire's disunity?'

'There's more, Priya. I was told that spies have found out that the Magadh emperor is planning to attack Vaishali. The parishad fears that the disharmony among the members of the confederacy will lead to his victory.'

'The weakness of Vaishali's army cannot be blamed on you!'

'The parishad has hit upon the solution to the discord and the military weakness, it seems. They conveyed their decision to me,' Ambapali continued. 'They have decided to appoint me as the nagarvadhu.'

'What!' Shocked, Priyamvada stared at her friend. This couldn't be true. 'How can they . . .'

'The vultures have been waiting for an opportunity to feast on my body, and now they hold me in their talons.' An ironic smile creased Ambapali's wan face. 'They call it a sacrifice for Vaishali's welfare. It was not a request or a suggestion, mind you. It is an order, and I am to obey it.' Her face contorted in grief.

Priyamvada had no words to console her friend.

'Was it my fault?' Ambapali whimpered pathetically.

'Of course not. These men assume they can own you— that is what is causing all the trouble,' said Priyamvada softly. She sat beside Ambapali and stroked her hair. 'You are the most beautiful and desirable woman in Jambudweepa. Everyone wants to own you.'

There was silence for a few minutes, and then Ambapali grabbed Priyamvada by the shoulders and began shaking the stunned girl. 'Did you hear what I said?' she demanded in a manic manner. 'I am to be the nagarvadhu, the Janpad Kalyani of Vaishali. Do you know what that means? I will be the bride of the entire city. I will be available to every man who can afford to pay for my services. Let no one be fooled by the glorified title. In reality, I will be nothing but a prostitute.'

She threw her head back and burst into loud laughter that had a hysterical edge.

Then, spent after the emotional outburst, the raj nartaki buried her face in her hands and sat silently for a while.

'So, you went to beg Satya for help,' Priyamvada said in a gentle voice. 'And he expressed his helplessness, as he always does.'

Ambapali raised her tear-stained face and looked at her friend. Priyamvada knew her so well. 'Yes, I rushed to him as fast as I could. He had told me once there were rumours of this happening, but I didn't think they would be true. He was aghast on learning about the parishad's decision. And you are absolutely correct about his response to my plea to get married. I know you will say I have no self-respect. What am I to do, Priya? I am desperate. I know of no other way to escape this predicament.'

'I have no words to express my anguish, Pali. I wish there was some way to overturn the decision . . .'

'The men in the confederacy have no reason to protect me. It is Satya who has hurt me the most. I will never forgive him for rejecting my love,' Ambapali said.

'Pali, my dear friend, what could poor Satya have done? He can't fight the king or the mighty men of the parishad. Be strong! Stop looking to him for help. It's your war, and only you can fight it.'

Suddenly, Ambapali's eyes flashed with anger. 'Yes, it's my war. I will fight it the only way I know. The parishad has given me two days to prepare for the ritual announcement.' She caught her breath before continuing, 'You have often told me it's impossible to change one's destiny, and you are right. I cannot change my destiny or the events that are unfolding, but I can definitely put a price on my body. I will put forth a few conditions before I agree to accept the post of nagarvadhu.'

There was a manic glimmer in her eyes as she straightened up and made for her mansion.

'Pali,' Priyamvada called out, anxious about her friend's mental well-being. Ambapali's tone carried an edge of desperation. 'Wait!' She hastened to keep pace with the agitated woman, who was striding determinedly ahead. 'What are you planning to do?'

'I am going to the palace to meet the king. I will put forth my conditions to him, so he can convey them to the parishad.'

'What kinds of conditions do you have in mind, Pali?'

'I want a palace of my own, where my writ will be law,' said Ambapali. 'I shall have the right to appoint my own staff with no interference. There will be no spies in my palace. I will decide the fees for my services, and who I permit to share my bed. Neither the king nor the parishad will have a say in any of these matters.'

'I wonder if the parishad will agree to these conditions,' Priyamvada said. 'It's common knowledge that the mahamatya has his spies in most places, Pali. A raj nartaki and a nagarvadhu entertain many nobles and dignitaries, not only from the republic but from other kingdoms as well. As a result, her residence is a hotbed of intrigue and politics. Tongues loosen under the influence of madira, and people are often indiscreet. They often talk about matters that should not be discussed. Many State secrets are likely to fall into the wrong hands. It's for this reason that the State appoints soldiers and staff with impeccable records. I doubt the parishad will agree to your condition.'

'They may try to bargain, but they have no choice if they want me as a nagarvadhu. In return, I will take the responsibility for taking care of the threats you mentioned. I will threaten to immolate myself in public if they don't agree. The people of Vaishali love their raj nartaki. I don't think they will want to watch me burn. The parishad will definitely not risk the displeasure of its citizens. Think about it, Priya. With the threat of an attack from Magadh hovering over them, an angry public will only aggravate the parishad's troubles.'

Priyamvada was horrified at the thought of Ambapali's immolation. But she did not see how the parishad would give in meekly to the raj nartaki's demands without such grim leverage.

'I have been humiliated, hurt and exploited by everyone,' raged Ambapali. 'I will not let them heap any more filth on me.'

'There must be another way,' Priya mumbled. 'I have been thinking, Pali. There is a simple solution to our problem. I am surprised that it hadn't occurred to me before.'

Ambapali halted and faced her friend. There was a glimmer of hope in her eyes for a few moments, and then her shoulders drooped with despair. 'There are no solutions, Priya.'

'Give me a chance, Pali. Listen to my plan, at least.' In an excited voice, she continued, 'The Vasant Utsav is just a couple of months away. There will be a dance competition once again. Scores of young girls will arrive to compete against you. All you have to do is to let them win. Someone else will be the raj nartaki and you will be free.'

'No, that won't work.' Ambapali shook her head. 'I will be the nagarvadhu in two days' time, and the parishad will have to appoint a new raj nartaki, anyway.'

Darkness had descended by the time the two women walked into the mansion.

'Don't go to the king now,' said Priyamvada. 'You can go in the morning. Let's sleep over the problem tonight.'

'Nothing will change in a few hours, my friend.' Ambapali laughed hollowly. 'They have sealed my fate. All I can do is to put a price on it.'

'Just one more night, please, Pali. Meet the king tomorrow.'

Priyamvada knew nothing would change, but she didn't want Ambapali to rush into a decision. It took reasoning and arguments, but she managed to persuade her friend.

'One more thing. Please keep this from Suvarnasena for the moment. I don't want her gloating over the prospects,' said Priyamvada.

'I am sure she has learnt of the development.' Ambapali's lips curled disdainfully 'That woman has spies all over town.'

Priyamvada clasped her friend's hands as they parted near Ambapali's bedroom. 'You must relax. Things will be better tomorrow.' Her words sounded feeble even to her ears, but there was nothing else to offer.

'Don't leave me alone, Priya.' Ambapali appealed as she turned to leave. 'Please stay and talk to me.'

They went out to Ambapali's private terrace. A gibbous moon surfaced from its sea of clouds. The marble chaise longue furnished with silk cushions beckoned invitingly, but Ambapali lay down on the thick mattress laid on the cool marble floor of the terrace. A subtle scent of flowers tickled their senses. Their privacy protected by the fragrant curtain of flowering vines, the two friends reclined amidst the multi-hued flowers growing in the beds along the parapet. Designed for a soothing ambience, the terrace was Ambapali's favourite place within the mansion. On hot summer nights, when the room felt claustrophobic, she escaped to the terrace to sleep under the open sky with the moon and the stars keeping a watch on her.

'It's so peaceful here.' She closed her eyes, inhaling the scents of citrus and flowers in the tranquil terrace. 'It's easy to forget all my worries when surrounded by so much beauty.'

'Would you like me to fetch you a glass of soma to soothe your nerves, or would you prefer aam or chandan panna?'

'A glass of maireya, please,' replied Ambapali. She preferred fruit and floral concoctions, but tonight was different. Her fraught nerves required something stronger.

Half an hour later, the wine had helped soothe her a little. 'I don't know what I would have done without you,' she said, taking another sip. Under the heady influence of the wine, life seemed almost pleasant. 'Do you regret coming here to live here with me?'

'Not for a moment have I regretted that decision,' replied the loyal friend. She had always felt fiercely protective of Ambapali.

'You are all I have. My father doesn't want to live with me, and my lover has rejected me. There's no one but you now.'

'I wonder if Suvarnasena has a family,' said Priyamvada, keen to change the direction of their conversation. 'I have never heard her mention one.'

'Speaking of the lady, where is she? I haven't seen her for a while. Not that I miss her,' Ambapali said. She was not used to drinking alcohol, and even the little she'd had was making her tipsy.

'She's indisposed—Nayantara told me.'

Nayantara—a domineering and spiteful person—had been appointed by Suvarnasena to act as the teacher's eyes and ears. Most of the dasis avoided her, and so did Ambapali.

'It's all for the good. I can't bear to have her nosing around tonight.'

'She's an unpleasant person,' agreed Priyamvada.

'But the unpleasantness is carefully concealed.'

'You are right. She's too clever to reveal her true personality. It took me a long time to see the greedy and venomous person hiding behind the mask.'

'She's not all evil. There are many good qualities in that woman.'

'Name a few,' challenged Priyamvada. She was happy Ambapali was distracted from her situation.

'She has an excellent knowledge of dance and the techniques of seduction,' Ambapali said, counting them off on her fingers. 'She's an accomplished flirt and an expert finance manager. She's also a skillful administrator.'

'That's true. She's managed your finances well. She runs this household efficiently and keeps the undesirable men away from you.'

'She also pushes me towards the moneyed shreshties and princes, which is something I detest. It's hilarious the way she plays up to Kumarabhadra,' Ambapali chuckled. 'She ordered me to entertain him one evening, but I couldn't stomach the repulsive touch and malodorous mouth. So, she began entertaining him herself.'

'You mean that old and toothless shreshti? There's a reason why she plays up to him. That man is one of the richest in Vaishali. He's flattered by her coquettish ways.'

'No wonder he gifted her a very expensive set of jewellery. Suvarnasena was showing it to me the other day. And that's just one of the few jewel sets he's gifted.'

'Should I try my charms on him?' Priyamvada batted her eyelashes and dimpled sultrily, and the two friends giggled. 'It could get me some expensive jewellery.'

'Suvarnasena would have no chance if you flirted with the man. You are a beautiful woman, Priya.'

'Nonsense!' Priyamvada was completely unaware of her own beauty.

'You won't have to use your charms on the old shreshti. I have observed several young men ogling you. I will introduce you to the right man, only after I am sure of their intentions,' Ambapali said.

'I am sure you will do that, but I want to try my hand at flirting like Suvarnasena.' Priyamvada mimicked the teacher's swaying walk and winked at her, sending Ambapali into peals of laughter.

The two women drank steadily and Ambapali turned more emotional as she downed more maireya, laughing and crying by turns.

'Beauty is a curse. It has ruined my life. It's brought me nothing but unhappiness.' Turning to her friend, the dancer asked, 'Do you think I am nothing more than a beautiful body?'

Surprised at the sudden turn of conversation, Priyamvada hastened to reassure her. 'Don't let anyone tell you that. You are the most intelligent and talented woman I have ever known.'

'Then why don't *they* see that? Why do they not understand that I have feelings, just like every other person? That I might want different things for my life.'

Priyamvada had no words to console the troubled woman. They sat shrouded in a veil of silence, struggling with their emotions. Several minutes passed, and then Ambapali sat up and squared her shoulders. Setting her jaw firmly, she declared, 'From this day, men may possess my body. However, no man shall reach my heart.'

The next morning, Ambapali presented herself at court. As she had predicted, the threat of immolation had the desired effect. Initially, there were objections from the parishad members when she put forth her conditions. The wiser ministers requested her to reconsider the terms, while the fiery ones rejected her proposal straight away.

'Devi, it is not right of you to make such unfair demands,' said the king. 'Won't you reconsider?'

She bowed reverently. 'With all due respect, Maharaj, is it fair to auction my body every night? Is it fair to force me into prostitution, just because my body distracts and disunites men? Has anyone considered my feelings or thoughts? The decision to make me a prostitute was made by the eminent members of the parishad. It is not my choice.' Her voice laced with bitterness, she continued, 'Every seller has the right to price his goods. Since I am being forced to sell myself, shouldn't I be allowed to quote the price?'

A deafening silence fell over the hall. No one met her eyes.

'Would any of you dream of placing a daughter or sister in this situation?' she challenged. 'I am someone's daughter. My father may be poor, but he is a proud man. Unfortunately, he is an insignificant citizen of this republic, and powerless to stop this auction. So, he must live in humiliation for the rest of his life.'

Ambapali saw several heads hanging in shame.

They asked her to wait in another room till the parishad reached a decision. Suvarnasena, who had accompanied her to the court, was aghast at Ambapali's daring.

'Have you gone mad?' she hissed.

'No, I have come to my senses, devi.' Ambapali turned her smouldering eyes to the woman. 'People have toyed with me too long. No more. Not without paying a hefty price. When I came here, I was an innocent village girl. In the past few months, I have learnt that money is the most important thing. It can control everything in the world. All I am doing is setting a price. What's wrong with that?'

'They can declare you a traitor,' said the teacher. 'They can put you in the dungeon or get you killed.'

Her statement seemed to amuse Ambapali. She threw back her head and laughed till tears stung her eyes.

'Do you think I am interested in living like a common ganika? I might as well be dead.'

Taken aback by the cynicism of the once docile girl, Suvarnasena was lost for words.

After a long and heated debate, the parishad members came to a decision. Summoning her to the hall, the chief minister declared that they agreed to all her conditions.

He uttered platitudes. 'Devi, you are Vaishali's pride. You are one of the most eminent citizens of the republic, and we would not want any harm to come to you.' The parishad had decided to grant her the use of the Shweta Shatadal Prasaad. She had free reign over her staff, and neither the king nor the parishad was to interfere.

The palace assigned to Ambapali was located at a distance from the city and suited everyone. The men who availed of the nagarvadhu's services would have the desired privacy, and Ambapali would have her private dominion.

It was a busy day for Ambapali and Priyamvada as they visited the mansion and discussed plans for the next chapter of their lives. Seclusion brought with it some unpleasantness. The palace was in a beautiful location, but it was also a favoured target of thieves. The two women agreed that they would need a sound security system to protect the mansion from undesirable elements.

The morning of Ambapali's initiation dawned fresh and beautiful. The birds chorused, buds bloomed and the air was crisp. It was a day designed for happiness, but gloom pervaded Ambapali's quarters.

As usual, Suvarnasena was unconcerned about Ambapali's feelings. 'Why are you looking so morose?' she demanded. 'You should be glowing with happiness.'

'There's nothing to feel happy about,' responded the despondent girl.

'Don't be ridiculous, Pali,' scolded the teacher. 'You will soon be a nagarvadhu. It is the dream of every courtesan. Do you realize what the position entails? Riches beyond your imagination will fill your coffers. You will have powerful men falling at your feet,' she gushed.

'You must have been sorry to miss out on the chance,' remarked Priyamvada caustically. 'You seem to be quite enchanted with the idea of the benefits that come with the post of a nagarvadhu.'

The sarcasm went straight over Suvarnasena's head. Sighing wistfully, she said, 'Unfortunately, the practice was halted for several years after a nagarvadhu committed suicide.'

Priyamvada and Ambapali were shocked to hear that. 'Tell us what happened,' Priyamvada said.

'The incident took place about six years ago. Kumudini was a sweet, simple girl from a poor family, and very beautiful. Men began eyeing her from when she was just eight years old. Her father was approached by many, old and young. All of them wanted to keep her as a concubine, but no one offered to marry the girl. Kumudini caught the attention of several setthis and even the king was keen on her. Finally, the parishad made her the nagarvadhu to keep everyone happy.'

'Poor Kumudini,' whispered Ambapali. The girl's tragic tale was a mirror of her own.

'Did she have no say in the matter?' asked Priyamvada.

'Does anyone have a say when the parishad decides something?' countered Suvarnasena. 'Kumudini could not handle the physical and emotional demands made on her. Three months later, she jumped into a well and died. She was only seventeen. Her five brothers paraded her body through the streets demanding justice. There was a huge outcry in Vaishali, and the Vajji confederacy was forced to halt the practice of appointing nagarvadhus.'

Priyamvada was aghast. 'Why then, or how, has this evil practice been revived?'

'The parishad consists of men with cunning minds,' Suvarnasena said, shrugging. 'They inserted a useful lacuna in the ordinance regarding the practice of appointing nagarvadhus. It states that a nagarvadhu can be appointed if there is severe fragmentation within the members of confederacy that can cause a threat to the State.'

She turned to Ambapali. 'Now, let's get you dressed. You are to look like a bride this morning.'

Priyamvada rolled her eyes as the woman continued to chatter.

'There is no need to be anxious. The rituals are pretty much like those of a traditional wedding,' Suvarnasena explained to her pupil. 'The only difference is that you will be given away to the State, instead of a man. I would have happily accepted the post of a nagarvadhu, had it been offered to me.' She sighed as she placed the choicest of jewellery sets in front of Ambapali to select from.

'What a pity indeed,' Priya said, shooting a sly look at her friend.

This time, her sarcasm hit the target.

'You don't value the offer because you can't imagine the power a nagarvadhu wields,' Suvarnasena said caustically. 'She is more powerful than a queen. Feted and revered by the nobles, a nagarvadhu can influence the very politics of the State.'

Ambapali wished the woman would stop talking. She had no desire to listen to the powers and privileges of a nagarvadhu. Her head was aching, and she felt wobbly on her feet as she got dressed.

'You look more beautiful than an apsara,' Priyamvada said as she assisted her friend towards the door.

A carriage, drawn by four white horses, was waiting for her. Festooned and bedecked, it befitted the status of a nagarvadhu. Ambapali's heart sank as she climbed into it.

Royal proclaimers had gone around town on horses, beating drums and announcing the appointment of Ambapali as a nagarvadhu the previous evening. As a result, the streets were lined with hundreds of people waiting to see the raj nartaki who was being elevated to the post of nagarvadhu after so many years. Jostling for a better view, they cheered and showered petals on her as she disembarked from her carriage. The procession had reached the abhishek pushkarni, where the ritual would take place.

Feeling like a sacrificial lamb, Ambapali walked towards the altar set up near the lake. She struggled to control the emotions welling inside, but ensured that her face remained neutral; a brave front.

The pushkarni was a heavily guarded area, with several rows of barriers. Soldiers stopped ordinary citizens from entering the area nearest the lake, which was reserved for rich and influential setthis and princes. Now, they showered gold coins on the woman who would soon be made available to them.

The abhishek pushkarni, with its clear water, was where kings bathed before being crowned. Surrounded by white marble steps all around, the water was believed to have healing properties. Ordinary citizens of Vaishali were not allowed to bathe in the lake. Even the parishad members were granted the honour only once in a lifetime, after they were elected ministers, at the time of their swearing-in. Ambapali was acutely conscious of the prestige associated with a bath in the lake. It was a sacred ritual, one that would elevate her status.

She was divested of all ornaments and told to change into a sheer white muslin antariya and a white kanchuki before taking a dip. Every curve of her body now clearly visible under the wet clothes, Ambapali felt herself shrinking with embarrassment under the penetrating male gazes. Her effort to hide her breasts behind a curtain of thick hair seemed futile. Even the priest was momentarily distracted at the sight of the woman before him. The others stared unabashedly.

Recovering, the priest chanted some mantras and sprinkled flowers in symbolic purification, after which she was led towards the decorated marble platform where the rest of the ceremony would take place. Like an automaton, she followed their instructions.

The king and the parishad had assembled on the platform.

Ambapali was asked to take a seat in front of the havan, where the priest was feeding the fire. He began to chant sacred mantras. She was instructed to pour ghee, honey, sandalwood and flowers into the havan kund. Her eyes filled with tears as she stood up and took the ceremonial seven rounds around the havan kund at his behest.

The symbolism didn't escape her. It was like a marriage, just as Suvarnasena had said. The bride was present, but there was no bridegroom, mused Ambapali as she threw the garland into the fire.

Seven vows completed the ceremony. They were the vows that would bind her forever. From the first vow, in which she promised to abide by the duties of a bride to the members of the gana parishad without bias or partiality towards a single person, to the last vow that demanded her to remain faithful to the confederacy and its laws, she parroted everything dictated by the priest. In the end, she was asked to pray to the Sun God for strength and perseverance.

In return, she could expect respect and honour from the State and the gana parishad, said the priest.

With those rituals, Ambapali was declared as the janpath kalyani nagarvadhu of Vaishali. She was now the bride of the entire city of Vaishali.

It was a declaration that her body was now for sale.

Fourteen

It was now four years since the day of the Vasant Utsav when Ambapali had been declared as the raj nartaki. In the very first year, she had realized the reality of the world she now inhabited. This was a world very different from the one she had left behind. It was a world besieged by greed, lust and selfishness. This was a make-believe world, not a real one. It had no place for virtue and vulnerability. She had stepped out of the protective cocoon spun by her father and friends. She now had to take control of her life and protect her interests. Bit by bit, she had shed her vulnerability and insecurity and donned an armour few could penetrate. Her sparkling eyes rarely twinkled with wonder and excitement. The smile never reached the eyes. The effervescence was a façade. Disillusionment and heartbreak can harden the most sensitive of hearts. By the fourth year, toughened by circumstances, she had turned into a perspicacious woman.

She was in the business of making men happy, one she handled with aplomb.

There were extravagant celebrations and ostentatious pageantry, all serving to burnish the status of one woman— Ambapali. Adulation of her beauty and talent, which had been confined to the adjoining kingdoms, now travelled to far-off places. Wealthy traders, princes of various clans, spoilt sons of rich men, State officials and travelers from all over the map arrived each evening with gifts of expensive jewellery, gold and silk. The young princes were ready to lay their lives for one glance from the empress of their heart.

The wealth that poured into her coffers rivalled that of the richest setthi of the region. It was more than the cumulative wealth of the parishad members and the king.

They came for all kinds of reasons. Some came for romance and entertainment. Some to trade information or strike important deals. Some to establish diplomatic ties. Some to spy.

Seasons changed. So did the agendas. One thing that remained unchanged was the ambition to visit the nagarvadhu's palace. Wine, music and wealth flowed every evening there, as did fun and gaiety.

The Shweta Shatadal Prasaad, built of white marble, stood in the centre of a lotus-filled lake, rich in fish and waterfowl. A sense of tranquility pervaded the place. It was connected to land by an arched and elaborately carved wooden bridge, which ended with ornate gateways festooned with flower-bearing creepers. Further out, the Sinh Dwar led into a large garden where fountains bubbled and exquisite sculptures of animals, gods and demons were strategically placed to create a beautiful ambience.

A medley of chirping birdcalls arose from parakeets, cockatiels, budgies and love birds nesting on the trees, while rabbits, deer and peacocks—all gifts from Ambapali's suitors— roamed fearlessly.

Scores of servants, soldiers and gardeners looked after the complex. The administration of the palace was in

Suvarnasena's capable hands, a responsibility that brought her great joy. Whether it was mediating a fight between the servants and the cooks, the recruitment of soldiers and dancers or the management of supplies, she carried out each task with remarkable efficiency. What she enjoyed most was the accounting of the expensive gifts that came each evening. It was an enormous task that required the gold to be weighed, coins counted, and the jewellery and artefacts to be evaluated and recorded. Few people in the republic could boast of handling so much wealth. With the help of an accountant, she maintained meticulously detailed account books.

Every evening, perfumed water was sprinkled around the complex, incense was lit along the path and the gates were draped with fragrant roses and jasmine. The marble palace shimmered in the light of hundreds of lamps. Musicians seated in the garden tuned their instruments, and soon the melodious notes of the evening ragas floated in the wind. Young girls greeted the princes and setthis as they arrived in palanquins and chariots.

The patrons were led into the enormous, extravagantly decorated hall in which was a stage where dance performances took place. The breeze from the river blew in through the large, open windows, lifting the soft, flowing curtains and bringing with it the scent of myriad flowers from the garden. There were low couches with silk cushions and bolsters for the men to sit and loll upon. Silver platters heaped with fruits and nuts, wine carafes and flower arrangements flanked each of the couches. The aroma of incense burning in brass holders filled the air.

Once the men had settled, they were served expensive wine and exotic food by seductively-dressed women. These

women, handpicked by Ambapali, were skilled in the art of
flirting, dancing and entertaining the visitors. They could speak
several languages, converse intelligently on many subjects, play
chaupar and were excellent dancers.

Wine, women, dance and music. There was enough to
keep the men entertained. Gambling was a popular activity.
People lost and made fortunes. The losers drowned their
frustration in wine, while the winners spent their winnings on
the beguiling women in the hall.

It was only after midnight, when most of the patrons were
drunk, that Ambapali made a regal entry into the hall. She
bewitched admirers with her smile. They vied with each other
for a place next to the nagarvadhu, sighing with longing as she
moved out of reach of their grasping hands. Sometimes, she
obliged them with a performance on the veena. Sometimes she
sat with a group of men and gambled, while the servants plied
them with food and wine. They willingly lost their money to
the enchantress.

Occasionally, she would consent to spend time in a private
room with a chosen few. Special dishes and rare wines were
served to them. Distinguished patrons fought and spent an
immense amount of money for the honour, undeterred by the
fact that very few privileged ones would be allowed into her
bed. The price of entering that bed was based on the whims
and fancies of the nagarvadhu. It was not money alone that
dictated her choice. The frustrated ones called her whimsical,
volatile and fickle. The fortunate ones remained bewitched.

Ambapali's personal chamber was sacrosanct. Simple and
unostentatious, it was a place that remained untouched by
lust and hedonism. The nagarvadhu had no control over the
raucous atmosphere of the rang mahal, but she was determined

to keep those elements outside the doors of her private chamber. The room was absolutely unlike what one would have expected from a ganika's chamber.

'I don't want to lose touch with the past,' she had told Priyamvada when they had first moved to the mansion, and her friend had tried to furnish the room with luxuries befitting her status. 'One day, when all this is over, I would like to get back to my simple life. This is a nightmare, and like all nightmares, it has to end someday.'

She slept on the floor, despite the enormous bed that occupied one side of the room. Her only indulgence was the huge, east-facing balcony that offered a mesmerizing view of the sunrise. No matter how late she went to bed, Ambapali rarely missed the magical hour. Her heartbeat never failed to quicken at the sight of the golden rays bursting on the horizon, their dazzle frightening away the darkness.

Someday, just like the rising sun, someone will wipe away the darkness in my life. She would draw a deep breath and prepare herself to face the new day and the challenges that came with it.

Fifteen

As time passed, Ambapali continued to fulfil her duties—smiling, entertaining and dancing. Dance, which had been her primary passion, was just another chore now. Nothing affected her anymore. Happiness, sorrow, frustration—she had seen them all. There were subtle changes in her personality as the months passed. From an unsure and gentle girl, she had matured into a confident and commanding person. Priyamvada's eyes had missed nothing. She could not come to terms with the transformation in her friend. Gone was the naïve village girl who delighted in simple things like plucking fruit from a tree or playing hide and seek. She remembered the wonder in Pali's eyes as the two of them had watched a beautiful butterfly emerging from a nondescript chrysalis.

The new Ambapali was a reckless, ruthless hedonist. The more her father and Satyakirti distanced themselves from her, the more arrogant and callous she became. The look in her eyes was unrecognizable. Those beautiful eyes that had twinkled in merriment were now dull and lustreless. Her smile never reached the eyes.

More surprising was the streak of cruelty that grew apparent in Ambapali. She had taken to going for hunts with her paramours, consorting with rash and violent young men, and ignoring the artistic ones. The blood sport seemed to bring her joy.

The generosity and philanthropy that had been part and parcel of Ambapali's nature had begun to dissipate. In the early days of her reign as a raj nartaki, and later as the nagarvadhu, she had won everyone's hearts by her kindness. No one went back empty handed from her abode. Beggars and the needy lined the temple she visited every morning, showering her with their blessings. Food, blankets, clothes—she distributed them without a second thought.

'We are privileged to have a roof over our heads and food in our bellies. These poor people have neither. Wealth is not for hoarding. It should spread happiness,' she had said when Suvarnasena protested the generous donations she made to various charities.

Not content with giving alms, she spent generously on the construction of new temples, homes for the homeless and free meals for the poor. But, over time, she stopped looking for opportunities to do good and was content with amusing herself. The turnaround in her friend's attitude pained Priyamvada, who had been proud of Ambapali's kind nature. The Pali she knew was a gentle, giving woman. She prayed that this was just a passing phase caused by emotional turmoil. The differences between the two friends were growing and their relationship had begun to fray.

Ambapali continued to try to provide for her father, though. The beautiful mansion she had bought for him had been furnished, but lay vacant because he refused to move there. She'd had many dreams when she bought it. Dreams of settling her father in the luxuriously appointed mansion with ample greenery all around. He had been a gardener all his life, and she had taken pains to create an environment he would like; yet, he resisted.

Once again, she tried to sway his decision.

'It's a beautiful home with huge gardens, located right on the riverbank. Besides, it is very close to the royal orchard. It is an exclusive neighbourhood too—only the richest of setthis and a couple of ministers can afford to build their houses there.' Ambapali sat at her father's feet, her eyes glowing with pride. 'You will love it.'

'That's very nice, my child,' said Dharma Datta, stroking her head absently, his eyes distant and sad.

Dharma Datta had seen the lurking ambition in Ambapali's eyes. She had changed. Her bearing was arrogant and her manner condescending. He wasn't sure he liked the changes in his daughter. He had heard people talking about her. Temptress. Enchantress. Bewitcher. Heartless. They had many names for Ambapali. Satyakirti's sensitive eyes had spotted the changes too, and he had gradually distanced himself from the woman he had once loved.

The doting father lived in denial for a long time, refusing to believe what people said. He loved his daughter too much to admit her flaws, but he could no longer ignore them. His illusions shattered, Dharma Datta still clung to unrealistic hopes that she would revert to her former self.

Soon after she became the raj nartaki, the proud man had decided to not take money from her, and now that she was a nagarvadhu, he had no wish to cash in on the opportunity. He continued to refuse financial help despite her persistent efforts.

'So, when do you want to move into the house?' she asked.

He remained silent. Ambapali was too perceptive to be deceived.

'You are not happy,' she complained. 'Your eyes belie the words you speak. Baba, you can't continue to live here in this tiny, dark and damp house,' she said. 'Your daughter is a rich woman now. The house I have chosen for you is magnificent. It has large grounds which you can turn into orchards. You can appoint a couple of gardeners and supervise their work. That will keep you busy. Believe me, Baba, you will be happy there.'

Irked by his hesitation, she continued, 'You don't have to work for anyone, anymore. You can be your own master. I will look after you.'

'Bless you, my child. I am touched by your concern,' he finally broke his silence. 'But I can't allow you to look after me. I will continue to toil as long as my limbs support me.'

'Your self-sacrificing attitude is helping no one. I am tired of your rigidity and uncompromising attitude. All I am asking for is a chance to make amends.' Anger sparked in her tone.

'What do you want to make amends for, Pali? You have done no wrong.'

'I feel guilty for leaving you all alone in this house,' she cried.

'You were forced to leave this house. You have done no wrong, my child.' He reached out to her.

'If I have done no wrong, why the punishment?'

'I have no wish to punish you. Why do you say that?'

'Then why are you denying me the pleasure of looking after you?' she said. 'I feel so helpless!'

Choking down tears of rage and frustration, she bit the inside of her lip so hard that she tasted the warm saltiness of blood. Her jaw tightened with the effort of holding back the tears. She cried, 'Why are you doing this? I have been hurt more than I can bear. You don't have to add to my wounds.'

Remorseful, he reached out for her hands. 'Pali, my child,' said Dharma Datta. 'I will die before I hurt you. All I have wanted is your happiness since the day I found you in the orchard. I understand your feelings, but I want you to understand my compunctions. I am an old man who has lived by certain principles. You can't expect me to abandon them at this stage of life. I am sorry, but I want to die in this house. I owe it to myself.' In a softer voice, he added, 'This house holds many memories for me. It is to this house that I brought your mother after our wedding. It is here that she breathed her last. This is where you grew up. How can I leave this house?'

There was a great sadness in his voice as he turned down his daughter's proposal one more time. He was poor, but a proud and sensitive man. There were so many things he could have said. The incident about his visit and the rude words uttered by Suvarnasena, for instance, but he had no wish to hurt his daughter. He left them unsaid.

Instead, he hung his head in silence. There were no words to express his anguish. Ambapali cast one last look at her father and stormed out of the house. Minutes later, he heard her whipping the horses hitched to the carriage. The sound of the horses' hooves beat a tattoo with the beats of his heart as Ambapali drove back to her palace. The royal gardener could no longer recognize his daughter.

She was a stranger.

One morning, when Ambapali had gone on a hunt with a Sakyan prince, Priyamvada decided to visit Dharma Datta. She knew that the father was worried about his daughter. As expected, Dharma Datta was delighted to see her. He bustled around the kitchen and returned with a plate heaped with food. A burst of aromas wafted through the room, whetting her appetite. There was a spinach preparation, lentils, shrimps fried to a crisp, venison and karambha topped with a generous dollop of ghee. It was quite obvious that the man had spent a lot of time in the kitchen. Priyamvada wondered why he had prepared so much food. Also, this wasn't the usual daily fare. A gardener couldn't afford to eat a meal this elaborate every day.

'Finish the food or I won't allow you to leave,' he said, placing the plate before her and sitting with a satisfied smile.

'This is a lot of food, uncle,' Priyamvada protested. 'I can't have it alone. Share it with me, please.'

'It's said that every grain of food has the name of a person written on it,' he said and smiled. 'My sixth sense has been telling me that someone would share the meal with me. Fried fish is Pali's favourite dish, and I was reluctant to enjoy the meal alone. God heard my prayers and sent you here.'

'But . . .'

'You may not recall the importance of this day, my child,' said Dharma Datta with a wistful expression on his face. 'Today is a special day. It's the day I found Pali under the mango tree. We have always celebrated this day as the luckiest one of our lives. I wonder if she remembers.'

Had Pali had gone on a hunting expedition for this very reason, Priyamvada thought. Had she done it knowing it would hurt the old man? Was it her way of exacting revenge? She couldn't imagine Pali being unkind to her father. Perhaps it had slipped her mind. Priyamvada wanted to make Dharma Datta happy. He watched with satisfaction as she polished off all the shrimps and licked her fingers clean.

'This is delicious!' she exclaimed. 'I will tell Pali that she missed a wonderful meal.'

'I don't know how she could have forgotten. This is the first time she is not with me on this day.' His eyes moistening, he took Priyamvada's hand in his own and asked, 'Tell me the truth, child. Is Pali angry because I refused to live in the house she bought for me? Is that the reason she's not come today?'

'No, uncle,' Priyamvada hastened to reassure the unhappy man. 'She had to go for an important event this morning. You know how they invite her and often she can't deny them her presence. In fact, I am here because she asked me to visit you today.'

Convinced by her lie, he said, happily, 'I knew it. Pali will never let me down.' Hastening to the kitchen, he packed some shrimps and venison in a clay pot and handed it to Priyamvada. 'Please carry this with you. I know she can afford shrimps and venison any time she wants, but they won't be prepared by her father's hands.'

'I can't remember my father, but I can imagine what he would have been like thanks to you,' Priyamvada said to the kindly man, overcome with affection.

Dharma Datta's words continued to ring in her ears as she travelled back to the palace. Although she had been coaxing Ambapali to visit her father, the last argument between the two seemed to have driven a wedge between them. Priya knew they were both hurting, but each one was waiting for the other to take the first step. Pali was being unreasonable. She resolved to take up the matter with her once again.

That was not to be. It was the month of Ashwin, a season Ambapali termed romantic. The rhythmic, gentle showers evoked her craving for the fritters prepared by her father. It was late evening, and the two friends were regaling each other with childhood anecdotes when Suvarnasena walked into the chamber, wearing a sorrowful expression. Priya narrowed her eyes and waited for the woman to speak. She was a better judge of human behaviour than Ambapali, and it had not taken her long to notice Suvarnasena's chameleon-like ability to change expressions to suit her purpose. She was instantly on the alert, trying to discern what had brought the crafty woman to the room. The woman's entry into their room invariably meant trouble. Taking Ambapali's hand in her own, Suvarnasena turned tearful eyes towards the nagarvadhu.

'My dearest child!' Suvarnasena wiped away the tears flowing down her cheeks. 'I have the unpleasant task of breaking sad news to you.'

Instantly alert, Priya pushed away the woman and hugged her friend in the protective circle of her arms.

'My father . . .' Ambapali's limpid eyes darted from one woman to another, as she tried to fight her rising fear. Her heart threatened to burst, as she shook Suvarnasena and cried, 'tell me it's not about my father.'

Priya's efforts to shield her friend from a shock failed, as she heard the woman's cold voice confirming their worst fear. She could discern the gloating note in Suvarnasena's words.

'I'm afraid it is. He is dead.'

At first unbelieving. Then aghast, Ambapali collapsed in her friend's arms. 'No! That can't be,' she wailed, rocking herself to and fro and weeping piteously.

Her deep, heartbroken sobs wrenched Priya's heart. She felt as if her entrails had been scooped out, leaving a hollow that could never be filled. Dharma Datta had been a father to her as much as he had been to Pali.

Struggling to control her grief, Priya squared her shoulders and pushed Suvarnasena out of the room, but not before seeing her victorious smirk. Pali's grief seemed to delight the wicked woman. Rushing to her friend's side, she took her crumpled, shivering body in her arms.

It was much later that she confronted Suvarnasena and learned the truth. Dharma Datta had been bitten by a venomous snake while working in the orchard. He died under the very mango tree where he had found Ambapali.

Sixteen

Varshakar's three-month reprieve had ended a while back; he had failed to keep his promise of presenting Ambapali at the Magadh court. In the meantime, she had become the nagarvadhu of Vaishali.

Bimbisara was not one to allow grass to grow under his feet, as the mahamatya attempted to work a miracle. Once he wanted something, the Magadh emperor was unstoppable. His ambition to have Ambapali as his raj nartaki grew with each passing day, as did his desire to defeat and conquer the Vajji republic. Its rich mines, fertile territory and the lure of trading opportunities fed Bimbisara's covetousness. The nagarvadhu was but another reason for war.

In the lull between the many exigencies of ruling, the emperor found his mind switching back to Ambapali. For the past few months, he had heard men extolling the talents of the beautiful woman. How she was intelligent beyond belief. How she danced like an apsara. That her rendition of the ragas on the veena could offer a challenge to Raja Udayan, the king of Kaushambi, who was the best-known exponent of the instrument.

I want her in Magadh by any means. He slammed a clenched fist against the wall. Unable to sleep, he had been pacing the floor of his chamber in great agitation. *I will offer her as much wealth as she desires*, he decided.

A few days later, he sent an emissary with an offer to Ambapali, an offer generous enough to tempt any woman. Or so he thought. His emissary returned to say that Ambapali had dismissed the offer angrily. 'How dare you bring such a proposal?' she had asked. 'Magadh has done its best to subjugate Vaishali and never succeeded. Your emperor is a greedy man who thinks money can buy him any woman he desires. Tell him this dancer is not for sale. He will have to conquer Vaishali before he gets me to dance in his court.'

Bimbisara was furious. *How dare she spurn my offer? Conquer Vaishali? If that is what she wishes, it shall be so. I will bring her in chains if required. I vow to possess Ambapali, body and soul, if that's the last thing I do.*

But first, I must find out if she is as beautiful as everyone claims, and for that, I shall have to visit Vaishali.

The more he thought about her, the more determined he was to meet the nagarvadhu of Vaishali. This time, he would let no one deter him from his decision. He would defy the mahamatya.

The sky had darkened as clouds gathered. His eyes glittering in the lights from the crystal chandeliers hanging from the ornately carved ceiling, he called for Varshakar.

'Pranam, Maharaj,' the mahamatya said in greeting. He knew exactly what the emperor was about to say.

Bimbisara was not likely to have forgotten about the promise, but that did not worry him as much as the thought of the emperor leaving for Vaishali. The time was still not ripe for a war with the Licchavis, who, after being fractionalized, had united once again. Engaging a well-fortified enemy at this time would be unwise. As he thought this, the dark and heavy clouds that had covered the sky gave way to a torrent of rain that poured over the city, its path lit with streaks of lightning. Not the season for romance or war.

The mahamatya had no intention of pandering to the whims of the emperor. Obsessed with the idea of possessing Ambapali, it was as though he had taken leave of his senses. The minister had gone through his arguments on the way to the royal chamber.

'I hope you recall the conversation we had and the subsequent promise made by you.' Bimbisara's voice was tinged with sarcasm. 'It's a long time since you made your promise, but the nagarvadhu is nowhere near Magadh.'

Varshakar bowed his head reverentially and replied in a regretful voice, 'My humble apologies, Maharaj. More essential aspects of the kingdom have kept me from keeping my word.'

'You think that bringing the nagarvadhu to our court is not an important matter?' countered the irate emperor.

The mahamatya respected Bimbisara for who he was: a shrewd and able ruler who had built up a formidable reputation for the Magadh mahajanapada, in diplomacy and on the battlefield. However, he could not bring himself to support this whimsical pursuit of a courtesan. The mahamatya's spies had reported Ambapali's reply to the emperor's missive. He chuckled at the woman's impudent response. It required courage to spurn an emperor's proposal. But there were more pressing matters at hand.

'With all due respect, Maharaj, I find it trivial compared to the measures needed to be taken to mitigate the problems that our subjects are facing. There has been famine in some areas.

Also, the land revenues have plummeted and the treasury is depleting rapidly.'

His words were calculated to shame Bimbisara for putting a woman above the State. They failed to do so.

'Mahamatya, you seem to have forgotten about my presence at every meeting at the sabhagrih. I am fully aware of the challenges we have been facing,' said the emperor. 'But the rains have been good, and that puts an end to the famine.'

'Although the rains have brought some relief, it will take some time for the farmers to get back on their feet. In the meantime, there have been reports of an increase in the activity of dacoits in the trading zones. Our spies have reported that the erstwhile commanders of Anga are regrouping to create unrest.'

Bimbisara began pacing restlessly around the chamber. This was an unexpected, disturbing development.

Anga, with its strategic location near the Bay of Bengal, controlled the trade and the routes to the seaports. The victory over Anga had brought enormous advantages to Magadh. Trade had multiplied, and wealth had poured into the treasury. Apart from commercial considerations, there was another reason for his keenness to keep Anga subjugated. Bimbisara's father had tried to conquer the kingdom, but Brahmadatta, the ruler of the prosperous mahajanapada, had humiliated and defeated him. The conquest, therefore, had been immensely satisfying.

No matter the reason, Magadh could not afford to ignore Anga. Varshakar knew this only too well. He had exaggerated the news about the unrest at Anga so the emperor would delay plans to attack Vaishali. There was disgruntlement among the generals in Anga, but it had always been there and would continue to persist.

Finally, Bimbisara said, 'I am confident that the yuvraj will take care of the insurgents at Anga. It will give him an opportunity to use his faculties.'

'With all due respect, Maharaj, the yuvraj will need an able adviser to deal with the rebels,' said Varshakar, who now saw a way to advance his career. Magadh had far too many able ministers, each one trying to rise above the other. At Anga, he would have no competition. The yuvraj, Ajatshatru, was an impatient young man with lofty dreams. More importantly, he had complete faith in the mahamatya.

'Why don't you go to Anga?' Bimbisara stopped pacing and turned towards Varshakar. 'You would be the right person to advise Ajatshatru.'

'It shall be as per your command, Maharaj.' The crafty man lowered his eyes to hide his glee. 'We will crush the unrest.'

Relieved, Bimbisara smiled. 'I want you back in Magadh as soon as you have quelled the rebellion. And then, we plan for the subjugation of Vaishali.'

'It will be under your reign shortly, Maharaj.'

'In the meantime, I will visit the city. Incognito.'

'You can't risk your life, Maharaj,' Varshakar protested. 'I will accompany you to Vaishali,' he suggested, though certain that the emperor would refuse the offer.

'Did I not order you to leave for Anga? I want no more delay. You are to leave right away.'

'I protest! You must not travel to Vaishali.'

Bimbisara held up his hand to silence the minister. 'My mind is made up, and nothing you say will change my decision.'

Grim-faced, Varshakar said, 'I will not try to change your mind, but you will need excellent guards to protect you. Maharaj, please allow me to choose the right men to accompany you to Vaishali.'

'There's no need for that,' said the emperor sternly. 'You may leave now.'

The mahamatya's brows were furrowed in worry as he bowed himself out of the emperor's chamber. Loyal to the throne, he felt that this obsession of Bimbisara's did not bode well for Magadh. He would have to get rid of Ambapali before she became a distraction for Bimbisara.

He did not think it would be difficult. There were enough spies in Vaishali to do his bidding. He would alert his best man there about the emperor's visit. The spy, Dhana Samant, operated as a cloth merchant, and over the course of eight years had entrenched himself in an affluent area of Vaishali with his large extended family. An innocuous-looking man in his fifties, rotund and genial, he had close contacts with several influential men in Vaishali, as well as access to the royal palace because he supplied clothes for the queen. Dhana would be the best man to monitor Bimbisara's moves and offer protection if needed. As for getting rid of the nagarvadhu, it would be child's play for him.

But eliminating Ambapali would have to wait till he returned from Anga, Varshakar decided. The most important task at the moment was to prepare the yuvraj to sit on the throne in a few years' time. Magadh needed a young and courageous man. The yuvraj had much to learn in terms of statecraft, and his training ought to begin as soon as possible.

While the mahamatya's thoughts were directed towards protecting the emperor and empire, Bimbisara's mind was occupied by the journey he would undertake soon. After some thought, the emperor settled upon one of his most trusted warriors to accompany him to Vaishali. Devavrata, a young man with brilliant control over his weapons and tongue, was the chosen man. One of the best warriors in the Magadh army, the young commander was devoted to Bimbisara. Deva was discreet, and, besides, with an excellent sense of humour, he was good company too.

Thrilled at the thought of his impending adventure, the emperor called for the young warrior.

Seventeen

It was the season of respite. First, the intense rains of Shravan and Bhadrapada gave way to the sporadic, gentle showers of Ashwin, and then to the cooler month of Kartik. The rains had retreated, and winter was quietly tiptoeing into the kingdom. It was the time of rejoicing and festivities, a breather before another round of hectic activities. The days began waning, and the nights grew longer. A mild chill lurked in the atmosphere, warning of the bitter winter months waiting around the corner.

Many summers had passed since Ambapali had left home, and she knew well now how life was full of uncertainties. People died. Friends left. But life went on. Life, for her, had turned into a constant tussle with emotions, with fresh challenges being thrown at her every day. Many were the lessons she had learnt, each of them killing a bit of her sensitivity. Despite her newfound dispassion, she had been devastated by the news of Satyakirti's marriage. She had been surprised herself at the storm raging in her bosom. She had ranted, cursed and cried, the changes in her mood surprising everyone around her.

The breeze was laden with a tinge of moisture as Ambapali whipped her horses into action. It was Satyakirti's birthday.

The wound reopened, and the hurt resurfaced. She couldn't decide if she should visit him, send a gift or ignore him. Her mind agitated, she called for the chariot and told the chariot driver to get down; she would ride alone. She wanted no one around her, not even Priyamvada.

Her hair tumbled out of its confines, falling around her shoulders, a curtain of black. Her eyes were red and puffy after the hours of weeping. Frenzied and wild, she looked nothing like the poised and ethereal nagarvadhu of Vaishali.

'Devi . . .' The chariot driver's protest fell on deaf ears. Worried, the man ran to inform Suvarnasena.

Hearing his shouts, Priyamvada raced out of the mansion. 'Pali,' she shouted. Ambapali did not look back.

She had no idea where she was going. All she knew was that she had to get away from everyone. Blinded by tears, Ambapali drove furiously towards the forests on the outskirts of the town. Satya was married. Satya had betrayed her, once and for all. He loved her no more. Her heartbeat drummed the message continually. Her breath coming in quick gasps, she continued to goad the horses to go faster. After a sudden burst of frantic riding, spent and tearful, she slackened her grip on the reins and allowed the horses to trot sedately till they reached the riverbank that lay just beyond the forests on the outskirts of town. There was a pleasant nip in the air, and she wrapped her uttariya around her shoulders.

The cool winter breeze and the profusion of wild flowers on the waterfront created a magical air around her. It was the perfect season for romance, she thought bitterly, as her heart ached with the loss of loved ones.

Ambapali dismounted and walked towards the riverbank. For a few minutes, she stood staring at the turbulent waters swirling and snaking determinedly past all obstacles. She considered jumping into the river and wondered if her death would bother anyone. Would it disturb the rhythm of anyone's life? Not likely. It would generate tumult and gossip for a couple of days before life resumed its course. Would it bother Satya? Perhaps! But he would go on with life and she would be relegated to history. No one was indispensable, least of all a nagarvadhu. Her death would, perhaps, make the ministers sigh with relief. Hadn't they blamed her for the disharmony within the council? Even though it had been their weakness; not her fault.

She sat on the bank in a contemplative mood. Ahead, the river continued to flow, undisturbed by her thoughts. Like time, it rushed inexorably towards its destiny. Never halting. Never hesitating. Always accepting. Therein lay its wisdom.

The message was simple. It was time to embrace destiny.

She was not a coward. Tossing all thoughts of suicide from her mind, she squared her shoulders and walked up to the chariot. She decided to head towards the royal orchards which lay close by. The trees in the orchard were dressed in multi-hued leaves, some green, some yellow. Dry leaves dotted the ground. There was a riot of colours around her. Flowers bloomed with renewed vigor and an intoxicating blend of fragrance flooded the air. The champa trees flaunted fragrant white flowers.

Leaving the chariot by the gate, Ambapali ambled towards the thicket of mango trees.

Memories deluged her mind as she sat under her favourite tree. This was where she had spent idyllic afternoons with Satya. She had danced to the tune of his veena. They had played the fool, whispered sweet nothings and raged against each other.

Her anger ebbed as the minutes passed. The serenity of her surroundings allowed her to think rationally. The constant flow of activity in the palace left no time for quiet contemplation. Peace descended as she reasoned with herself now. Their parting had been inevitable. He hadn't spelt out the reasons, but she knew them anyway. She was wedded to an entire city. She couldn't be the wife of one man. She was a ganika. A prostitute. The nagarvadhu was meant to bed men, not to marry them. She had wealth and riches, but she would never have a family.

Although she had known the impossibility of their union, the news of Satyakirti's marriage coming so soon after she had lost her father had made it more difficult to accept. The shock of her father's sudden death had brought back a part of her vulnerability she assumed she had lost.

Dharma Datta had been working in the royal orchards when he suffered a snakebite. There had been no one around, and he had died alone among the trees. It had been a lonely death for the man, Ambapali knew. Her visits to her father had decreased over time. Unhappy with his daughter's ruined life and how much she had changed, he had distanced himself from everyone. His unexpected death probably came as a relief from his prolonged suffering, worry and guilt. He must have embraced it with happiness, she knew.

As days turned into weeks, and her grief refused to let her rest, she had got their home repaired and furnished, and often returned there when she was looking for peace. It was her refuge—a place where she could escape when seized with hopelessness. It comforted her to be there.

Dejection weighing her mind, she had been drawn towards the teachings of Sakyamuni. It was Priyamvada who had taken her the first time to the enlightened one's sermon, and she had been so impressed by his teachings that she never missed a sermon whenever he visited the town. There was a constant tussle between her heart and head. While the head rejoiced in worldly offerings, the heart pined for a normal life. She wanted a loving husband and children, a home that would brim with happiness. Instead, she lived in an enormous palace with all the comforts of life but experienced no happiness. The people who presumed to own her dictated her life.

In one of his sermons, the enlightened one had spoken about the path to happiness

'People suffer because they misperceive certain things. They crave and cling to these misperceptions, which causes a state of dissatisfaction.'

What is it I crave, Ambapali questioned herself. *Is it Satya?*

But Satya was married now. He had married Urmimala.

Ambapali had decided not to attend the wedding—she would not have been able to bear the humiliation and pain. She had sent expensive gifts to the couple though.

I have to forget the past and begin afresh. Baba is no more. I can't bring him back to life. Satya has moved on, and so must I. She would have to accept the truth. Life was not about stagnation. It had to continue to move. The river had taught her that, she decided, staring into the distance. Lulled by the tranquility in the mango grove, she mulled over Sakyamuni's words. *Dukkha is the suffering that comes when we want things to differ from the way they are.*

It was near dusk, and the sky was growing dark in the distance, but she continued to sit under the tree. A dry leaf pirouetted down in the breeze, spinning through the air on its downward journey. It blew past her face and landed lightly on the ground. Sighing, she picked it up.

The mango tree, under which she sat, was special. It had been her confidant. This was where Dharma Datta had found her. This was where he died.

She was reluctant to give up the silence and peace and return to the flashy palace with its solicitous servants and fawning admirers. If only it were possible to live here forever. Life would be so much simpler.

Her beauty was her biggest enemy. It had been the cause of all her unhappiness. It had brought her nothing but sorrow and taken her father and friends from her. Often, she toyed with the idea of disfiguring herself. No one would want a disfigured nagarvadhu.

Wrapped in her musings, Ambapali failed to notice the two men watching her intently. They stood behind a tree, very close to her.

They were tall and powerfully built. Their attire proclaimed them to be prosperous traders. One of them was older and strikingly handsome. An impressive moustache added to his majestic aura. Dressed in a crimson silk dhoti and a fine uttariya, he looked like a rich setthi. Pinned on his turban was an elaborate jewel crafted from expensive emeralds and pearls, and a solid gold kayabandh adorned his waist. He looked like a man who was used to being obeyed.

His companion was younger and stouter. His conduct was deferential. 'There she is,' whispered the companion. 'They call her the most beautiful one on earth. She is Ambapali, the nagarvadhu of Vaishali.'

'They are right,' replied the senior of the two, captivated by the sight of the beauteous woman sitting under the large mango tree. 'She truly is ethereal. I have seen no one as beautiful as her.'

The last of the sun's rays cast a magical spell on the orchard. The colours of the sky transformed, illuminating the clouds in the west with orange-red sunlight, while those in the east remained stained blue and indigo. Twilight painted the forest in enchanting colours. The woman appeared like an exquisite sculpture in that light. 'Now that you have seen her, we should leave this place. It would be unwise to linger here any longer, Arya.'

'Wait! Let me drink deeply of her beauty. My eyes are reluctant to stray from her face.'

A white silk antariya tied deep below her navel, and a transparent embroidered uttariya thrown carelessly around her shoulders, her hair cascading, Ambapali looked like a nymph who had lost her way.

It was easy to recognize the light of rapture in the dark brown eyes of the older man. His companion sighed and sat down under the tree. 'Let me know when you are ready to leave,' he said.

'Not in this lifetime,' said the other. 'I want to carry her away with me, to relish her forever.' There was a wistful note in his voice.

Then, the dark shape of a reptile caught his eyes. It had emerged from a hole near the mango tree and was snaking swiftly towards the woman.

Like a flash of lightning, he leapt towards her. Unsheathing his sword, he severed the black snake near the woman's ankle.

He was too late. The deadly snake had already bitten Ambapali.

She fell into a swoon as the poison began to take its effect. Two puncture marks showed the spot where she had been bitten. He took off the uttariya and bound it around her ankle. Extracting a bejeweled dagger from within the folds of his clothes, he quickly made an incision on the afflicted area.

'Arya, wait!' shouted the companion, as the man began sucking out the poison. 'Don't endanger your life. Let's take her to a vaid.'

Paying no heed, the man continued sucking and spitting out the poison from the swollen ankle. Bit by bit, he sucked out the poison and Ambapali stirred.

A smile of satisfaction lit up the man's face before he fell back in a heap. He had saved the woman's life.

'Arya!' shouted the companion. There was urgency in his voice. 'Devi,' he shook the shocked woman. 'In saving your life, my friend seems to have ingested a lot of the poison. He needs immediate treatment.'

His words galvanized Ambapali into action. 'My chariot is standing just outside. Carry him to it,' she urged. 'My home is not far, and I know a good vaid.'

Dharma Datta's house was not too far from the mango grove and they drove there at a breakneck speed. Minutes later, having helped the companion lay the man on a bed, she drove off to fetch Vivaswat.

'There's a lot of poison in his body,' Vivaswat said. He had treated many cases of snakebite. It was a regular occurrence in the village, especially during the monsoon. 'You did the right thing calling me so quickly. Another half an hour and he would have died.'

An hour later, having administered his treatment, the vaid gave instructions on the dosage of the various herbs. There were many restrictions that had to be followed. 'He requires complete rest and should remain in bed for the next three days. The asavas and other medicines have to be given at the right time. Any carelessness can have grievous results.'

'Please don't worry, Arya, I will be here to look after him,' said the companion, as he walked with the vaid to the door.

'Thank you for everything. At the time of crisis, I can think of no other person but my friends and you,' said Ambapali. 'I will not be able to get over my guilt if something happens to this man. I would have died if he had not sucked the poison out of my body.'

'My only regret is that I couldn't save your father.' Vivaswat shook his head sadly. The two men had been good friends. 'He was dead by the time the other gardeners found him.' He placed a loving hand on her shoulder.

'No one can change destiny,' said Ambapali. 'Baba was destined to die in the gardens he loved so much. I am sure he must be happy wherever he is now.' She wiped her tears with the uttariya. 'I will accompany you to your house so I can collect the medicines.'

The drive to the vaid's house was a silent one. 'Won't you come inside and meet Satya and Urmi?' asked Vivaswat as he got off the chariot. 'They will be so happy to see you.'

Ambapali hesitated. She was not ready to face Satya. 'It's late,' she said finally. 'I should get back to the palace. Priyamvada will be pacing around in anxiety. And please don't share the snakebite story with Satya. It will upset him.'

'Rest assured. I do not discuss my patients with the family.' The vaid entered the house.

Urmimala, who had seen Ambapali, rushed out just as she turned to leave. 'Pali!' she exclaimed. She reached up and hugged her friend. 'I am so glad to see you.'

His wife's excited chatter brought Satyakirti outside. Ambapali paled at the sight of her former lover. They stood staring at each other in silence. Remorse and guilt were etched on his face, while hers was reproachful. An impenetrable veil of unspoken emotions hung between the two of them. Urmimala continued to talk excitedly.

'You can't go away,' she said, reaching for Ambapali's arm. Her exuberance was a cover for the awkwardness she felt. 'I have so much to tell you.'

'Not today, please Urmi,' Ambapali said. 'I will meet you some other day.'

'Let her go,' said Satyakirti, putting a hand on his wife's arm. 'Pali is a very rich and important woman, Urmi. She will not be comfortable in our humble house.'

Ambapali was outraged by the acerbic comment. 'How dare you!' she thundered. Her body was trembling with emotion. The feelings she had bottled up rushed to the fore. 'How dare you say that? It is you who let me down. Not once, not twice, but several times. How could you marry Urmi?'

'What do you mean by that statement? Why shouldn't Satya have married me?' raged Urmimala. 'What could he have done when you turned him away from the gate of your palace? In fact, I have loved him for a long time. He never noticed because he was in love with you.'

'That's a lie. I never turned him away. Despite my pleas, none of you attempted to meet me. Don't deflect your guilt by blaming me,' said Ambapali, livid.

'It's the truth,' Satyakirti intervened. 'I couldn't get over my remorse for turning down your request for marriage. Guilt haunted me for several days. My family admonished me, saying I was a coward.' His face reflected a gamut of emotions, one after another. 'I went to your palace to speak to you.'

'You came to my house?' Ambapali was stunned.

'Yes! I was stopped at the gateway by a guard. He informed Suvarnasena, who came out of the house and greeted me. She remained courteous till the time I asked for you. Your teacher ordered me to remain standing near the entrance while she checked with you. She went into the house and returned after a few minutes, saying, "Pali is busy, she does not want to meet you." I was so hurt, but I couldn't do anything but go back.'

'Why don't you tell her the humiliating things she said?' asked Urmimala. 'Suvarnasena—'

'No, Urmi!' Satyakirti interrupted her mid-sentence. 'It doesn't matter. What has been done can't be undone. I wouldn't have spoken about this had Pali not blamed me.'

'She should know the truth,' insisted his wife. 'Suvarnasena was vicious, and she insulted Satya, saying he was a gold-digger.' Urmi's chest heaved with emotion. 'She accused him of trying to influence you so he could live in the palace, and she also—'

'Stop!' Satyakirti clamped his hand on Urmi's mouth. 'I don't want to hear of those things again. Why rake up the past?'

Urmimala removed his hand from her mouth and continued, unfazed, 'Not just Satya, she turned away your father, too. He went to meet you several times, and each time he returned without seeing you. Not only did that woman refuse to let him enter the palace, she threw a bag of coins at him, saying it should satisfy him. He flung it back at her, of course, but the poor man was devastated. He lost his will to live, separated from you.'

'I can't believe this,' muttered Ambapali. 'Baba did not tell me anything.' Ashen, she sat down heavily on the ground. 'Why didn't Baba and Satya tell me about their visits?' she repeated dully.

'They wanted to save you the pain, I guess. Everyone knew the difficulties you were facing. They didn't want to add to them,' Urmimala replied gently.

'Even Priya?'

'Do you think Suvarnasena would have risked Priya knowing about Satya and your father's visit to the mansion?'

'What prevented you from informing me of my father's death? You didn't feel it your duty to break the news?' Ambapali asked bitterly. 'Where were you, when I needed you most?

There was a moment's silence, and then Urmi replied, 'We knew you would be devastated to hear of his death and would need your friends around.' She wiped her tears and continued gently, 'We had gone to you, but she turned us away saying she would break the news herself. We waited for a while, hoping to catch a glimpse of Priya, but she was nowhere to be seen.'

Ambapali suddenly looked fatigued. Too much had happened in the past few hours. A close encounter with death is enough to shake a person, but she had to deal with the ordeal her saviour was facing. And now, this information about Suvarnasena's treachery. Her world had upended and she felt like an emotional wreck. 'That woman has ruined my life. I might be able to forgive her for humiliating Satya and my father, but how can I forgive her for not allowing you to be with me when I needed my friends?' She buried her face in her hands and wept softly. 'She is responsible for my misery.'

'Come inside, Pali,' begged Urmimala. 'You don't look well.' She tugged at the stricken woman's hands. 'Stay for a while.'

'No, Urmi,' she said, firmly but gently. 'I have some unfinished business to deal with.' She got to her feet. She was done grieving. It was time for action now.

Her face was thunderous as she got on to the chariot and rode away, leaving her anxious friends staring behind her.

Eighteen

The two strangers exchanged notes in Ambapali's village house. The older man, weak from the after-effects of the poison, lay on a rough mattress placed on the floor.

It seemed eons since, dressed as mourners, they had crossed the cremation grounds and entered the city through the Mukti Dwar, along with other mourners. Late that evening, they had made their way to Samvarta setthi's mansion. Samvarta was one of the eminent traders of Vaishali. He was also one of the spies Varshakar had planted in the city over the past decade. Some of them had established themselves as traders, while others masqueraded as workers, labourers and peasants; some ran wine taverns. These were choice places for gathering intelligence, since wine always loosened tongues and inebriated officials and soldiers would often reveal State secrets. Many Magadh ganikas had also proven to be invaluable sources of information.

The men had spent a long time discussing the developments at Vaishali and gathering intelligence. Bimbisara had plans of stealing into Ambapali's palace the next day, but he did not reveal this to the setthi.

'The fewer people we involve, the better it will be,' he told Devavrata. 'The nagarvadhu's palace is visited by many prosperous merchants every evening. We will enter the place along with them. It should be a simple task if I dress like a wealthy trader. You will come as my assistant.'

Destiny, however, had other plans. Wandering around the orchard the very next evening, they ran into the nagarvadhu and he had saved her life.

Bimbisara retched as the poison acted upon his system. 'Maharaj, you must allow me to inform the setthi to arrange a comfortable and safe place for your stay,' begged his companion. 'This house is not fit for you. We can move to Samvarta dev's mansion tonight.'

'Don't worry about me, Devavrata,' the older man said as he sat up on the bed. 'I am quite comfortable here. This place is a godsend. It's the ideal hideout for us. No one will think of looking for us in this isolated house. I wanted to meet Ambapali and fate has brought me right to her abode. It is more than I could have hoped for. I can have my fill of her presence till I recover, and then we can leave Vaishali.'

'I am concerned about your health, Maharaja,' said Devavrata, who gazed at the emperor anxiously as he continued to wheeze. 'The dampness in this house will delay your recovery.'

'What happened to your optimism, Deva?' Bimbisara closed his eyes wearily. 'All I need is a couple of days. I will be fine after some rest.'

'The good part is that there are guavas in a tree at the back of the house,' the young man said, giving in to his master's stubbornness. 'I will fetch some for you.'

'You will encounter another snake, and that will be the end of our mission,' quipped the emperor. 'I love the fruit, but I won't be able to suck out the poison from your wound.

Wait for me to recover before you embark on an encounter with reptiles.'

'I would—' Devavrata began, then stopped as Bimbisara raised a hand in warning. The sound of hooves had drawn his attention. Unsheathing a dagger from its scabbard, the young soldier peeped out of the window. He heaved a sigh of relief at the sight of Ambapali's chariot. Minutes later, she burst into the house carrying a basket.

'I have brought you the medicines, and there is some milk and fruits in the basket,' she said casting an anxious look at Bimbisara. 'Is he feeling better?'

'Thank you, devi. You are very kind,' Devavrata said as he joined his palms.

'Please bear the discomfort tonight,' she said. 'I will return in the morning and make proper arrangements.'

'We are comfortable enough, thank you. We are in your debt for providing us with this shelter.'

'It's I who am indebted to your friend for saving my life. I am in a hurry now, but I will return very early tomorrow,' she said. She was smiling, but Bimbisara could tell that Ambapali was distressed. Her face was flushed, whether because of the exertion or some strong emotion, he could not decide.

'Is anything the matter?' Bimbisara asked. 'Can we help?'

'It's something I have to handle myself.' Squaring her shoulders, she turned to leave the room. She hesitated for a moment near the door. 'Have you ever had to deal with betrayal?'

The emperor remained silent. He had seen enough betrayals to last a lifetime, but he could hardly tell her that.

'Devi, it is natural to feel betrayed when someone we care for does something hurtful. The way I deal with the hurt is to ask myself two questions: first, does the betrayer care for me? Second, does the betrayal affect me? If the answer to the first is yes, I forgive. If the betrayal affects me, I take action.'

'What if the betrayal has hurt someone you love?

'In that situation, I would take action. I consider it important to protect the people I love.'

'That was very helpful, Arya.' Ambapali folded her hands. 'You have given me the answer to my dilemma. I have to avenge someone I love. Now, I must leave.'

'It's very late. Do you want me to accompany you to your palace?' Devavrata offered.

'Thank you, but there's no need for that. Stay with your friend. He needs you more.'

And she was gone, leaving the fragrance of flowers behind her.

'I wonder who has betrayed the lady,' remarked Bimbisara.

'She did look troubled,' the young man said. 'Life can be difficult, even for a nagarvadhu.'

'It's not easy for anyone, especially for a nagarvadhu. She has to deal with undesirable men and their shenanigans every day.' The emperor remained silent for a few minutes. Finally, he said, 'She spoke of betrayal. I wonder what kind.'

* * *

Her jaw clenched, Ambapali drove her chariot to the palace. The drive had cleared her mind, and she was set for confrontation.

Priyamvada came rushing up as she entered the palace. 'Where did you vanish, Pali?' she asked. 'We have been so worried.'

'Where's Suvarnasena?' Ambapali said through gritted teeth, her chest heaving with emotion. The riding whip in hand, she strode into the house.

'Pali,' Priyamvada trotted behind her, concerned. Taking the whip from her friend's hands, she said, 'Relax! Let me ask someone to fetch you a cooling drink.'

Ambapali's eyes were ablaze. Rage flowed through her like lava. Fists clenched, she ground out the words, 'No! I must deal with that woman.'

Priyamvada noted the stormy look on her friend's face and wondered what had happened.

'So, you are back?' Suvarnasena asked. She had crept silently into the room. 'I am shocked by your irresponsible behaviour. Would you be kind enough to inform us where you have been?'

'How could you?' shouted Ambapali. Anger thrummed through her veins. 'Does your greed know no limit?' The atmosphere crackled with tension.

The teacher's steely eyes studied her with a predator's unwavering attention. 'I am shocked at your insolent behaviour. I forbid you to speak to me in that tone.'

'Forbid? You can't forbid me anything.'

'Pali, please . . .' Priyamvada interposed soothingly, placing herself between the two women. Never had she seen her friend in such a temper.

'You keep out of this,' warned Ambapali, pushing her away. Her dark eyes smoldering, she continued, 'This is between Suvarnasena and me.'

'To what do I owe this honour?' shot back Suvarnasena, unperturbed by her pupil's words. 'I have worked hard to establish you as a nagarvadhu. It is thanks to me that you are a rich and famous person today. If people flock to this palace, it is because of my efforts. Do you think you could have done any of this on your own? You were a village bumpkin with no sophistication. All you had was a beautiful face and voluptuous body, which is not such a rare thing. It is I who honed and polished a worthless piece of stone and turned it into a dazzling diamond.'

'I was—'

'Let me finish,' Suvarnasena held up her hand and continued, 'Do you think it is easy to run an establishment as large as this? I work twenty hours a day to keep the wheels turning without pause! All you do is sit and amuse the patrons, for which you are gifted enormous amounts of gold and wealth. It's I who keeps an account of everything, resolves each issue, sorts out differences between the princes and setthis, manages the servants and the guards. Without me, you are nothing more than a ganika. And you have the audacity to shout at the teacher who taught you everything and helped you rise to such heights? You are the most ungrateful person I know!'

Suvarnasena's eyes were filled with rage.

Ambapali knew it was emotional blackmail, but she could also recognize the truth in the teacher's words. Simmering with outrage, she countered, 'You are mistaken, devi. This is not about ingratitude or audacity. This is about my life. This is about self-respect. I acknowledge the things you have done for me, but you forget that I had no ambition to be a raj nartaki, let alone a nagarvadhu. I didn't want this wealth and fame. All I wanted was a simple life. You forced me to become a raj nartaki and separated me from my father and friends. You drove away each and every person who loved me. You ruined my life! If I am nothing more than a ganika, it's because of you. I will forever hold you responsible for my unhappiness.'

'I have done nothing of the sort,' retorted the teacher coolly. 'It's not I who changed the course of your life. Your selection as raj nartaki was the parishad's decision, as was the elevation to the post of nagarvadhu. I had nothing to do with either.'

'It's you who forced me to take part in the competition, so you are the root cause of all of it. I forgave you for that, but I will never forgive you for keeping my father and Satya away from me.'

'You are mistaken. I didn't keep your father or Satya away from you.'

'Didn't you turn them away at the gate? You told them to leave, saying I was too busy to meet them. Isn't that the truth?' Grief had replaced the anger in Ambapali's voice. 'You humiliated my father. He lost his desire to live because of you.'

Priyamvada gasped with surprise.

'Who told you I turned them away? Was it Satya?'

'Satya is too much of a gentleman to tattle against a woman. It was his wife who told me everything. How could you do this, knowing I loved him?'

Like a chameleon, Suvarnasena changed colour. Realizing that Ambapali had learnt the truth, she swiftly altered her tone. From belligerent, it segued into a wheedling one. 'Pali, I meant no harm. Believe me, I acted in good faith.'

'Do you think I am so gullible as to believe that? Thanks to you, I am no longer a naïve and trusting girl. Your callousness has turned me into a cynical woman. I will no longer be taken in by your smooth talk.'

'Listen to me, Pali—'

'I have always listened to you, and now it's your turn to listen to me! These are smaller incidents when compared to the time you stopped Satya and Urmi from conveying the news of my father's death. You derived inhuman satisfaction in breaking the news in a cold-hearted manner. He was the only family I had. Do you realize what his death meant?' bellowed Ambapali, her anger returning. 'I would like you to pack your things and leave by tomorrow morning.'

She turned and walked towards her room. Horrified by the sudden turn of events, Suvarnasena trotted behind her. 'Where do you expect me to go? I closed my dance school to be with you. Where will I go now?' she cried.

'I am not throwing you out on the street,' said Ambapali, turning to her. 'I will give you money to restart your school. You can keep all the jewellery and money that you have pilfered from my coffers. Yes, I know about that.'

Suvarnasena turned ashen at the accusation. The nagarvadhu could send her to prison.

'For the last few years, you have been siphoning away both cash and gold. There is enough for you to live a luxurious life. Yet, I will sanction money for your dance school.'

'Forgive me for all the wrongs, Pali,' Suvarnasena begged with folded hands. She had no wish to lose the golden goose and was deploying every weapon in her arsenal to change Ambapali's decision. 'I will serve you faithfully. Please don't turn me out.'

Ignoring her pleas, Ambapali stormed into her room and slammed the door. She threw herself on the bed. Then, seized by grief, she wept bitterly. Why did everyone let her down?

She woke with the sun shining into her eyes. The drapes had not been drawn the previous night, neither had she changed her clothes. The enormity of her actions last night hit her like a sledgehammer.

There was a timid knock on the door. After a few moments of hesitation, Indumati entered her bedroom. She had brought with her a fresh juice and the news. Suvarnasena had left. The information that she had carried away several big boxes didn't bother Ambapali. Instead, an overwhelming sense of relief washed over her.

Gone were the days of enslavement. No more pushing. No more prodding. The decisions would be for her to make and take. She would be at the helm of her life. At last. She would have to forget Satya and every unpleasant incident in her life. She would start afresh.

Her heart sang a small, bittersweet ditty. *I am free.*

Nineteen

An hour later, Ambapali directed her chariot toward her father's home.

That morning, she had spent considerable time over her toilette. Her soft white muslin antariya, tied below her navel, was clasped with a filigreed gold waistband, and a delicate blue uttariya with golden threads was thrown carelessly over one shoulder.

A dozen gold chains adorned the luxuriant curls that had been parted on the side and fashioned into ringlets. A large tikli with radiating beaded strings covered half her forehead. Her neck was weighed by several strands of the purest pearls, held together by a pendant of rubies. Bracelets and bangles covered her wrists.

'You look gorgeous!' whispered Priyamvada, awed.

'Happiness makes people look more beautiful,' replied Ambapali, smiling. 'Somehow, I feel truly able to move on from Satya and the past now. Knowing that he tried to reach out to me makes me feel better, even though things didn't work out. Perhaps they were not meant to.'

Priyamvada smiled and hugged her friend. 'It's been such a long time since I saw you so happy and carefree.'

'I feel unshackled and light. I am ready to begin afresh, without Suvarnasena, without the memories of the past haunting me.'

'Where are you going now, Pali?' asked Priyamvada. 'If you are going to the village, I would like to accompany you. I want to meet the man who saved your life and thank him.'

Ambapali had told her all about the stranger who had saved her.

'I will take you tomorrow, Priya,' Ambapali said. 'Today, can you send word to all my old employees—Lilavati, and the others. I want them reinstated with immediate effect.'

'That's an excellent idea. Lilavati can take charge of the things handled by Suvarnasena. She's a very loyal and honest person. I am sure she will be happy to work for you, Pali.' Priyamvada adjusted her friend's uttariya. 'In the meantime, enjoy yourself with the trader.'

Anticipating a playful slap, Priyamvada skipped out of her friend's reach.

Still smiling, Ambapali drove her chariot out of the palace gates. With her, she was carrying enough fruits, nuts and food to last a couple of days.

People stopped and stared as she galloped through the town, smiling and waving at them. They rarely saw the nagarvadhu, who was usually surrounded by a posse of bodyguards who kept the commoners at a distance. Taken aback to see her smiling and unguarded, they raised their hands and cheered.

From time to time, she slowed down and showered some karshapanas on the poorest of the lot. Her mood upbeat, she hummed under her breath.

On reaching the house, Ambapali found the stranger sleeping. There was no trace of his companion. She sat quietly near his bed and stared at the man.

Although in his forties, the stranger was strikingly handsome with chiseled and aristocratic features. The broad chest and rippling muscles added to his manliness, as did the square and determined chin edged with a well-kept beard. His eyebrows were thick and well-defined, and the forehead prominent. The sharp, amber eyes were now closed in repose. If there was any incongruity, it lay in the cruel twist of his thin lips.

He looked majestic, even in sleep.

Sensing her presence, Bimbisara blinked awake and gaped at the woman sitting near him. The sun's rays from the window fell on her face, adding to its radiance. She looked more beautiful than he remembered. His throat dry, he croaked, 'Devi!'

'Pranam, Arya.' She smiled and folded her hands in greeting. 'Did you sleep well? Was the room comfortable? Did you eat? I hope you are feeling better.'

Bimbisara cleared his throat and said, 'So many questions! The answer to all is in the affirmative.' His eyes twinkled with mirth. 'It looks like you have dealt with whatever was troubling you last evening.'

'How do you know?'

'Your smile lets out the secret. And you look relaxed.'

'You are right. I feel light and happy this morning.'

'Happiness suits you. It makes you radiant and adds to your beauty. I have never seen anyone as beautiful as you.' His words were flirtatious. 'And I have come across many women in the course of my journeys.'

Ambapali was no stranger to compliments but, for some reason, these words from him made her blush. She rose abruptly, saying, 'I brought you some food.'

'But there are enough fruits to last us a couple of days,' he protested as she placed an enormous basket near his bed.

'There is no need to stay here for that long—' she began, drawn towards the eyes that were the colour of molten copper.

Bimbisara was surprised at her words. 'Ah. No, devi, I won't inconvenience you for long,' he said. His voice hardened. 'I will go away as soon as Devavrata returns.'

'You have misunderstood, Arya,' she hastened to reassure him. 'I want to take you to my palace as soon as the vaid allows it. It will be much more comfortable for you there.'

'Oh, I couldn't . . .'

'No, Arya.' She held up her hand. 'I won't listen to any objection. You have saved my life and there is little I can do to repay you. Please don't deny me the privilege of hosting you for as long as you are in the city.' Ambapali put her palms together. 'You will not be unhappy there, I promise.'

'I . . .'

Ambapali thought she understood the reason for his hesitation. 'I see. Staying with the nagarvadhu may not be appropriate.'

'Please don't say that devi,' Bimbisara said quickly. He stood up unsteadily and had to grab her hands for support. For a few moments, they stared at each other. A hot flush shot up her neck and Ambapali withdrew her hands. 'I would be glad to stay in your palace for as long as you wish,' he said.

Tongue-tied, she stared at the handsome man who towered above her. His presence filled the space. It brought vitality to the room. This was no ordinary man, Ambapali realized. Why was she so affected by him?

Ambapali looked away towards the window, eyes alighting on the profusion of wildflowers outside and the myriad of bees. For so long she had neglected herself, forgotten to take joy in the course of nature. Now she could feel happiness stirring within her.

'Then it's settled.' She smiled brightly. 'I will speak to the vaid and we will decide on the next course of action.'

There was a silence for a few moments.

Observing the enormous quantity of food she had brought, Bimbisara joked, 'Is this meant to feed a battalion of soldiers? I hope you do not expect me to eat everything.'

'We have to get you back on your feet,' she said. 'Didn't you hear the vaid saying so? I am not willing to hear any excuse.' It had been a long time since she had looked after anyone, Ambapali realized, and she was enjoying herself. She bustled around the kitchen and returned with a pot of broth and a platter of fruits. 'Finish these.'

'I can't eat so much,' he protested.

'Sshhh! Just eat!' She placed a finger on her lips. 'I will be forced to feed you if you don't help yourself,' she threatened, her eyes dancing with mirth.

It was a novel experience for Bimbisara. It had been ages since he was bullied by anyone. Ever since he was crowned at fifteen, he had ordered everyone around. 'You are a heartless woman, devi. A beautiful one at that. How can I disobey you?' he said.

He ate under her watchful eyes, amused at her concern.

'I am confused, Arya,' she said, raising an eyebrow. 'Looking at your clothes, one would assume you to be an important person. How come you have neither a horse nor servants with you?'

She was leading him towards dangerous ground, and Bimbisara had no wish to tread on it. 'You have misunderstood, devi. I am an ordinary person, with no claim to importance.'

'Well, I know nothing about you, not even your name.'

Bimbisara stared at her for a moment. He had discussed the details of their assumed identities with Devavrata, but he fumbled. It was difficult to look her in the eye and tell a lie. He turned his gaze away.

'My name is Indrajeet Varman,' he said. 'I am a trader of perfumes from Avanti. But my dealings extend all the way to Gandhar and beyond. This may seem like bragging, but my perfumes are sold in the bazaars of Misr and Basra.'

'Do you travel a lot?' she asked wistfully. Full of romantic notions, the idea of travelling to far-off lands appealed to her.

'Well, my business takes me to many places. It can be quite tiring, actually.' His creative mind skillfully conjured up a convenient backstory.

'I have never gone beyond Vaishali, but I would love to see other places, other cultures,' she said, sighing.

'Perhaps you will.'

'Is this your first visit to this city?'

'I have come here a few times.'

'In that case, you must be familiar with it,' she said. 'Do you have friends here?'

Bimbisara wished she would stop probing him. With each question, he was sinking into a quagmire of lies.

'Unfortunately, a trader has no friends. Making friends requires time. We are like driftwood, floating from one place to another. I have some good friends at Avanti,' he replied.

He steered the conversation away from himself, saying, 'Devi must have many friends.'

Ambapali toyed with her uttariya, struggling to control her emotions. She spoke finally, voice heavy with grief and regret. 'Is friendship even possible as we grow older? The innocent friendships of our early years are the only ones that stand the test of time. I had my childhood friends, who were very dear to me. We were all happy together until I attended the raj nartaki's performance at Vasant Utsav. That evening changed the course of my life.'

'Are you not happy that your path has led you to wealth and acclaim?' he asked.

'No!' The tremor in her voice conveyed more than words ever could. 'It has taken away everything and every person I hold dear. No amount of wealth can compensate for the love of your father and friends.'

Then, unwilling to show weakness to the stranger, she turned her face away to hide the eyes filled with unshed tears. She had let her guard down, Ambapali realized, and she wasn't sure why or when. Brushing away the stray tears that had escaped, she squared her shoulders and faced him again.

Bimbisara's eyes had missed nothing. Behind the restraint, he glimpsed hints of a tender and sensitive woman. He was enchanted by her. He stretched out a hand and patted her shoulder. There was compassion in his touch.

Determined to change her mood, she smiled and said, 'I protest. You are a difficult man, Arya. You have eaten nothing.'

'And you are a tyrant, devi.' He reached out for a bunch of grapes. 'You will share these with me.'

'You are the one with poison running in your blood.' Her radiant smile ousted the gloom of the room.

'That's a serious charge,' he countered.

They continued to banter. Deva, who was about to enter the house, halted at the threshold and cleared his throat to signal his presence. As ordered by Bimbisara, he had visited the central market and bought a measure of the most expensive perfumes, delicate essences guaranteed to tantalize the senses.

As he had approached the house, he had heard snippets of conversation and the sound of laughter that followed, full of effortless joy. The companion had never heard the emperor laugh in such a carefree manner. The weight of a crown doesn't allow such liberties. He paused and smiled; his heart full of happiness for the emperor.

'Enter!' ordered Bimbisara. Ambapali looked at him, curiosity stirring again. His response sounded much like a royal command. Realizing his slip, the emperor made haste to repeat, in a much softer tone, 'I am awake, Deva. Please come in.' Turning to her, he winked. 'He assumes I sleep the entire day.'

Devavrata's keen eyes took in the easy companionship between the emperor and the courtesan.

'I have carried out your instructions,' he said in reply to Bimbisara's raised eyebrow.

Ambapali looked at the man she knew as Indrajeet.

'Devavrata is a capable young man,' Bimbisara responded to her silent query. 'He went out to the market in connection with our business. As expected, he's managed all the transactions satisfactorily.'

'Devavrata, I hope you haven't sold *all* your wares,' Ambapali said, dimpling at the young man. Like most affluent young men and women of the city, she indulged in perfumes.

'I wouldn't have dared to do that, devi. I have kept aside several for you.' Devavrata hastened towards the outer courtyard and returned with a bag. With a flourish, he began to display all the different essences he had purchased that morning.

Ambapali examined the perfumes with excitement. She opened each container and sniffed at the contents delicately. 'What a lovely collection! I'm spoilt for choice,' she declared. 'I would like to buy all of them, Arya.'

'You cannot buy them.'

'Aren't you selling them?'

'Yes, I am selling them, but I won't sell them to you.' Amused, Bimbisara watched her face fall in disappointment. He chuckled. 'They are a gift,' he said. 'We also produce several kinds of tailas and lepas. I will remember to bring some more the next time I visit Vaishali.'

Time glided past on well-oiled wheels as they shared the broth and fruits.

'I have brought something to keep you amused,' she said, disappearing into the other room. She returned with a chaupar, pawns and cowries. 'I hope you like playing chaupar.'

'Indeed, I do,' Bimbisara said, busying himself with the cowries. It had been a long time since he found the time to indulge in one of his favourite pastimes. 'I am impressed by your thoughtfulness, devi,' he said.

'An ailing person's mind must remain engaged, so he doesn't spend too much time thinking about the illness. That's what my father believed.'

'Your father is a wise man. Does he live with you in the palace?'

Ambapali's eyes misted over, as she responded in a low voice, 'He's no more.'

He tried to apologize, but she waved it off.

'I brought him a lot of sorrow,' she said.

'No daughter can bring sorrow to her parent!'

'My father could never come to terms with my being a nagarvadhu. It devastated him.' Tears flowed down her cheeks. 'He died of snakebite. It would have been fitting if I had died of a snakebite under the same tree.'

Her words shocked the emperor. Once again, he cast about for words to comfort the woman. 'You can't allow grief to cheat you of your life.' He reached for her hand and patted it comfortingly. 'I lost both my parents when I was very young,' he said. 'We have to live in the belief that they are now in a better place.'

'Let's not talk of sad things.' Ambapali forced herself to snap out of the gloom and turned her attention to the chaupar with a wan but determined cheer. 'I'm sure you can't beat me at this.'

'Will you bet on that?' His eyes twinkled with mirth.

'I don't like gambling, but this one time I shall.'

'What will you give me if I defeat you?'

'Don't be too sure of winning,' she teased. 'I am quite good at it.'

'In that case, you have nothing to fear.'

'All right, whoever wins can ask for anything,' she said. After a brief hesitation, she hastened to add, 'Within reasonable limits, of course.'

They played three rounds of chaupar, and each time, he trounced her. 'You must have cheated,' she declared. 'How could you win each game?'

'Don't try to wriggle out of your promise, devi,' he teased. 'According to our wager, I can ask for anything, not once but thrice.'

'I believe in keeping promises,' she retorted. 'What do you want?'

'There is no hurry, devi. I will ask for my reward at a suitable time.' His enigmatic smile conveyed a lot more than the simple words. 'I trust you won't forget the promise.'

'I never forget a promise nor do I go back on one,' she said.

'Is there a veena in this house?' The image he had of Ambapali seemed incomplete without the instrument and the anklets. 'I wanted to hear you playing Raag Asavari. It's one of my favourite ragas.'

'No, there isn't! I'm glad you reminded me. I will carry my instrument the next time I come here.'

They spent an idyllic evening. Bimbisara couldn't recall the last time he had enjoyed himself so much. His responsibilities rarely allowed him the leisure to indulge in things he loved.

Ambapali, too, was happier than she had been for a long time. The ugly shadows that seemed always to hover around her had disappeared.

I should spend more time in this house. It makes me happy. It makes me forget I am a nagarvadhu. But will it be the same once Indrajeet leaves? Why do I feel so drawn to this stranger? Is it because Satya belongs to Urmi now? Am I searching for a replacement? If so, why a stranger? I could choose anyone from the wooers clamouring for my attention. God knows there are enough of them.

These thoughts crowded her mind as she rode away in the chariot. The sun was low on the horizon, and birds were flying home across a sky that was a vivid orange.

Twenty

It was long past sunset. The sky was an inky blue expanse speckled with stars. The night wrapped around the trees like a dark blanket. The lamps enveloped the room with warmth. His hands clasped behind his head, Bimbisara lay on the bed, daydreaming. Ambapali's blushing beauty was so different from the image of her he had carried to Vaishali.

An hour passed. He walked to the door and peered in the dark, wondering what was holding up Devavrata. He had sent the soldier on a mission to Samvarta setthi. As the night wore on, an apprehensive Bimbisara began pacing around the courtyard that fronted the house. Questions began to replace the pleasant thoughts of Ambapali. What if Deva had fallen into enemy hands? Would they torture him? The emperor was preparing to walk to Samvarta setthi's mansion, though he was in no condition to do so, when he spotted a shadow hurrying towards the house. It was Devavrata.

'Pranam, Maharaj,' he panted.

'What took you so long?' said Bimbisara, his tone sharp with worry. 'I was wondering if they had caught you.'

'I escaped by a whisker, Maharaj. I was on my way back when I realized that I was being followed. I think it was a Vaishali soldier, but I am not sure.'

'You haven't led him here, I hope.'

'No, Maharaj, I took a very long detour to shake him off.'

Bimbisara looked around cautiously, but it was too dark to determine if someone had followed Devavrata back to the house. Deva might be right—perhaps he had gotten rid of the person—but it was not a chance he wanted to take. They would have to move to a Magadh agent's house as soon as possible.

'Let's go inside and discuss the matter.' Bimbisara pulled Devavrata inside and shut the door.

Outside, a shadow peeled itself away from a tree.

It was Pundrik Varman, a spy who had fallen out of favour and into a complicated web of greed that led him to where he currently stood. Once a keen young soldier of the Vajji republic, he had been tapped to be on the elite intelligence division for Vaishali. Nepotism threw a spanner in his glowing career. Much to his disappointment, he had found himself superseded by an inefficient relative of the senapati.

Things had not gone well on the home front. His wife, who had been ailing for a long time, succumbed to her illnesses. Frustrated, Pundrik sought refuge in alcohol. He took to visiting drinking houses in the seedy lanes of the city. His vices continued to grow. Wine, gambling and ganikas took a toll on his health and wealth. By his late forties, his failing health and nefarious activities resulted in a serious setback to his career. Seniors who used to have nothing but praise for his work now looked down on him.

It was while he was in a gambling den that the idea
occurred to the frustrated spy. He could work as a double
agent and earn good money. In the course of his work, he
had to travel to adjoining kingdoms. Pundrik's wife was
from a small village near Rajgrih, so he had a valid excuse
for his frequent trips to the Magadh territories. Over time, he
developed many useful contacts. He knew many of the nayaks
and dandanayaks in the Magadh army. It was not too difficult
to establish his credentials and reliability. Pundrik began
trading information for cash, passing on secrets to Magadh
while keeping his seniors in Vaishali supplied with updates on
Magadhan activities.

His eyes and ears were naturally kept open for any
opportunity. He had recognized Devavrata when he passed
him at the market and suspected that something was brewing.
Certain that he had hit the jackpot, the spy began following the
young man. He was surprised when the Magadh dandanayak
halted at the small house in the village. Was it a safe-house?
Was the dandanayak on a mission? Perhaps Devavrata could
lead him to other Magadh spies. It was invaluable information.
It would certainly bring him a hefty reward from the Vaishali
senapati. But he would have to discover the reason for the
Magadh dandanayak's presence in the city. His reward would
be proportionate to the importance of the mission.

A little short-sighted, he failed to recognize Bimbisara
from a distance and was wondering if he should creep closer
when Devavrata re-emerged from the house. His mind made
up, the double agent began shadowing the young man. Across
the village and along the fields, he followed, maintaining a
reasonable distance from the Magadh soldier, until they found
themselves in a sordid part of town.

Where is Devavrata going? wondered Pundrik. Humming under his breath, the young man walked carelessly along the cramped and dirty lanes of the sleazy quarters. Their drains overflowing with dirt, the smelly lanes were packed with tiny tenements on both sides. Ill–lit and noisy, the area housed several drinking houses and cheap ganikas who were patronized by labourers, masons and riff–raffs. Sounds of boisterous arguments, drunken laughter and coarse singing were peppered with female tirades and laughter.

The double agent was instantly suspicious. It was not an area into which dandanayakas ventured unless they were on a mission. Pundrik rubbed his hands with glee. This was big.

Suddenly, his mind was assailed by doubt. What if he passed the information to his seniors, and they took the credit? They could, then, claim the reward. No. He had no wish to be cheated of the recognition due to him. He would bypass the junior officer and directly approach the Vaishali mahasenapati with the information, he decided. There had been several reports that the Magadh emperor was preparing to attack Vaishali. Perhaps Devavrata's mission had to do with the war preparations.

Devavrata continued to walk through the alleys till they had passed the sleazy parts and reached an area frequented by soldiers and minor tradespeople. The lanes were a little wider and not as dirty. The houses on either side of the lane were bigger, the drinking houses less crowded and the ganikas fewer. Reaching the end of a lane, Devavrata hesitated in front of a tavern. He cast a cautious look around before darting inside. Pundrik followed the dandanayak into the drinking house.

A medium-sized room in the front served as the watering hole, while the proprietor used the rest of the house as a residence. A few oil lamps spread small circles of dull light around the room. Pundrik scanned the handful of customers and ganikas scattered around the room.

Hiranya, the owner, a dark and hefty man with protruding teeth, had been a Magadh spy for a long time and knew most of the soldiers and spies who worked for Vaishali. Pundrik's entry so soon after Devavrata's was enough for him to figure out that the spy was shadowing the dandanayak. He didn't miss Devavrata's imperceptible nod as the young man took a seat in an unlit corner of the room.

The owner saw Pundrik pause near a ganika, who smiled invitingly at him. The ageing spy's eyes lit up at the sight of the different wines. From maireya to medaka, from prasanna and mahua to asava—there was a wide choice of drinks. Deciding to make the best of the situation, he ordered wine and some roasted meat to go with his drink. The medaka that arrived in a clay pot was of superior quality, he noticed, pleased.

One of the ganikas walked up to him and simpered, 'A handsome man like you should not be alone.' She ran her hand over his chest and he shivered with delight. 'Won't you buy me a pot of prasanna?' she said, pouting fetchingly.

Pundrik stared at the sexy woman, his hands itching to feel her voluptuous body. 'I am happy tonight,' he said, stripping her with his eyes. 'Ask for anything you want.'

'That's a generous offer. Don't go back on your words.' She drew closer and fondled him.

'I won't,' he murmured, closing his eyes to savour the sensation of her fingers. Wine and women! He had the best of them now.

While the ganika flirted with the Vaishali spy, Hiranya walked over to Devavrata. The dandanayak asked for maireya, which was a code for Hiranya to detain the man who had followed him into the drinking house.

An hour passed, but Devavrata made no move to leave the place. Pundrik wished he could accompany the ganika back to her house. He was aroused beyond control, but pleasure would have to wait. He couldn't afford to lose sight of the dandanayak. In the meantime, he drank some more medaka and flirted with the woman.

'Let's go,' she whispered in his ear. 'I can't wait to feel you.'

'Nor can I,' Pundrik replied hoarsely. He paid her some money, after which she allowed his hands to stray over her body. Getting bolder with each passing minute, the spy continued to fondle her.

One by one, the customers began leaving till only the four of them remained. The ganika, bored and sleepy, was getting impatient. Pundrik wondered if he had been mistaken about the dandanayak being on a mission. He darted another look at Devavrata, who was asking for another round of maireya in a drunken voice.

'Let me fetch you another drink, after which we will leave,' said the ganika determinedly. 'You can have the rest of the medaka at my house.' Swinging her hips, she walked towards Hiranya.

A few minutes later, she was back with a large clay pot of wine. She poured some in Pundrik's pot and gazed into his eyes, which were bloodshot with lust and wine. A few sips of the drink later, Pundrik's lifeless body collapsed on the ground. Placing a small purse with money in Hiranya's hands, Devavrata stepped out of the tavern.

It was close to dawn when Devavrata returned. Bimbisara, who had been waiting anxiously, raised an eyebrow questioningly.

'Pranam, Maharaj.' Devavrata smiled tiredly and folded his hands. 'We took care of the spy. He won't be able to tell anyone about us.'

'That's excellent!' the emperor said and walked away, happy that he could focus on the nagarvadhu.

Twenty-One

Ambapali's private garden at the back of the palace was the fruition of her dream project. It boasted several arbours with myriad fruit- and flower-bearing trees, lotus ponds and fountains crisscrossed with walkways. One of the first things she had done after moving into the mansion was to employ a battery of gardeners to landscape the area, sparing no expense.

A small marble temple with a statue of Nataraj situated right in the centre of a lotus pond was her spiritual sanctuary. It acted as her refuge when she was troubled. There, alone, surrounded by the greenery and the heady scent of flowers, she would sit for hours meditating or musing over a myriad of thoughts, trivial and serious.

The garden was out of bounds for the staff and visitors. While the gardeners worked there during the day, evenings saw Ambapali strolling along the labyrinthine paths that led through the rose garden and arbours. The marble platform in front of the temple was where she practised playing the veena. Even Priyamvada, her closest friend, did not venture to the temple without a nod from Pali.

The only time people had been allowed to wander around the garden was when she invited them once for a special soiree. A tiny amphitheatre at one end of the garden served as the venue for her performance, along with several talented musicians. The scent of nocturnal flowers flooded the senses along with divine music. The beauty of the garden served as a perfect background to the dreamlike experience. It had been a magical night, as wine and an extravagant spread of food enhanced the effects of the music. Never had the city seen such a unique celebration of senses. The guests wandered around the garden, enchanted by its beauty. The soiree and the garden became the talk of the town.

That was the first and the last time Ambapali opened the garden to visitors.

It was in that garden that Bimbisara found himself the next morning.

He had been woken up by Devavrata at the crack of dawn, informing him of Ambapali's arrival. The sun had barely risen and the eastern sky was a jumble of rose-and-yellow tones when they started for the Shweta Shatadal Prasaad.

'I wanted an early start, so you can enjoy the beautiful ride to the palace,' she explained. The truth was that she didn't want to attract the attention of passers-by. As usual, she had not brought along the chariot driver.

The early start suited Bimbisara as well. Despite the disguise, he had no wish to risk recognition.

Priyamvada had ensured that the drawbridge of the rear gate was lowered to receive the nagarvadhu's guests. Ambapali didn't want to announce Indrajeet's arrival at the palace, though she knew that it would be difficult to keep him hidden from the prying eyes within.

Dismounting at the rear gate, the three of them walked down the drawbridge. They were greeted by Priyamvada as

they made their way to the upper floor of the eastern wing,
where the guest rooms were located. Realizing their need
for privacy, Ambapali had instructed them to be given two
adjoining rooms of ample size at the end of the passage in the
unoccupied flank of the building. They were lavishly furnished
and had large garden-facing terraces.

Over the next three days, they spent a lot of time together,
talking for hours. Ambapali was reluctant for him to leave the
room because of his health.

'I am not an invalid, devi,' he protested. 'Remaining
confined to a room makes me feel like a caged bird, especially
when I gaze at this beautiful garden. It tempts me to disregard
your restrictions.'

They were sitting in the shaded part of the terrace, which
provided a delightful view of the garden.

'You are a free bird, Arya. I dare not dream of caging
you.' Her laughter was like the tinkling of bells. 'Why don't
you tell me about your journeys?'

That wouldn't be difficult, Bimbisara thought, relieved
that she hadn't asked him a personal question. All he had to do
was to draw on his imagination.

She flooded him with endless questions. She wanted to
know about the places he had seen and the people he had met.
Bimbisara wove interesting tales of his adventures in faraway
lands. Some of them were fictitious. Many were based on his
experiences.

Ambapali listened with rapt attention to his tales of voyages
through rough seas that were full of strange sea animals, some
of them large enough to capsize boats. The stories narrated
the perils that sailors and merchants faced. Merciless pirates,
tumultuous tempests and dangerous dragons peppered the tales.

The adventures took her through dark and dense forests inhabited by man-eating tigers and lions, pythons and anacondas, cobras and kraits. She shuddered with fear and excitement, and he enjoyed watching her reactions.

He told her of divers who faced dangers to collect corals and pearls embedded in the seabed. He described the mountains of Simhaladweep that yielded blue sapphires, and the blood-red rubies that came from Brahmadesh, the pearls found in the seas around Chin, the exotic wines of Misr and Gandhara, and the splendid horses of Kambhoja.

Ambapali's curiosity was insatiable.

'I don't think a lifetime is enough to hear about your adventures,' she sighed. 'Stories are poor substitutes for real experience, I know. If only I could travel to those wondrous places.'

'Wishes do come true,' he said enigmatically. 'You may travel someday.'

Her eyes shining, she turned to him. 'Arya, please tell me about your visit to Misr.'

He had never visited Misr, but that didn't prevent him from spinning a thrilling yarn about his travel through a desert on camelback. He told her about crossing the desert, parched with thirst and deluded with mirages. He narrated stories about his confrontations with ferocious bandits. As days went by, he began enjoying the story telling. He felt proud of his spinning skills.

Ambapali began to ignore the patrons who came to the palace, rarely responding to their messages. All she wanted was to spend time with Indrajeet. Days passed, and her fascination for the man continued to grow.

He didn't flatter her with flowery verses, nor did he make amorous demands. All he did was to provide her a peep into a world of fantasy. Ambapali had heard many stories from her father, but they had lacked the imagination and details that made Indrajeet's stories so interesting. Dharma Datta's stories had been about gods and demons, never about journeys.

'Life would be so interesting if you could stay here forever,' she said. 'I have never felt so alive. Every night I go to bed thinking of the stories you've told me. Each morning I jump out of the bed, raring to hear more. Your stories have opened up a new world for me. A world I couldn't even imagine. Now, I can see myself wandering through the very places described by you.'

They were walking around the garden. She patted the deer that was nuzzling her hand in search of food.

'I am honoured by your words,' he said gallantly. 'It's been wonderful to spend time in this beautiful palace, devi. I would love to stay here forever, but I can't. We can't always do the things we wish, unfortunately. Life has to go on. You have your patrons to look after, and I have my business. It's impossible to predict the future, of course. Our paths may cross again, someday. And then we will pick up the threads. I will have fresh stories to narrate.'

A wistful look crossed her face. 'You will have fresh stories, but I will have nothing new in my life.' Plucking a flower from a bush, Ambapali began tearing the petals in a frenzied manner. 'I don't want to continue this life. It's not what I want. This luxurious palace, admirers, wealth and servants. I don't want them. I have never craved for these. I wanted an uncomplicated life. Will I be able to break these shackles ever?' She turned anxiously towards him.

'It's our mind that creates shackles,' he repeated the words spoken by Sakyamuni in one of his discourses. The Magadh emperor had sought the wise one's advice whenever the sage stayed at Grudhkuta. 'We can break them whenever we want. All we require is a lot of determination.'

It set her thinking. 'Can we really break the shackles?' she asked.

At that moment, he wanted nothing more than to hold her in his arms and kiss away the furrows on her brows. It had taken him an enormous amount of restraint to keep his emotions in check. The time was not yet ripe for that. He didn't want to drive her away with his ardour.

Slowly and surely, the Magadh emperor had fallen in love with the woman whom he had wanted to punish for refusing his offer to make her the Magadh raj nartaki. He loved her as he had never loved any other woman. Ambapali, too, felt her heart succumbing to the stranger's charm.

'You are in love, Pali,' remarked Priyamvada as she styled her friend's hair one morning. She scrutinized her friend's face in the polished metal mirror. 'You are glowing. Indrajeet has pierced your armour.'

'You are wrong.' Ambapali protested.

'I am not wrong. The blush on your face is a giveaway.' Priyamvada tied a couple of jasmine strings around her friend's hair. She was happy to see the twinkle had returned in her eyes. 'Any fool can see the changes in you, and I am definitely not a fool. It's not your fault,' she teased. 'He's an impressive man. I am half in love with him myself.'

'It's his caring nature, not his looks, that made an impression on me. I don't know of any man who would risk his life for a woman he didn't know.'

'Well, I am happy that Indrajeet has drawn you out of your shell.'

'Everything seems like a dream. I feel worried it won't last.' Ambapali clutched Priyamvada's hands in hers. Her eyes troubled, she said, 'My heart can't bear another betrayal.'

'Everything will be all right. Trust your instincts. They will not let you down.'

The nagarvadhu's feelings for her guest had been noticed not just by Priyamvada but a few others in the palace, including a few servants still loyal to Suvarnasena, who reported to her every incident that took place in Ambapali's domain.

Suvarnasena had been smarting ever since she was thrown out of the Shweta Shatadal Prasaad. She wanted to avenge the humiliation. Ambapali had provided her with enough to restart the dance school and it was doing well. Eager parents had enrolled their daughters, hoping they would find fame as a raj nartaki. Suvarnasena had renovated her mansion and was living well, but this did not satisfy the woman. She had wanted to be known as the force behind the nagarvadhu, with all the power and money that came with it. Ambapali had deprived her of that, and for this, she would never forgive her former protégée. She was determined to find a way to hit back. Suvarnasena's access to the council members worked to her advantage. The ones spurned by Ambapali were seething with rage. One of them, Krishnadev, an aged minister, had taken a serious dislike to Ambapali. Rich and influential, he had been denied the pleasure of the nagarvadhu's exclusive company.

Not all the riches offered by him could buy him a night of sensual pleasure. He had promised a reward if Suvarnasena could bring the haughty woman to her knees.

So all Suvarnasena had to do was to find a way to kindle the fire. Word would reach the king, and Ambapali would be destroyed forever. But there had to be a strong reason for that to happen.

Twenty-Two

The season was on the verge of changing as the cold months of winter made way for pleasanter weather. The dormant seeds lying in the womb of the earth awoke from their slumber, stretched lazily and prepared for a new life. It was the season of love and rebirth. A season of hope and dreams.

A waxing gibbous moon hung tenaciously in the sky, casting a soft glow into Ambapali's room.

Her mind buzzing with a dozen thoughts, she tossed restlessly on the bed. Everything had changed since Indrajeet had entered her life. She was no longer in control of her emotions. When she had become the nagarvadhu and Satyakirti had refused to marry her, the very thought of love had evoked bitterness. But Indrajeet had stirred deeply buried emotions. Her heart brimmed with hope and she had begun dreaming of happiness once again. She felt her body tingle with desire each time it brushed against Indrajeet. Her heart missed a beat at the sight of his lean and muscular body. She wanted to possess him. She lusted for him as she had never lusted for any man.

She knew the love and passion wasn't one-sided. The past few years had brought her in close contact with men, and she had learnt to read them. She was aware Indrajeet desired her.

The pair were no longer satisfied by word plays and innuendos. It now required immense will power to control their ardour. That morning, they had come very close to succumbing to their emotions. Lust was an emotion Ambapali had rarely experienced after she and Satyakirti had parted ways. And now, she felt her mind return adamantly to fantasies about a man she barely knew. In the mellow spring, her dormant desires had awakened once more. A different kind of heat was making her sleepless that night. Her body was demanding the feel of Indrajeet's arms around it. Her lips were craving for his kiss.

As a courtesan, she was no stranger to love and lust. Sleeping with men was one of her duties as a nagarvadhu, which she performed with dispassion and disinterest. It was a mechanical parting of legs, allowing the man to satisfy his lust. Her participation had remained minimal.

Why was she experiencing such attraction for a man she had met just recently? Was it just physical attraction? She enjoyed his company, there was no doubt about that. But did she perhaps want more?

This couldn't be happening to her. This couldn't be allowed to happen.

Perspiring, she got up and walked out to the balcony. The cool breeze did nothing to douse the heat, nor did the marble floor. Her body feverish with desire, she walked out of her room and strolled towards the pool. Its water looked cool and inviting. Without a second thought, she plunged in. She shivered as her body hit the cold water. The shock of it made her skin tingle. It calmed her mind. Ambapali flipped onto her back and floated lazily, allowing her body to adjust itself to the cold.

She continued until the desire ebbed and her mind regained control. Suddenly, her sharp ears caught the resonance of strings. Someone was tuning a veena. It was her veena. The one gifted to her by Satyakirti. The one she held sacred.

It was placed in the gazebo near the temple, which was forbidden to everyone.

How dare anyone touch her instrument?

Livid, she stepped out of the pool, preparing to confront the offender. It was then that the notes reached her ears. Spellbound, she listened to the faultless rendition of Raag Madhuvanti. It was one of her favourite ragas. It was also a raga that had been perfected by Satyakirti. He had taught her to play it as well. Memories of those happy times flooded her mind, and she closed her eyes.

It's the gamaka that renders beauty and uniqueness to the raga, making it exquisite, Satyakirti had taught her. The veena was the only instrument on which all the gamakas could be played.

Water dripping from her clothes, Ambapali walked towards the gazebo, her ears tuned to the raga. Although the technique was flawless, the rendering lacked finesse. It was the gamaka that the player hadn't perfected.

She saw the man playing the veena, and her heart flipped. His eyes closed, Indrajeet was sitting cross-legged on the floor with the resonator on his left thigh. He was using his left hand to play the frets while he plucked the strings with the right hand. Ambapali noticed his long and artistic fingers that were teasing the strings. She hadn't heard of a trader being a musician. There were so many facets to the man she harboured in her mansion. Each time she unpeeled a layer, she found another one. Her eyes rested on the rippling biceps of his arms; her body yearned to be held by them. She couldn't imagine a trader with such a well-muscled body.

He had told her that his business took him on many voyages. Perhaps a trader was often required to protect his ware from dacoits. That must be why he had such a strong physique.

Her heartbeat sped up as she gazed longingly at his well-toned body. Those wide shoulders that were meant to be cried upon, the torso that was an excellent place to rest the head, and those lips . . . she felt faint with desire at the thought of being kissed by them. The thought of his fingers straying over her body made her shudder with yearning.

She shook her head, willing the thoughts away. From a vilambit laya, a slow beat, the tempo had risen to madhyam, medium, and then drut, fast, evoking different types of emotions in her. Her mood ascended from the dreamy heat-laden trance to a slow awakening of senses and then a feeling of pulsating exhilaration as Indrajeet continued to play. He was good. But he could be better.

I will have to teach him the gamakas, she decided.

He hit the crescendo and then everything was quiet. Sensing a presence, he opened his eyes.

'Ambe!' he whispered. For a moment, Bimbisara wondered if he was dreaming. Her wet clothes clinging seductively to the body, an ethereal-looking Ambapali was standing before him. Dazed by the vision, he put down the veena.

Drops of water sat like dew on her trembling lips. The white mulmul antariya, now transparent, clung to her hips, and the wet kanchuki was a scant cover for her breasts. The uttariya had been discarded when she dived into the pond. He felt his body react with desire. A strange tightness in the chest made breathing difficult.

Ambapali drew closer.

'Go away,' he breathed out, closing his eyes.

'What if I don't want to?' she whispered, as she ran a finger lightly down his face, tracing his features. Her finger moved like a feather down his forehead to stop at his lips, leaving a trail of fire in its wake. Teasing. Tantalizing. Stirring his senses.

I am not a virgin, he told himself; nor will she be the last woman. I have lost count of the women I have slept with. This is what I wanted. To enslave and ravish her. I am a husband to many women. I am a man who has fathered several children. Why this hesitation?

'I don't know if I can hold back,' he warned in a voice thick with desire. The waves of heat rose between their bodies. He shuddered, trying to stop himself.

'Sshhh!' she said. 'I don't want you to hold back. Why are you trying to suppress your desire?' Her eyes glittered with want. Ambapali felt herself melting in the blaze of his eyes. Her arms snaked around him and then he felt her lips settling on his. Soft, sensuous and lustful.

Giving up all resistance, he tightened his arms around her pliable body, breathing in her scent, his tongue exploring her mouth. His hands moved impatiently down her body, peeling away the clothes. First, the girdle holding the antariya was discarded, and then he peeled away the kanchuki. His fingers wandered over her. Sometimes tender. Sometimes rough. They explored each curve and hollow. Their movements grew more frenetic, and he felt himself going taut with desire.

'Ambe,' he whispered into her ears. 'I want you.'

She lay still for a while, reminded of another who had called her by that name. She gave herself a mental shake to get rid of the memories. Satya was in her past. This was her present. This man, who lay by her side, was hers to love and cherish.

She used every trick taught by Suvarnasena to seduce a man. Her skilled fingers wandered over him in desperate urgency. Searching, seeking and goading. His feverish breath melded with hers and he groaned. Wrapping her legs around him, she opened herself in welcome and gasped at the impact.

He didn't want it to end. And when it did, it was just perfect. He had come to conquer, but she had vanquished him.

Ambapali felt an avalanche of emotions rushing through her. Later, she lay back, a satisfied smile hovering on her lips. Raising herself on an elbow, she gazed tenderly at the man lying next to her. She realized that it wasn't just her body she had given him. He now held her heart in his hands. She loved him. Was it gratitude for saving her life? No. It couldn't be. The surge of emotions for him went beyond mere thankfulness.

They lay side by side, limbs entwined. Replete and sated. She drew a deep sigh and closed her eyes.

Life would never be the same for either of them.

Her feelings were confusing. She had loved Satya since she was just a girl, but she knew now that her love for him had not been an all-consuming one. It had been tolerant and resilient. It had lacked the intensity she now experienced. This was as sudden as it was inexplicable.

The sudden resonance of the veena string woke her up a couple of hours later. Ambapali sat up and covered herself. She stretched languorously. Indrajeet's fingers glided across the strings and, minutes later, the melodious notes of Raag Bhairav filled the garden. The rendering began with a relaxed and slow-tempo alapana, rising thereafter. His nimble fingers moved smoothly, like the flutter of butterfly wings.

What a glorious way to wake up, she thought joyfully.

Unable to restrain herself, she began dancing. It had been so, even when Satyakirti played the veena. She could not stop her feet from matching the rhythm of the music. Her movements fluid, mood upbeat, she continued to dance to his tune. The rhythm intensified and so did her steps, till the notes reached the crescendo and ended triumphantly. Exhausted, Ambapali collapsed with a satisfied smile. It was the nearest thing to bliss. This was the way she would like to spend her life.

Bimbisara was taken aback by how he had played. He had been playing the veena for a long time, yet never had it been as inspired as it was that morning. Was it the environment? No. The garden of the royal palace at Rajgrih was as beautiful, if not more so. It must be the emotions that welled in him that morning.

Bimbisara wanted to forget he was the mighty emperor of Magadh. He wanted nothing to do with the intrigues and intricacies of an empire. He wanted to forget that he was a pretender who had arrived in Vaishali on a mission. He wanted to be a commoner, free to live the way he wanted. To be with his love.

'Ambe,' he said, putting down the instrument. 'I am the happiest man on earth.'

It was the most beautiful morning. Dawn was breaking and life stirred. The early rays of the sun cast a golden glow, waking up the flowers. Bees hummed and wooed the blossoms. Laden with the scent of dewy flowers, the wind rustled approvingly. Heaven had descended in Ambapali's garden. Everything was just as it had been, yet something had changed. The gloom in her heart was replaced with joy.

She felt light as a feather. She was in love.

Hand in hand, whispering words of love, the two of them walked back to Ambapali's private chamber.

Twenty-Three

Suvarnasena was intrigued. Her spies had reported that a merchant named Indrajeet was staying at the Shatadal palace. They informed her of Ambapali's preoccupation with the man. If he was a wealthy merchant, she had never heard of him, and she knew almost every prosperous merchant in the city and beyond.

'Devi is so besotted with the man that she remains locked in her chamber with him all day and night,' whispered Ratnaprabha. The woman had been employed as a masseuse by Suvarnasena. Her job included monitoring the goings-on in the nagarvadhu's palace. 'It's been more than twelve moons since he arrived with a companion.' Ratnaprabha extracted paan from a pouch tucked in her waistbelt and pushed it into her mouth. She chewed on it for a few moments.

'Get on with the story!' shouted Suvarnasena, impatient to hear the details. 'I don't have the entire day to spend with you.'

Ratnaprabha crammed the paan firmly inside her left cheek. She loved gossiping, and the prospect of sharing juicy titbits with her employer delighted her. The money she was paid didn't hurt either. Suvarnasena was a stingy woman, but she was desperate to discover the cracks in Ambapali's household. She was eager to find some reason to act against the nagarvadhu. And this made her part with a coin now and then.

With a wicked gleam in her eyes, Ratnaprabha began speaking. 'In the meantime, the patrons continue to be entertained. The dancers and musicians perform. Wine is poured, dice rolled, gambling continues. Everything continues as before. Everyone is told that the nagarvadhu is unwell. Patrons are disappointed, but life goes on.'

Suvarnasena digested the information. She wondered if the woman was exaggerating. In all the years she'd known her, she had never seen Ambapali open herself up to any man— apart from Satya. 'Ambapali has not left her room at all?' she asked doubtfully.

'In the past few days, the lovers have gone out only once. They left the palace through the private gate and went hunting. Every evening, they emerge from devi's chamber to stroll through the garden or swim in her pool. It's like they can't have enough of each other.' The masseuse winked vulgarly.

'What is he like, the merchant?'

'Oh, he's handsome enough to make a maiden swoon. Those muscular arms! Even I would have succumbed to his charms if I were younger,' she said, grinning. 'No wonder that the nagarvadhu is smitten by the man.'

Suvarnasena looked away thoughtfully. 'What makes this man special, I wonder? Ambapali has been courted by hundreds of men. I have never seen her get attached to any of them. And mind you, she can count some of the most handsome rakes of Vaishali among her wooers. She has rejected hundreds and slept with dozens.'

Ratnaprabha shrugged. 'I don't know. He's not young. The man is not a year less than forty-five, if you ask me. Perhaps it's his experience with women that makes him so attractive. All I can deduce is that he's cast a spell on our lady.'

Suvarnasena was not convinced. She had never seen Ambapali waver from her loyalty to Satyakirti. So strong had been her love for her childhood friend that no prince or setthi had found a place in her heart. The woman had given her body to them, but her heart remained untouched. So, who was this man?

Worried that the stingy woman would not pay for the information, Ratnaprabha hurried to make the story more interesting. 'There's something fishy about the whole affair, if you ask me. He looks majestic and moneyed, but the man has brought no servants or attendants with him. A trader would carry some goods, wouldn't he? I wonder if there's a secret he wishes to hide.'

'Well, if there is a secret, you will have to discover it,' Suvarnasena told the masseuse. 'I can pay only if you bring me valuable information. The news that Ambapali has fallen in love is of no use to me. She has every right to fall in love or sleep with any man of her choice. Tell me about this companion of his.'

'The companion is one of a kind. He's young. Couldn't be a day over twenty-five, but he's not interested in women. Can you imagine? The dancers employed to perform in the palace are as beautiful and sexy as the apsaras in Indrasabha, but he's not shown any inclination to bed them. Rambha and Urvashi have tried several times. Such is the man's reputation that the girls have wagered that the one who sleeps with him will win a handsome amount of money. One by one, they have tried and failed. They told me that the man rebuffed their advances. I have known no man who can resist their charms.'

Ratnaprabha sat back triumphantly. If this news didn't arouse Suvarnasena's curiosity, nothing would.

Suvarnasena knew all about Rambha and Urvashi. After all, she had handpicked them for the nagarvadhu's palace. She had selected only the most beautiful women, trained in the art of seduction. It was her idea to name them after the apsaras in Indralok. To evoke a simulation of Indrasabha, the hall had been decorated and furnished like the real one. Like the eleven celebrated apsaras that inhabited Indralok, Suvarnasena had chosen eleven girls. It was impossible for men to fight their allure, she knew.

Ratnaprabha was right. There was something fishy about the two men who had turned up at the nagarvadhu's palace. A masseuse was in the best position to extract information. Not only did she have access to all the rooms, but she also had the privacy and the opportunity to gather titbits while massaging the dancers, when they were relaxed and unwary.

The only issue was that the nagarvadhu didn't trust Ratnaprabha. Ambapali had appointed her own masseuse, who was a loyal and tight-lipped woman.

'Keep your eyes and ears open, woman,' Suvarnasena instructed the masseuse. She pulled out a coin from a pouch lying nearby and handed it to Ratnaprabha. 'If the information is important enough, I will make this worth your time.'

The woman cackled happily. 'Trust me, devi. No one can hide a secret from this masseuse.'

Ratnaprabha was back the very next week. She had been ferreting around for additional information in the Shweta

Shatadal Prasaad, and now the woman could barely hold back her excitement as she entered Suvarnasena's house.

'What is it now?' Suvarnasena groused.

'I know you are busy, devi. But I have important news. The merchant remains locked inside Ambapali's chamber, but his young companion is out the entire day. I have seen him leaving the palace in the morning and returning late at night.' The woman paused to see the teacher's response to that bit of information. Satisfied with the gleam of interest in her eyes, she continued. 'I found an opportunity to search the rooms during his absence, and guess what I discovered?'

'Come to the point, woman,' snapped Suvarnasena. 'I don't have the time for guessing games.'

'Well, there were a few pieces of jewellery among his possessions. I found solid gold kayabandh, a five-string pearl necklace with a pendant inlaid with precious stones, and a pair of earrings.'

'What's unusual about that?' snorted the teacher. 'These days I find men loading themselves with all kinds of jewellery. Why shouldn't the companion of a wealthy merchant own a few expensive pieces?'

'Devi, a Magadh jeweler crafted these pieces. I know enough about jewellery to recognize the origin of a piece. I say so with complete confidence.'

'Those two men are traders. It's not unlikely that they bought jewellery in some other kingdom during their travels.'

'That may be true, but how do you explain the pouch of Magadh karshapanas hidden under the mattress?'

'Magadh karshapanas?'

'Yes, silver coins with four punch marks. A few had the typical symbol of the sun and six arms engraved on them.

There were others with engravings of the six-armed wheel, the bull, the sun, the fish and the crocodile symbol. Anyone with a little intelligence can see that these are from Rajgrih. I could steal a few, so you can show them to an expert. Believe me, devi, there's more than what meets the eye. I suspect them to be Magadh spies.'

The teacher knew a treasury employee could surmise the origin by looking at a coin. He could tell the name of the village, town and the identity of the mint where it was struck.

'I forbid you to steal anything from the man's room,' Suvarnasena's voice rose sharply. 'We don't want them to suspect anything. At least, not till we have enough evidence to haul them before the king.'

The teacher thought for a few minutes and then barked, 'What has Ballabh been doing? Has he been sleeping all this while?' Ballabh had been employed by her ostensibly to guard the palace, but his real job was to report on the people who visited the nagarvadhu. 'Why hasn't he noticed anything suspicious about the two men staying in the place?'

'Pardon my saying this, devi, but he is a thick-skulled fool with more brawn than brains.'

'I want you to ensure that Ballabh follows the companion when he goes out in the morning. I want a detailed report about where the fellow goes, whom he meets, and what he does throughout the day.'

Ratnaprabha nodded happily. She liked nothing better than commanding the minions to do her bidding. In the past couple of years, she had consolidated a place for herself in the palace. Her services as a masseuse were much in demand among the dancers employed by the nagarvadhu. In the meantime, her stock as a spy had gone up in Suvarnasena's coterie. Blessed with a pair of sharp eyes, a gift of the gab and an intelligent mind, she had proved herself invaluable.

Grudgingly, the teacher dug into her pouch and handed another coin to the masseuse. 'This is for Ballabh. Your reward will come after the work is done.' She waggled her forefinger warningly. 'Remember, I want complete information about the companion's movements.'

And so it was that Ballabh found himself tailing Devavrata early the next morning.

It was after he had walked for a while that Devavrata sensed he was being followed. Over the past three days, he had contacted many men and women working as spies for the Magadh intelligence division. He wanted to make the best use of his time while the emperor was engaged with the nagarvadhu, and so the dandanayak had worked on gathering information about the Vaishali army commanders and ministers.

That morning, he was on his way to keep a rendezvous with one of their most important informers. The man who worked for Samvarta setthi, had been successful in making inroads into the Vaishali intelligence unit. If Devavrata truly was being followed, he would need to do something about it immediately.

The venue selected by the agent was a temple atop a hill on the outskirts of the city. Its remoteness meant it was usually deserted. A trained warrior, Devavrata was comfortable walking long distances. What he didn't like was the idea of walking along isolated paths that were fringed with jungles. His senses heightened, he could distinctly hear the footsteps of his pursuer.

He bent down, pretending to adjust the strap of his footwear. The steady sound of footsteps behind him stopped too. The wooded area on either side of the path provided ample cover for a person to dart into the undergrowth and escape. It also provided enough cover for a killer to hide. Regretting that he had not accepted the horse offered by Samvarta setthi, Devavrata quickened his steps. Suddenly, the dandanayak turned around and looked directly at the stocky beggar behind him. The move took his pursuer by surprise. Flustered, the beggar paused and then walked past. The fellow was dressed in tattered clothes and a turban concealed half his face.

What a bad disguise! Deva smiled to himself. Beggars didn't walk on isolated roads. They crowded near temples and markets, where there were people who might part with a few panas. Besides, the stalker was too hefty to pass off as a beggar.

What worried Devavrata was the unmistakable shape of a dagger outlined in the cloth tied around his waist. He could fight the man, but he had no idea if there were more people hiding in the forest, waiting to ambush him.

On an impulse, the dandanayak decided to resort to his earlier trick of leading the pursuer into Hiranya's drinking house. That way, he could leave the matter in Hiranya's capable hands. Decision made, the young man turned around and began walking the way he had come.

His quarry's sudden turnaround took Ballabh by surprise. Ratnaprabha's instructions had been precise. He was not to harm the man, just follow him and note the people he met and places he visited.

'Ensure that he doesn't realize he is being followed,' the masseuse had asserted.

The oaf vacillated for a few minutes.

Why was he walking in a different direction? Perplexed, Ballabh resumed walking behind the quarry. It was at this point that both the pursued and pursuer spotted a bullock cart coming from the opposite end of the path. The two sturdy bulls were going at a good speed, and the bells around their necks rang rhythmically. The cart passed the two men and went ahead for a little distance before stopping by the side.

The cart driver got down and, taking a pitcher of water from the undercarriage of the cart, began drinking.

Minutes later, Ballabh felt himself being pushed to the ground. The assailant stuffed a piece of cloth into his mouth to keep him from shouting, and then his arms were tied behind his back. He felt himself being pushed into the cart, which was loaded with hay. Everything happened in a flash, leaving him dazed and incapable of handling the sudden attack.

Minutes later, Devavrata heard the rhythmic tinkling of the bells again. He turned back to see the cart racing away on the path.

His pursuer had disappeared. Perplexed, he shook his head and continued walking.

Twenty-Four

It turned out to be a very eventful day for Devavrata. One which had required him to remain alert, right from the moment he spotted his pursuer to keeping his rendezvous with Samvarta setthi's man.

He narrated the morning's incident to the spy, whom he met soon after his pursuer disappeared. 'I have no idea who the man was, why he was following me and where he went,' Devavrata said.

'I don't think that Vaishali's spy network is aware of your presence in the city. I've had my ears to the ground. The man who followed you a few weeks back was eliminated in Hiranya's drinking house before he could pass the information to anyone. So, who was following you this morning?'

Devavrata shook his head. 'I think it proves we are mistaken that no one knows of our presence in the city,' asserted the dandanayak. 'How else can one explain it? His pathetic disguise indicates he was not a skilled spy, though. And if the man was not a member of the Vaishali security setup, who was he? How did he know that I was staying in the palace?'

'He could be a servant of the nagarvadhu's palace,' said the spy. 'He may have been planted by someone wanting to monitor the goings-on there. Warning bells must have been sounded when they saw you arriving at the palace. That's my guess.'

'That would be the most logical explanation. It would be easy for a servant to monitor our moves.'

'It would be dangerous for Maharaj to remain there any longer. Convince him to return to Magadh immediately.'

'I could try, but I am not sure how he will react,' Devavrata said. He wasn't too happy about the prospect of making the suggestion to the emperor. He knew it would annoy him. 'What puzzles me is the disappearance of the spy,' he said after a few moments. 'One minute he was behind me and the next he was gone without a trace. It was as if he had vanished.'

'There is just one possibility. Once he realized you were aware he was following you, he could have escaped in the cart that passed by you. The cart driver must have been instructed to remain in the vicinity. There might have been a pre-arranged signal between the spy and the cart driver.'

Devavrata nodded his head. 'You're right. That is the only explanation.'

'Samvarta setthi wants you to meet him as soon as possible,' the man said. 'Is it possible today?'

The dandanayak said it was, and the two headed to Samvarta setthi. Devavrata told him about the man following him in the morning. 'I wonder if the cart was there on purpose,' he said.

'The cart driver was our man,' the setthi set Devavrata's mind at rest. 'As you know, we have been keeping an eye on the palace for a long time. A couple of days back, I received instructions from the mahamatya. Aware that the emperor is residing at the palace, Arya Varshakar instructed me to tighten the security there. One of our spies saw the man dressed as a beggar following you, and he acted swiftly. The man is now in our custody. He is a soldier called Ballabh, who was employed as a palace guard by Suvarnasena.'

'Suvarnasena? Wasn't she the nagarvadhu's mentor? Why has she appointed spies in the palace?' The possibility of their identity being revealed was troubling Devavrata. 'Do you think she suspects we are from Magadh?'

'It would seem so. Suvarnasena feels she was insulted by the nagarvadhu and wants to get her revenge somehow. Our interrogation reveals that there are several men and women who spy for her in that palace. What is worrying is that Suvarnasena is in close contact with a minister called Krishnadev.' The setthi got up to pace the room. There was silence for a while, and then he stopped and faced Devavrata. 'It will be impossible for us to protect Maharaj if word gets around that he is here. I will make all arrangements for him to leave for Magadh tonight. You have to convince him that it's necessary.'

'It will be—'

'There is no time for hesitation.' Samvarta setthi's voice hardened. 'We had no advance intimation of Maharaj's visit, so the arrangements here are far from adequate. Besides, his presence has to obviously remain a secret, which makes it doubly difficult for us to provide security. The more people we involve, the more dangerous it becomes. Can you imagine what will happen if the Vaishali intelligence learns he is here? Short of attacking Vaishali, we cannot save the maharaja if you don't act swiftly. Even an attack may be too little too late.'

Devavrata nodded. He knew what the setthi was saying was right. 'I will try to persuade the emperor.'

'We are fortunate that Suvarnasena's lackey wasn't a skilled spy. It may not be so, the next time,' warned the setthi. 'Assuming that your cover has been blown, the Shweta Shatadal must be under surveillance. And I suspect that Suvarnasena's spies are keeping a constant watch on the two of you. It would be safer for the maharaj to slip out at night. They may alert soldiers if they see you leaving, and that could lead to an ugly confrontation. One we should avoid. I am sure you don't want a swordfight with a posse of Ambapali's guards. I don't think the maharaj would want Ambapali to know his identity at this point in time.' Observing the troubled expression on the young man's face, he continued, 'What we need is a quick and quiet getaway.'

'It's not going to be easy to leave the palace undetected. The palace has dozens of servants and other staff. There are soldiers stationed outside the entrances. How are we to leave without being seen?' Devavrata asked.

Like a conjurer, the setthi produced a detailed layout of Ambapali's palace. The man's thoroughness impressed Deva. No wonder the mahamatya entrusted the most dangerous missions to him.

'How on earth did you get hold of this?' he asked, poring over the sketch.

'It's easy to get anything if you have the money and the brains.' The setthi sat back with a smug smile. 'I feared such a situation the moment our emperor moved to Devi Ambapali's palace. Intrigues and conspiracies are not restricted to courts—we can find them everywhere. More so in places where the powerful stay.' Pointing at the drawing, he said, 'I want you to study this layout and tell me how you propose to get the emperor out of the palace.'

Despite scrutinizing the diagram for a while, the young man failed to come up with a workable plan.

'There doesn't seem to be any unguarded gate,' he said. 'The rear gate is locked and guarded. It has a drawbridge that can be lowered only from the guard's room. Besides, it's used only by tradespeople and for deliveries during the daytime. Going out from there is impossible. As for the main entrance, it is locked after the departure of the patrons, and is heavily guarded through the night.' The young man had, in fact, carried out a painstaking inspection of the palace to locate any possible exits in case of an emergency. There were none that were not risky. Ambapali's palace was a well-protected fortress.

'Look closely, Deva. There is a gap that can be used for your escape.'

'The palace is situated right in the middle of a lake.' Devavrata shook his head. 'I give up, Arya. Why don't you tell me the plan since you seem to have thought of everything?'

'The Shatadal palace was owned by a clan chieftain at one time. Like most old palaces, Devi Ambapali's palace has a secret passage. It has not been used for decades, so most people don't know about its location.'

Samvarta setthi pointed out the secret passage and narrated his scheme for Bimbisara's escape. Despite all attempts, Devavrata could find no fault with the plan. Satisfied, he let out a sigh of relief.

The two men spent some time fine-tuning the details of Bimbisara's journey to Magadh, after which Devavrata left for the palace in a carriage that the setthi had arranged for him.

An arduous task awaited him there, he knew. Convincing the emperor to leave would not be easy.

Bimbisara and Ambapali had spent the evening engaged in a lively discussion. The topic was music, which they both loved. Earlier that evening, she had delighted him with a scintillating rendering of Raga Tilak Kamod on the veena.

'Ambe, you surpassed yourself this evening,' he said. 'It brought a feeling of buoyancy to my heart. I am amazed at the effect of music on my moods. Your rendition of Raga Lalit filled me with such intense despair last evening,' he said.

They had finished a very satisfying meal a while ago and were enjoying a drink on the terrace.

'You are not the only one, Arya. According to my music teacher, there are different emotional responses to different musical scales. For instance, a raga with shuddh swaras, natural notes, causes a calming effect on our mind, but a raga with komal swaras, flat notes, can have a melancholic effect. It can cause emotions of sadness and longing in the listener.'

'You are such an interesting woman, Ambe. Beautiful beyond description, and intelligent beyond comparison.'

'What about loving beyond words?' she teased.

He threw back his head and laughed. His expression suddenly changed from mirthful to sombre. The amber eyes burning with passion, he said, 'The truth is that I have no words to describe you. You have bewitched me, woman. I want to lie in your lap and gaze into your eyes all night. Isn't it strange that we were absolute strangers a few weeks ago, and now I can't imagine living without you? I want to whisk you away from this palace and keep you with me forever.'

She was carried away by the magic of his words. Not very long ago, she had dreamed of hearing the same words from Satya. He had never said them. Instead, Satya had married her best friend. And now, this man, a stranger, was offering her the

chance to live those dreams. But suddenly, she was afraid of
the offer. She was afraid of her dreams being shattered. Afraid
of waking up one day and finding it all gone.

Ambapali shook her head. 'No, Arya. That can't happen.'

A look of annoyance crossed his face. 'Why can't it
happen? Don't you love me, Ambe?'

A timid knock on the door interrupted the conversation.
Wishing it away, the emperor waited for her reply.

'Someone's at the door,' she said as she stood up. But he
caught hold of her hand and pulled her down against himself.

'Why are you trying to evade my question?' he asked
sharply. 'Didn't you instruct the servants to not disturb us?'

'I did. So, it must be something important.'

'Nothing is more important than your reply. I want to
know if you love me enough to spend the rest of your life with
me.' Her hesitation irritated him. 'Whoever is at the door will
go away.'

She ignored his protests and opened the door to find an
anxious-looking Devavrata standing outside.

'I am sorry for disturbing you, devi,' he said. 'It is of
utmost importance that I speak to Arya immediately.' The
young man's expression conveyed more than the words
could.

'Who is it, Ambe?' the emperor asked from the terrace.

'It's Deva,' she replied. 'He wants to have a word with
you, Arya.'

'Tell him to go away. I will speak to him in the morning.'

'It's an urgent matter, he says.'

Annoyed, the emperor strode to the door and faced
Devavrata. The nagarvadhu withdrew to the terrace to give
them privacy. In the short time she had known him, Ambapali

had realized that her lover was domineering by nature. She liked Deva and didn't want to embarrass him by being present at the scene.

'What is so important that you couldn't wait till morning?' thundered Bimbisara. One look at Devavrata's ashen face and he softened. A trivial matter wouldn't have caused the young dandanayak to rush to him, he realized. It had to be something that needed urgent action.

'I apologize, Maharaj.' Devavrata closed the door and cast a look towards the terrace where Ambapali was sitting. 'It's a matter of utmost importance,' he said softly. 'We must speak in private.'

'Let's go to your room and talk,' suggested the emperor. Devavrata's anxiety had not escaped him. 'You go ahead. I will join you in a while.'

The emperor walked back to the terrace.

'What is it, Arya?' asked Ambapali. 'Deva looked quite disturbed.' She scanned her lover's face.

'It's about an important consignment which was to have arrived this morning,' Bimbisara invented an excuse. 'Deva has discovered that a group of bandits seized the packages. Not just that, they killed one and injured a couple of my men.'

'You must inform the security forces so they can catch the bandits.'

'Don't fret, Ambe,' he said quickly. It would be fatal if she were to take an interest in the matter or seek the help of a minister. 'I don't think that would be necessary. Since the incident happened in the forests on the outskirts of Kapilavastu, we will have to inform our counterparts there. They will take the action required.'

'Will you have to leave Vaishali?' She was disturbed by the thought of his leaving.

'I don't think so. Let me discuss the matter with Deva. Maybe he can handle it.'

'You can use my chamber,' she said. 'I will go to Priya's room.'

'I have no intention of disturbing you, Ambe.' He wrapped her in his arms and kissed her on the forehead. 'We can do the talking in Deva's room. If we finish quickly, I will return. Else, I will sleep in my room tonight. Don't wait for me.'

'Come back soon, Arya,' she murmured. 'I find it difficult to fall asleep without you by my side.'

He tightened his grip and planted a kiss on her waiting lips. A tremor rode through her body. Sighing with pleasure, she closed her eyes. 'Return soon,' she whispered.

The emperor strode into Devavrata's suite, where the dandanayak was pacing anxiously. 'Maharaj, someone has discovered your presence at Vaishali. We will have to leave at once.' The words tumbled out of the dandanayak's mouth, making his distress clear. On his way back to the palace, he had realized the need to exaggerate the warning to convince the king.

'Stop blabbering and speak slowly,' instructed Bimbisara. 'Drink some water. It will calm your nerves.'

Nodding obediently, Devavrata poured water into a glass and gulped it down quickly. Patiently, Bimbisara waited for the young man to speak. The matter must be quite serious to rattle Deva, he thought. He was usually unflappable, a trait that had helped him win many battles on the field and in court.

Drawing a deep breath, the young dandanayak related the events in an orderly manner. 'Samvarta setthi has made all the arrangements. All we have to do is to steal out of the palace unseen,' he ended.

Once Deva had narrated everything, the emperor knew he had to acquiesce. It was too dangerous to remain in Vaishali.

Twenty-Five

The darkness intensified, and so did the silence around the palace. The two men waited, each lost in his own thoughts.

The emperor was distraught that he was leaving Ambapali without bidding farewell. But he dared not listen to his heart. It would be impossible to steal away if Ambapali was awake. She would ask him a hundred questions and he would have to continue lying to her.

He was not free to love. The kingdom came first. Ambapali would have to wait till he conquered Vaishali; only then could he take her with him to Magadh. Bimbisara was so confident of her love that he refused to entertain the thought that she could spurn his offer of marriage. But matters of the heart had to be kept in abeyance for the moment. Once again, as always, he steeled his heart, forcing his mind to dictate his decisions.

It was well past midnight now, and stillness reigned over the palace. In the rang mahal, the drunken soirees had ended. The sound of anklets and music could no longer be heard, nor the sound of laughter. The last of the carriages had trundled out of the palace as the remaining patrons departed.

Another hour passed. Exhausted dancers, musicians and minions went to bed. Save for the guards, not a soul stirred.

The occasional hoot of an owl or the bark of a dog were the only sounds breaking the stillness of the night. Outside, the darkness was absolute as they stepped out of the room. The corridor was lit by a few lamps. Devavrata took the lead, dagger at the ready to fend off any attack. He doused each lamp as they passed, plunging the passage into darkness. Down the corridor they walked, their ears cocked for any sound. Their exit would be through the ancient temple, close to the rear gate. A flight of stairs from the sanctum sanctorum of the temple led to the edge of the lake, he had been told by Samvarta setthi.

The challenge was to cross the small open patch of ground in front of the temple. Anyone who cared to look out of the southern window would see them quite easily. But it was a chance they had to take.

Devavrata's skin crawled with fear as the emperor gestured his readiness, and the two of them sprinted towards the temple. It was only after the two of them had made it into the temple that he exhaled.

A couple of lamps burning in the sanctum sanctorum threw more shadows than light. The secret flight of stairs lay right under the deity. The two men turned the heavy idol along its axis with difficulty, trying to suppress the twinge of guilt that stabbed their conscience.

The welcome sight of a heavy trapdoor under the idol was a relief. Although the setthi had told him about the secret exit, Devavrata was not prepared to believe it till he'd seen it. At last, their escape seemed possible.

The trapdoor revealed a flight of stairs disappearing into a gaping and dark hole. In the dim light of the temple lamps, they could see crudely hewn stone steps. A dank and foul smell emanated from the dark passage. Devavrata descended first, brushing aside cobwebs, a temple lamp in hand. They could hear the idol churning back to its place once the trapdoor had been closed.

The air grew cold and clammy as they groped their way down the steep steps, sending shivers down their spines. Dust tickled their nostrils, making them sneeze. Bimbisara hitched up his uttariya to cover the lower half of his face, and Devavrata followed suit.

As they reached the bottom of the steps, Bimbisara stumbled. His foot had hit something lying on the ground. He peered into the darkness and lowered the lamp to examine the object. In the flickering light of the lamp, they saw a skeleton. Either it was the remains of someone who died while trying to escape, or someone had dumped the body there.

Devavrata shuddered. The bones were a reminder of the dangers that faced them.

They had to crouch low to get to the small door that lay at the end of the passage.

'Is the door locked?' Bimbisara asked in a muffled voice.

'It has a rusted lock which won't require too much effort to break,' Devavrata whispered in reply. He inspected the lock and then used his dagger to leverage an opening.

At last, the lock fell apart, and they opened the door. Devavrata blew out the lamp as they stepped outside. They stood on the narrow, sandy bank of the lake. The emperor breathed deeply of the fresh night air.

It was dark and quiet all around. The placid lake stretched before their eyes, reflecting the lazy beams of a waning crescent moon in the sky. The view wiped away all the apprehension in their minds. Captivated by the sight, Bimbisara sighed. He was going to miss the Shweta Shatadal Prasaad as much as Ambapali.

The pragmatic Devavrata was the first to turn his mind to the issue at hand. 'Now to cross the lake,' he said. 'Maharaj, we may have to swim across the lake to reach the path beyond. Samvarta setthi's man is waiting there with a carriage.' Swimming in the cold water in the dead of the night held no appeal to the young man.

'What if it turns out to be our lucky night?' jested Bimbisara. His mood had lightened, now that the two of them had gotten away undetected. 'What if we find a boat moored nearby?'

'Wishful thinking!' Devavrata said.

'Look to your right, Devavrata,' instructed the emperor, whose quick eyes had noticed a couple of small boats moored a little distance away from where they were standing.

'What a wonderful sight,' exclaimed the young man, as he hurried towards the boats.

In the dim light of the moon, he examined them. The wood had warped, and the bottom was covered in debris. There was a foul smell in the crafts, but they would have to do.

Selecting the better one of the two, he began unfastening the ropes. Spotting the single oar lying nearby, he turned it in his hands. It would serve.

'Let's go,' said Bimbisara. He stepped into the boat and Devavrata pushed it into the water. 'We have no time to lose.'

The dandanayak smiled to himself as he began rowing energetically. It had been a risk-laden escape, but they had made it to the lake. All they had to do now was to cross to the other end and they would be safe.

As they reached the middle of the lake, Devavrata felt wetness at his feet. Looking down, he saw water seeping into the bottom of the boat. The floor of the craft was filling up with water.

'The hull is leaking, Maharaj,' he warned. 'It will sink before we reach the bank.'

'Don't be disheartened, Devavrata. A swim will do us good.' Bimbisara chuckled, amused at the expression on his companion's face.

Tying his uttariya around his waist, the emperor slipped quietly into the water. Devavrata dived in a minute later. Like an exhausted dancer, the boat began to sink slowly and gracefully.

The lake seemed to stretch endlessly as they swam in the cold water. After what seemed forever to Devavrata, they reached the opposite bank. A chorus of frogs croaked in welcome as they stood up, shivering in their wet clothes. Luckily, they didn't have to look far for the setthi's man. Dressed in tattered clothes, he was sitting under a tree by the side of the path. He appeared like a genie as soon as Devavrata stepped forward.

'Pranam, Arya,' he greeted Bimbisara with folded hands. 'I will be back in a moment.'

Saying so, he sprinted off energetically towards the thicket on the roadside. Minutes later, he reappeared in a ramshackle wagon drawn by a pair of miserable-looking animals.

'Has this been sent by Samvarta setthi?' Devavrata asked indignantly. He was outraged at the audacity of the man.

Bimbisara, however, didn't seem to care. He had already climbed into the hay-covered rear of the wagon.

'It's not my fault,' whined the driver. 'I was ordered to bring this wagon to you.'

Grumbling, Devavrata clambered beside the driver and the wagon rolled towards the setthi's mansion. He rubbed his hands together to bring some warmth to them. All he wanted was to get to a warm place and rest for a while.

The same thoughts must have been racing through the cart driver's mind, as he prodded the horses to move faster. At last, they reached the large mansion where the setthi lived. He emerged from within as soon as the cart halted. Folding his hands, he greeted the emperor and led them inside.

'Couldn't you send a chariot or a comfortable carriage for the emperor?' Devavrata rebuked the man. 'Don't you realize how cold it is? How do you expect the emperor of Magadh to travel in such a shabby vehicle?'

'Forgive me, Maharaj,' the setthi said with folded hands as he led them to a luxuriously furnished chamber. The room was warm and comfortable. Fresh clothes had been laid out on the bed, and a table groaning with the weight of food and drinks awaited the two men. 'A luxurious carriage travelling through an isolated area at this time of the night is likely to attract attention. Hence, I was forced to send that old wagon. It might have been uncomfortable to travel in, but it was safer.'

'You did the right thing. Any intelligent man would have done the same,' Bimbisara responded with a smile and glanced meaningfully at his companion.

Realizing his foolishness, Devavrata blushed and lowered his head. He had much to learn from the wise setthi.

'I would like to leave for Magadh as soon as possible, before sunrise if that can be arranged,' the emperor said after he had changed into dry clothes. He sipped madira from a jeweled cup and continued, 'I shall soon return to this city as a victorious ruler.'

'We shall await that day, Maharaj,' the setthi said.

Garbed in fresh clothes and worries erased from his brow, Devavrata entered the room. He was in time to hear the setthi line out the next steps of the plan.

'Maharaj, I have arranged for a boat and a couple of trusted men to accompany you to Magadh. It is the same route that you had used while entering Vaishali. My men, dressed as mourners, will lead you to the boat.'

'Although I hate to leave the city as a mourner, that's the safest way, I guess.'

'The Mukti Dwar is the least guarded entry to Vaishali. Since it opens into the cremation ground and is used only to ferry the dead on their last journey, the security system is lax,' said the setthi. 'People are superstitious about using a gate meant for the dead, and the guards that are there are lazy and greedy. It has become a convenient entry and exit point for smugglers and other criminal elements.'

Samvarta setthi poured some more wine into Bimbisara's cup. 'Not many hours remain for sunrise. Please rest awhile. It's going to be a stressful journey to Magadh.'

At the crack of dawn, six men made their way to the cremation ghat. Chanting mournful verses, they carried a bier through the Mukti Dwar. They passed the sleepy guards at the gate with no hindrance. The emperor and Devavrata, dressed in the coarse clothes of peasants, followed the bier as mourners.

The business of death had already begun at the cremation ghat with a few pyres at various stages of being burnt. Biers continued to arrive. Flames leapt high, and the air was thick with heat and fumes. In no time, entire existences were being reduced to mere handfuls of ash by the angry flames.

The wails of mourners filled the air. Some buried their grief in silence. The smell of death gripped everyone in its embrace.

Devavrata hastened his steps, discomfited by the grim reminder of the temporariness of human life. Though in his early twenties, he had seen many deaths on the battlefield. Yet, the sight of a dead body continued to disturb him. He let out a sigh of relief when they reached the isolated far end of the ground. Soon, more bodies would arrive and more pyres would burn.

The bearers set down the bier. Lying under the pristine white cloth was a dummy—a bundle of straw shaped like a human body. The men wordlessly pointed out a boat that was anchored some distance away. Well-made and durable, the boat that would take the emperor back to his capital bobbed in the black morning waters.

In the Shatadal palace, the rising sun's rays hit Ambapali's bed. She rubbed her eyes and stretched herself languidly. The space next to her was empty. Indrajeet's discussion must have lasted longer than he had expected. She rose out of the bed and eagerly made her way towards Devavrata's room.

It was vacant. She ran to the garden. She searched the gazebo. The veena was where it always was, but there was no trace of her lover. Perturbed, she rushed from one end of the palace grounds to the other. At last, giving up her search, she threw herself into Priyamvada's room.

'Priya, he's gone.' Her voice broke. She buried her face in her hands.

'Have you looked in the garden? What about Devavrata?' Priya shook her distraught friend to get answers out of her.

'I can't find Devavrata.' Ambapali raised her tear-stained face. 'They have both vanished without a trace.'

'Pali, wait here till I return,' said Priyamvada, stepping out of the room.

She asked everyone. Neither the guards nor the servants had seen the two men leave. They seemed to have disappeared into thin air.

'Devavrata wanted to discuss something important last night. He said it was an urgent matter.' The words burst out of Ambapali's mouth when Priyamvada returned to her. 'He seemed quite upset. When I asked if it was something serious, Indrajeet mentioned bandits. He said they had waylaid his men and stolen all his goods.' She wrung her hand in distress. 'I hope he's not gone to the forest to confront them.'

'He wouldn't have gone without informing you. And why wouldn't he seek the help of the security? They have vanished as suddenly as they arrived. The entire thing seems odd, Pali.'

Ambapali shook her head. 'You forget that I brought them here.'

'Let's be rational, Pali. No guest leaves the host's house without informing them. Besides, they have not left from the front gate. Why would they sneak away, and from where did they leave?' Priyamvada reasoned.

'Let's wait for some time. It could have been an emergency, and they may have had to leave in a hurry. Indrajeet wouldn't have liked to wake me up if it was late,' Ambapali defended her lover. She refused to believe he had deserted her. 'I am sure he will return. He loves me. He told me so.'

Priyamvada hugged her friend but remained silent. She had her doubts about the trader returning.

A week went past, each day increasing Ambapali's distress. No one had seen or heard of Indrajeet. Yet, she refused to believe he would never return. She started at every sound, running out to the balcony every time she heard someone arriving. Sleepless and anxious, she lost her appetite.

Priyamvada could not bear to see her friend's condition. 'Get a grip over yourself, Pali,' she exhorted. 'The least Indrajeet could have done was to send word through someone.'

'What if he's in danger? What if the bandits have captured him? What if . . .'Ambapali's voice trailed away uncertainly.

'How long will you delude yourself? We know next to nothing about the man,' Priyamvada hardened her voice. She wanted her friend to accept the reality. 'The more I think about the matter, the more convinced I am. Indrajeet is not an honourable man. He's a rogue. He fooled you.'

Ambapali shook her head and said, 'You are mistaken, Priya. He loved me. I know he did.'

'Love! It's just a convenient word. He tricked you, Pali. He never loved you. He wouldn't have stolen away if he did.'

'I don't believe it. There must be a reason for him to have done so.'

But as the weeks passed with no sign of the merchant, she was forced to face the truth. Indrajeet had cheated her. He had used her. He would never return.

She was shattered.

'Why am I abandoned by everyone I love? My father, Satya and now Indrajeet. Why have I been doomed to lead a loveless life?' she asked pathetically.

Priyamvada had no words to console her distressed friend.

The news of the merchant's disappearance had spread like wildfire through the palace. There was consternation. Who were these men? Where did they come from and why had they left without informing anyone? Where and how did they go?

The news made its way to Suvarnasena. First, Ballabh had returned babbling about being kidnapped and interrogated by masked men in a cellar. Now, this. Strange things were afoot, Suvarnasena thought. The noose around the nagarvadhu's neck was tightening. All she had to do was to give it the last tug.

It was time to confer with Arya Krishnadev, she decided. The happenings in Ambapali's palace would interest him, and the rewards were likely to be generous.

Before she could reach the Arya, though, more shocking news emerged from the nagarvadhu's palace.

Twenty-Six

As the weeks passed, Ambapali remained listless. The more she tried to analyze Indrajeet's conduct, the more she despaired. His deception took a heavy toll on her.

'Why couldn't he tell me he had to leave?' she sobbed. 'He was a merchant. I wouldn't have stopped him from his travels. But he stole away at night like a thief. Why?'

Priyamvada suspected that the man's disappearance had nothing to do with his business. There was something more to it. Did he have an ulterior motive for entering the palace? Was he a spy? Was he hiding from someone? She shuddered at the possibilities. She had no intention of expressing her suspicions to Ambapali, though.

'Some people aren't comfortable with goodbyes,' Priyamvada consoled her friend. But the excuse sounded hollow and unconvincing, even to her ears.

Priyamvada's mind was occupied with other worries too. The discontent of the patrons was beginning to make itself manifest. There was still wine and gambling, dancing and music, but the princes and setthis were complaining of the nagarvadhu's absence and calling for her to present herself. Their grumbling had grown more strident in the past few weeks. The excuses offered by Priyamvada were no longer being accepted, and they took out their frustration by harassing the other dancers. The situation was getting untenable. It was time Ambapali snapped out of her gloom and paid attention to her responsibilities, Priyamvada thought, overwhelmed.

'You have to forget him, Pali. He's not worth the tears you are shedding. No man is worth the tears. Life can't end with the death of a love affair,' Priyamvada said. 'It's getting difficult to manage affairs. You must make an appearance in the rang mahal tonight. One performance from you will make everyone happy.'

'I can't,' Ambapali protested. 'I am not feeling well.'

'Please, Pali! Lilavati and I can't manage without your cooperation.'

Finally, Ambapali agreed.

News that the nagarvadhu would be performing that evening spread through the city. Lilavati made special arrangements for a lavish feast for the patrons.

Her face wan, Ambapali walked into the packed rang mahal. The first item was a group dance, which she performed with the other dancers. It fetched loud appreciation and applause from the audience. They clamoured for a solo recital. It had been a long time since they had seen her dance, they said. She agreed, but her performance lacked spirit, and the patrons were disappointed.

Over the next few days, Ambapali continued to make perfunctory appearances at the rang mahal. Slowly, the number of patrons began dwindling. They found other avenues for entertainment, grumbling about the apathetic and disinterested nagarvadhu.

Their discontent was the last thing on Priyamvada's mind. She was worried about her friend's health. Ambapali had lost her appetite and was losing weight. There were dark circles under her eyes. She complained of nausea at the sight of food. The cooks worked hard to prepare her favourite dishes, but she left them untouched. She behaved irritably with the servants and rebuked them for minor mistakes. Ambapali had also grown very emotional and burst into tears at the slightest pretext.

This could not continue, decided the devoted friend. She sent for Vivaswat, who was a father figure to both the women. The vaid checked Ambapali's pulse and asked some searching questions. He shook his head and drew a deep breath before speaking.

'Pali is pregnant,' he said. 'I will give some medicines to promote appetite, but she must start eating regular meals or else the baby will suffer.'

Shocked, Ambapali sat up with alarm. 'There must be some mistake,' she cried. Her face crumpled at the thought of bearing her treacherous lover's child. 'This can't be true.'

Priyamvada felt a surge of sympathy for her friend. The woman had suffered enough tragedies to last a lifetime. To have loved a man who stole away in the dead of night was painful enough, but carrying his child was the final blow.

'I don't want this child. Can you do anything to help me be rid of it?' Ambapali asked desperately, clutching at his hand.

The fatherly vaid had a soft spot for the girl he had known since she was a child. He knew that any one of the nagarvadhu's patrons could have sired the child. The baby would never bear the name of its father. That was the sad truth of Ambapali's life. Yet there was little he could do.

He prised her fingers away gently. 'I am afraid it is a little too late for that.'

'What will I do, Priya?' Ambapali raised her tear-streaked face.

'You will eat and get strong,' Priyamvada said, forcing a smile on her face. She took her friend's cold and clammy hands in hers, and continued, 'You will give birth to the baby and shower all your love on it. We will bring it up together. It will be your reason to live and be happy.'

After the initial shock, Ambapali began to accept her situation. Despite her reservations, she could not help feel a surge of affection for the tiny life growing in her. Her mood oscillated from one end of the spectrum to the other, alternating between weepy and jubilant, excitement and anxiety.

Ambapali kept away from the rang mahal, refusing to comply with requests for a performance. No amount of money offered by the setthis could force her to make an appearance.

The news couldn't remain a secret for long, particularly not when there was soon visible proof. The entire palace was buzzing with excitement, and then it spread through the city. The nagarvadhu was pregnant, people whispered. There were countless speculations about the father. The princes and setthis who had bedded her wondered if she was carrying their seed in her womb.

Suvarnasena was flabbergasted. She hadn't expected Ambapali to be so foolish as to bring an innocent, fatherless child into the world. Like many others, she speculated about who the father was. A prince? Or was the folly a result of her brief dalliance with the foreign merchant?

Like Suvarnasena, Satyakirti was shocked when he heard the news.

I must look after her, he decided; that's the least I can do. While he had not often met Ambapali or Priyamvada over the last few years, he had not forgotten them. They had, after all, been friends from childhood. When he told Urmimala the news, she urged him to visit Ambapali.

'It's time to let go of all the resentment and guilt,' Urmimala told her husband. 'In Pali's present condition, she needs the love and support of her friends. We are her only family.'

'Marriage has turned you into a wise woman,' Satyakirti joked. 'My wisdom must have rubbed off on you.'

'In that case, shouldn't you be doing the right thing, my wise husband?' Urmimala said. Finally, Satyakirti agreed to visit her palace.

Carrying a basket of fruits, dressed in his best clothes, he appeared at the palace gates one morning. That was as far as he went. He lost his nerve and, leaving the basket of fruits with a guard, returned home without meeting Ambapali. Later, he asked Urmimala to visit the palace and check on Pali's health.

A delighted Urmimala went, carrying some homemade sweets.

It was an emotional meeting. The three women realized how much they had missed each other. They hugged each other and cried. It had taken her a long time, but Ambapali had finally accepted reality. Destiny had laid out a path for each of them, and it had forced them to follow that path. She had walked on it with indignation, Satyakirti with resignation and Urmimala with happiness. Whatever had happened thereafter was no one's fault. She was ready to embrace the present now, though; she wanted her friends back in her life.

'I have become very emotional lately,' Ambapali laughed through her tears. 'Tears flow freely these days.'

'Pregnancy does that,' remarked Urmimala as she wiped her eyes. 'But the emotions can wait,' she continued. 'I want a tour of the place.'

As her friends took her around, Urmimala's eyes widened with wonder at the magnificence of the palace. She wandered around Ambapali's chamber, admiring everything.

'This is like a dream, Pali,' she exclaimed excitedly. 'You are fortunate to be living here, Priya.'

'Would you like to exchange places, Urmi?' teased Pali. She was happy to see her friend after a long time. 'I don't mind leaving all this and returning to the village.'

'I wouldn't trade Satya for anything in the world. Not even for a palace and wealth,' declared Urmimala. Once she got started on her beloved husband, nothing could stop the woman's chatter.

Priyamvada, who had been watching Ambapali, noticed an expression of sadness flit over her face. 'I think Pali is going to have a daughter,' Priyamvada said, attempting to change the subject. 'I can imagine what a beauty she will turn out to be. Imagine the heartbreaks she will cause.'

'No, Pali looks too radiant,' declared Urmimala. 'I am sure it'll be a boy. Do you have morning sickness?'

'Well, initially . . .'

'There you are. Severe morning sickness indicates you are expecting a boy.'

'That's a silly way of predicting it.'

'No, it isn't. That's the method used by the wise old women in the village. If you crave salty, sour and spicy foods, you will have a son, but craving sweets points to a girl. So, what do you crave?'

'Stop this nonsense, silly woman,' Priyamvada swatted Urmimala's hand.

'I don't mind answering her question,' said an amused Ambapali. 'I've been craving sour and spicy food,' she said.

'There you are!' exclaimed Urmimala. 'What did I tell you? It's going to be a son for our friend. Have you decided on a name, Pali?' she asked, excitedly. 'Do you want me to make a list of names?'

The three friends strolled out to the garden, chatting. They reminisced about their childhood and exchanged the latest gossip.

'You must come more often,' Ambapali said.

'I will continue bothering you till you are tired of me,' promised Urmimala as they hugged each other.

'Never!' declared the nagarvadhu. 'I haven't enjoyed myself so much for a long time.'

True to her promise, Urmimala continued to visit her friend, bearing gifts and loads of advice.

Months passed and Ambapali was impatient to hold her baby. It was an incredible feeling. Love suffused her each time it kicked inside. It felt like a host of fluttering butterflies had crowded the pit of her stomach.

Finally, one night, after a long, painful labour, the baby was born. And just as Urmimala had predicted, it was a boy. Both Priyamvada and Urmimala were present during the birth, holding their friend's hands, encouraging her to give one last push. They were the ones who took the baby from the old midwife.

'Is he . . .' Ambapali raised her head from the bed to look at the baby.

'He's perfect! A miniature version of his mother.' Priyamvada's eyes sparkled with excitement. 'Mark my words, Pali, he'll fill this house with laughter and happiness.'

'Absolutely true, he's the most beautiful baby I have ever seen,' Urmimala cooed. 'I am sure he's going to be a heartbreaker,' she declared.

'He will grow up to be a kind person, just like his mother,' said Lilavati, as she swaddled the baby. 'He'll make you proud, devi.'

Ambapali was overwhelmed by love for the tiny being. Her sun rose when the baby smiled and eclipsed when he cried. The vaid found himself summoned to the palace at the slightest sign of discomfort in the baby.

Often, when the baby slept, Ambapali pored over his features, trying to find some resemblance to Indrajeet. It saddened her to think that the boy would never know his father.

'It's time we gave him a name,' Priyamvada said when the baby turned six months old. Till then, everyone had called him by whatever name they fancied. For Ambapali, he was Surya; Chandra for Priya. Urmi called him Varun. Lilavati named him Daksha and Indumati called him Arjun. The cheerful boy responded to all the names.

'You are right, we should decide on a name,' agreed Ambapali. She watched fondly as her son gurgled and kicked his chubby legs. 'He will be confused by the dozens of names people have given him.' But no name was good enough for her precious baby, she felt.

The three of them argued over many names till Priyamvada finally said, 'I think it would be best to take the baby to the Buddha's sangha to get him blessed with an appropriate name.'

The women set out with the baby for the Buddhist monastery. They were disappointed to find that most of the monks were away. They had decided to return another day

when they chanced upon an old and ailing bhikkhu. Left
behind because of his inability to walk, the toothless monk
was moaning softly. There was no one around. Moved by
his plight, Ambapali offered him water. She supported his
emaciated body while he drank thirstily from the earthen cup
she held to his dry lips.

'Who are you, kind lady?' he asked after she lay him back
on his worn blanket.

'I am Ambapali, the nagarvadhu of Vaishali,' she replied.
'Do you want me to bring you something?'

'No devi, the monks have gone to beg for alms and should
be back soon.' He gave her a toothless smile. 'What brings you
here?'

'I came to seek blessings for my son, but Bhante
Chandrakirti is not here.' Bhante Chandrakirti was the head
of the monastery and a gifted man.

'He's accompanied the others to the city. Why don't you
wait here for a while?'

She pondered for a few minutes, and then, laying her son
near the old monk, she requested, 'Will you bless my child,
and give him a name, Bhante?'

He was surprised at her request. His lips trembling with
emotion, the monk placed a wrinkled hand on the baby's
head. 'I will never forget this gesture, Ambapali. I am but an
infirm old monk, yet you requested me to bless your son.'

Eyes shut, he contemplated for a moment and then said, 'I
name him Vimal—the pure and unblemished one.'

'Vimal!' Ambapali repeated the word a few times. 'It's a
beautiful name. We shall know him as Vimal. Thank you,
Bhante. You have done me an immense favour.'

'What a wonderful name,' seconded Priyamvada. Taking the baby from her friend, she began cooing, 'You are Vimal, the purest one.'

Happiness made Ambapali's skin glow and eyes sparkle. Motherhood added to her beauty and transformed her. When Vimal began walking, she decided it was time to start entertaining her patrons in the rang mahal.

Once again, the palace echoed with her laughter. Once again, she donned her regalia. The news that she had started dancing in the rang mahal travelled across the city. It brought back the princes and the setthis to the palace.

Years passed in the blink of an eye. Basking in the love of his mother and Priya, Vimal grew into a gentle and cheerful boy. He and his mother would often visit the monastery. Ambapali enjoyed its serene atmosphere and Vimal enjoyed spending time with the monks. By the age of five, he could recite the verses, play the veena and displayed a flair for art.

The little boy had taken a particular shine to Bhante Chandrakirti, and would follow him around the sangha, chattering incessantly.

'Your son is an intelligent and curious boy, devi,' Bhante Chandrakirti said one day.

Ambapali preened at the praise. For the past two years, she had made efforts to teach her son the lessons she had learnt as a child.

'He needs a guru, someone who can guide him and make him grow into an upright man,' advised the monk.

The monk's words put Ambapali in a dilemma. She was reluctant to send him to a gurukul. All this while, she had protected her son from unpleasant questions. Once he started attending a school with other boys, it would be impossible to protect him from their cruel remarks. She finally decided to appoint a teacher who would stay in the palace. Priyamvada helped her interview several people, but they found none worthy of the child.

The answer came to her one morning. It sent her rushing to Chandrakirti at the sangha.

Prostrating herself at his feet, she said, 'I have been thinking about your advice, Bhante. It is only today that I found an answer, and so I have come to you with a request.'

'Rise, child,' said the monk. 'Tell me what you want.'

Encouraged, she told him her desire to put her son under the tutelage of a young monk called Suhaskirti. His compassion and wisdom had impressed the nagarvadhu. The request put Chandrakirti in a quandary. It was unusual for a little boy to stay in the monastery, and he could not allow Suhaskirti to stay at Ambapali's palace.

Sensing his hesitation, she said, 'I am aware that it is an unusual request. But I have spent a long time deliberating the matter. Vimal is very drawn to the sangha and adores Suhaskirti. I believe it would be best if Vimal took his lessons from him.'

'I understand, devi. But Suhaskirti cannot stay at your palace. He's a monk and has many duties and restrictions. Also, we do not remain in one city for a long time. There will be times when he may have to travel or could be busy with other work, especially in Vaishali.' The monk paused. 'Besides, there might be things you want him to learn, things like hunting, which a monk cannot teach.'

'The first problem can be solved by Vimal's coming to the monastery, Bhante. I will send him here every morning. As for the periodic interruptions, I don't think it will disrupt his studies significantly. And I am skilled at the hunt; I will teach him when the time comes.' Ambapali looked expectantly at the monk.

'Please give me some time to think about it, devi.' Chandrakirti folded his hands together.

It didn't take too long for the monk to reach a decision in her favour. And so, Vimal found himself at the sangha every morning. On days of special gatherings or sermons, the lad would stay with the monks in their peaceful and orderly monastery. The more time he spent there, the less he wanted to return to the luxuries and clamour of his mother's palace.

Twenty-Seven

A resplendent harvest moon bathed the sky in a warm, milky glow. Astrologers predicted it was the season of new beginnings. For farmers, the moon marked the change of seasons to one of joy and celebrations. Of feasting and revelry.

But, for the citizens of Vaishali, the moon meant yet another night of suffering. War was at their door. The Magadh army had laid siege to the city. The grounds just outside the gate were teeming with soldiers. It was three months since the enemy had entrenched itself in makeshift camps outside the city gates. Their intention was to knock down the gates and breach the walls. Slowly but gradually, they were chipping away at their defences.

The Vaishali senapati sent large contingents of the army to drive the enemy away. They failed to make a dent in the mighty Magadh army. Demoralized and wounded, the soldiers returned, their numbers greatly diminished.

No one knew how long they could keep the Magadh forces at bay.

Trade had come to a grinding halt. The treasury was emptying at a rapid pace as the confederacy recruited men and bought horses and weapons. To cope with the financial crisis, the parishad raised taxes to unprecedented levels. After all, States—especially embattled ones—cannot run on an empty treasury. Soldiers cannot fight on empty stomachs.

Soldiers died. Women wailed. Cattle collapsed for lack of fodder. Orphaned and hungry children roamed the streets. Hunger haunted Vaishali. The only satisfied lot were the birds of prey circling over the scenes of ruin.

Almost all men, young and old, had been recruited to fight. Labourers, carpenters, masons, artisans, everyone joined in the war efforts. Some went willingly. Some unwillingly. With no formal training and no discipline, they were a ragtag bunch of men. They had a purpose, but not the skills to be warriors. Having never battled, the novices wasted ammunition and turned tail on sighting the might of the Magadh army.

Like many rich citizens of Vaishali, Ambapali donated liberally to the treasury. She set up food distribution camps to feed the hungry, distributed blankets to the old and ailing, and paid for medicines for the wounded.

While Vaishali continued to suffer, the soldiers in the Magadh camp were in a buoyant mood. Confident of victory, they waited for their emperor's order to storm the city. It was just a matter of a few days.

This time around, Bimbisara was determined to fight to the finish. His plans of attacking Vaishali had been delayed several times. First, he had to quell the rebellion in Anga, and then Magadh was attacked by a combined force of two minor kings. He had attacked Vaishali only after he had dealt with the other irritants, but the delay had seen some positive elements. His commanders had done well in preparing for the war. The ancillary units had fought hard. Spies had gathered crucial information about the army, and several vishkanyas who had been planted in the city had been successful in killing a few able generals and ministers of Vaishali. Bimbisara, proud of his son Ajatshatru's prowess, had appointed him the supreme commander of the Magadh forces. The hot-blooded young yuvraj was determined to claim a role in the conquest this time. He had prepared hard for the battle, conferring with the able commanders of Magadh and devising a strong battle strategy with them.

There were vested interests behind the attack on Vaishali, though. Ajatshatru had dreams of ousting his father, and was being encouraged by a group of cronies with ulterior motives.

A few years back, the mahamatya had been insulted by the king in the court, and had long waited for revenge. The Magadh senapati, Kirtimadhav, had fallen out with the mahamatya over his sister's marriage with the mahamatya's son. The two had been romantically involved, and the senapati's sister was pregnant, but the mahamatya refused to bless their marriage and called her a harlot. Soon, the personal feud had taken a serious turn, and the matter reached Bimbisara. The girl had committed suicide and the anguished senapati demanded justice from the king. There was disruption in the court as ministers took sides. Despite his competence and political skills, the mahamatya was not a popular man, and he found himself isolated. Goaded by the circumstances, Bimbisara had sent him away to a distant province for a couple of years. When he was finally recalled to the capital, the mahamatya found himself sidelined.

Disappointed with his stagnation in the court, the mahamatya put his weight behind the prince. He had been Ajatshatru's mentor for a long time and knew the prince was ready for the throne. The canny mahamatya was sure his loyalty would bring him handsome returns at the right time.

Bimbisara was completely unaware of these machinations. He was focused on conquering Vaishali, and dreamed of carrying away only one thing to Magadh. Let the others plunder and loot the city, or claim credit for the victory. Ambapali would come with him.

Samvarta setthi had kept him updated on Ambapali's activities, and the emperor was aware that she had given birth to a son. Instinct told him it was his child. He dreamt of the day that he would ride home victorious, with her by his side. His son was a Haryanka prince and would be brought up like one.

* * *

The sabhagrih at Vaishali buzzed with worried voices. They debated on the next step forward. Should an envoy be sent out with a peace offer? Should they continue to try and fight? The clan rulers voiced their suggestions.

'We have run out of resources. There seems no other way than to accept defeat,' the chief minister declared.

'Is there no alternative?' the king asked, though he knew there was none.

'There is no hope of beating back the Magadh army, your Majesty. We can only try to prevent the city from being plundered and the women from being ravaged by appealing to Bimbisara,' said the senapati, his shoulders slumped with hopelessness. The reverses of the battle haunted his nights. His soldiers were dying even as they sat in the sabhagrih, discussing ways to end the battle.

'There is something he will be loath to refuse,' said the raj purohit.

'What do you have in mind, Arya?' asked the king. His weary eyes held a flicker of hope. 'The treasury is empty. We have nothing. What can we offer?'

'I know Bimbisara wants the nagarvadhu. We could send her to him as an emissary of peace. She is an astute woman. She could find out if we can offer something in return for peace.'

'You think that will satisfy him?'

'It is worth an attempt. We have to try all possible means to buy peace.'

'Will Devi Ambapali agree?' asked the senapati. It seemed an absurd idea, but it held a glimmer of hope for the desperate men.

The idea seemed to appeal to the parishad. 'We can only try,' said the chief minister.

'Present the nagarvadhu here in the morning,' the king ordered before the ministers dispersed.

In her palace, unaware that the parishad was toying with her life once again, Ambapali snuggled close to her sleeping son and sighed contentedly.

* * *

At the Magadh camp, the royal astrologer drew up charts to predict an auspicious day for the final push and advised the emperor to wait.

Magadh's spies continued to bring reports of the worsening conditions and depleting resources within the city. They informed the king of the despair that overshadowed the meetings at the sabhagrih. It boded well for Bimbisara.

But the Magadh commanders noted the flagging spirits in their camp. The troops were getting restive. Away from home for far too long, their appetite for war was waning with each passing day. The sordid promise of rape and plunder were the only things that kept them going.

The stars did not favour an attack, but tensions were at a high. The commanders conferred with the yuvraj and suggested that the gates be razed immediately so the attack could begin. The mahamatya joined forces with them.

'Yuvraj, we have to act now,' said Varshakar. 'I know that Maharaj is waiting for an auspicious day to be announced by the royal astrologer, but dispirited soldiers can't win a war.'

'It's easy enough to batter down the massive gates with our war elephants. Once we gain entry, I don't visualize any hurdles in storming the city,' said Ajatshatru, convinced. 'But mounting an immediate attack would be tantamount to disobeying Maharaj. We will have to convince the emperor about the need for immediate action.'

'Maharaj has appointed you the supreme commander of the army. It is you, Yuvraj, who has to speak to him about the change in plans,' said Varshakar, his perceptive eyes not missing the prince's uneasiness at the prospect of facing his father. 'Do not fear. Maharaj is wise enough to recognize the wisdom of the suggestion.'

Encouraged by the mahamatya and the senapati, Ajatshatru put the suggestion before the emperor. 'Maharaj, after much deliberation, the commanders and the mahamatya suggest that we launch an attack on the city immediately. The soldiers are getting restless.'

Taken aback, Bimbisara remained silent for a few moments before reacting. 'Are the commanders and the mahamatya not aware of the raj jyotishi's caution? Is there any specific reason for hastening the attack?'

'No, Maharaj, just that our troops need a reprieve. It's been several weeks since they have been camped in the marshes.'

'I am aware of that,' Bimbisara snapped. He guessed that the mahamatya had pushed Ajatshatru to come to him with the suggestion. In a softer voice, he continued, 'Son, I am as eager as you are to get this battle over with, but now is not the time. Let's wait till the astrologer gives a signal. I will address the troops tomorrow.'

Unhappy at the rejection of his proposal, Ajatshatru left.

Alone in the royal tent, Bimbisara mulled over what his son had said. One reason he had wanted to delay the attack was that he wanted to transport Ambapali and her son to safer territory before the soldiers went on a rampage. He had already attempted once to get her to Magadh and had failed. The emissary had been insulted and thrown out of her palace.

Why should I go down in history as a coward who deserted her home for safety? She had riled. *'Give me one good reason to do so.'*

When told that the Magadh king had requested her presence, she had laughed derisively. *'Ask him to come personally and explain why I should do so. He's Vaishali's enemy, and I have no wish to heed to an enemy.'*

Bimbisara knew she would not agree to leave Vaishali unless he went personally and explained everything. He had wanted to meet Ambapali and reveal himself as Bimbisara, the man she had loved, but the preparations for the campaigns had kept him from doing so. He knew it would be difficult for him to explain why he had resorted to falsehood, and a niggling doubt had made him uncomfortable. Would she forgive him and agree to leave Vaishali? Now was no time to brood. He had to act immediately, and take his chances with her.

Bimbisara knew it would be impossible to control the troops once they entered the city. The mansions and palaces would be their first targets for plundering. And even if ordered to stay away from Ambapali's mansion, there was no guarantee that the troops would remember his words amidst the ferocity of battle and its aftermath. No. The task of getting Ambapali out of Vaishali had to be carried out by him. Only he could do that job. Bimbisara decided he would visit the Shatadal palace that very night. He summoned Devavrata, the one man he could trust with his life.

The dandanayak asked no questions when told to be prepared to leave the same night. He knew of the worries that hounded the emperor's mind. The news of Ambapali's son had reached his ears, and he, too, was eager to protect her from the Magadh soldiers.

As planned, the two men stole out of the camp in the dead of the night and made their way to the boats anchored at a distance. Bimbisara had dressed as a soldier. All they carried with them were their arms and a change of clothes.

The boats were heavily guarded. The guard commander looked suspiciously at the two men, who said they were on a royal mission. Battles required subterfuge and intrigue, the commander knew. He asked no questions, but demanded to see the royal order. It was only after they had flashed a permit with the emperor's seal that he allowed them to take a boat.

This time, they had no way to inform Samvarta setthi or seek his help. Taking their chances, they landed near the cremation ghat that led to Vaishali. A dire sight greeted their eyes. The war had caused enough deaths to keep the fires blazing day and night in the mourning ground. The high-pitched sound of keening sent goose pimples creeping over the emperor's skin. He had seen many deaths, but the scene at the cremation ground was eerie enough to make him shudder.

Bimbisara was struck with remorse for a few minutes. It was because of his actions that people had died. For the past few years, whenever Gautama Buddha stayed at Rajgrih, the emperor had made time to attend his sermons. The enlightened one had repeatedly pointed out the futility of war and bloodshed. You have no right to take away what you can't give. Only God may give and take life, he had said.

The Magadh emperor stood rooted to the cremation ground.

I will wage no more battles after the subjugation of Vaishali. I will do penance for all the misery and deaths caused by my actions. I will try to atone for all my sins.

The battle of Vaishali will be my last battle.

Thus resolved the emperor.

Twenty-Eight

In a pensive mood, the emperor followed his faithful commander out of the cremation grounds. At that moment, he wanted to give up his crown, wealth, and power—everything. He wanted to hand over the kingdom to Ajatshatru, who was impatient to occupy the throne. But that would have to wait. First, he had a promise to keep.

The desire to see his son hastened his steps. Several springs had passed since he had met Ambapali. The child must have grown. Did he badger his mother with hundreds of questions, like most children his age? Did he resemble his father, or was he like the mother? Did he ever call for his father? What did Ambapali tell him when he asked for his father? Did she love him still, or did she have a new paramour? His mind swirled with questions.

In the Shatadal palace, the nagarvadhu was tossing in her bed, unable to sleep.

The shortages of the war had hit the palace, and lately, the rang mahal was falling silent, as princes prepared for war and setthis saw their profits plummet. No one had the money to spare for extravagance. Only a reckless few, who lived day to day, kept the rang mahal running. She had been forced to trim her expenses by letting a few servants and guards go.

Soon she would have to let many more of her servants go, as her coffers ran low. The Magadh emperor had brought untold ills to the prosperous city, she thought. They lived in uncertainty, not knowing when the siege would end or when the Magadh soldiers would launch the final attack. Bimbisara's victory would cause mayhem, she knew. They needed to plan ahead.

Ambapali didn't care for herself, but she was worried about her son. He would be safe at the sangha, she decided. No one, not even the Magadh soldiers, would dare to attack a monastery. Even a monster like Bimbisara was a follower of the Buddha.

I will send him to the monastery early in the morning, she resolved.

Dawn was a few hours away, but Ambapali remained restless. A strange premonition of disaster overwhelmed her. She walked to the terrace and stared at the garden beyond. The place looked magical in the moonlight. The sight brought back many memories of love and lust. Wistfully, she recalled the evenings spent in the gazebo with Indrajeet. It was like a picture gathering dust, fading with time. Yet she continued to cling stubbornly to those half-forgotten memories, dredging them up from time to time.

The scent of flowers was strong as she stared into the distance, her thoughts far away. Suddenly, a shadow crossed her line of vision. It was followed by another. Two figures. Were they patrolling guards or intruders? No, their movements were stealthy. Guards would not move that way. They could be bandits. Hunger was turning honest men into thieves. There had been several cases of robbery in recent weeks. Alarmed, she was about to call out for the guards when one of them looked up.

Shocked, she withdrew behind the curtains and stared back at the man. *Is that Indrajeet? But it can't be. I am imagining things. My mind is playing tricks.* She peered into the darkness from behind the curtain. It *was* him.

With a strangled cry, she stepped back from the terrace. Her heart hammered against her ribs.

Controlling the surge of emotions, Ambapali rushed to the door. He was there before she could step out.

With a sob, she rushed into his waiting arms. 'Oh, Indra!' she choked out. 'Is it really you? I can't believe you have come.'

'Hush, darling!' He stroked her head as she continued to sob. 'I will take you back with me.'

'What took you so long?' she cried. 'I had given up on you.'

'Don't cry, Ambe, I am here now.' There was urgency in his voice. 'We have to leave quickly before anyone sees us.'

'Leave? Where to?'

'Ambe, any delay can lead to my death. We have to move quickly.'

'I don't understand. Why should anyone kill you?' She clung to him.

'We can't linger. My life is in danger.'

'You are safe in Shatadal,' she said, drawing herself up with pride. 'No one will dare to lay a hand on you. I will protect you with my life.'

'No, you wouldn't be able to protect me. I won't be spared, and neither will you.' Bimbisara realized she would not act until he revealed his identity. Aware of the strong reaction the truth would cause, he lifted her face, forcing her to look into his eyes. 'I am the Magadh Samrat Bimbisara.'

She laughed. *A fine prank indeed*, she thought. But as she looked at him, she realized he was serious. She stared speechlessly at the man she loved. Her voice hoarse with fear, she whispered, 'You are not a trader?'

'No.' He hung his head, unable to meet her eyes. 'I . . . I lied to you, Ambe.'

'It can't be,' she whispered, backing away from him. He made a move to hold her, but she shrank away from his touch. 'Don't come near me,' she hissed. 'You deceived me.'

'Come with me, Ambe,' he pleaded. 'I will make you the queen of Magadh. Our son will be a prince.'

'He is not your son. He's mine. Mine alone. You have no right over him,' she said fiercely. 'I am no queen and my son is no prince. We are citizens of Vaishali and you are our enemy.'

'I love you. I want to give both of you everything I can. Any happiness I can,' he pleaded. 'Let me take you both to safety.'

'Go away before I summon the guards.' She clenched her fists to control herself.

'The Magadh soldiers will be all over the town soon, looting and killing. It will be impossible to control them, Ambe. Do you want our son to be killed? Don't you love me anymore?'

His words made her hesitate. Calling the guards would mean his death. She loved him still, Ambapali realized. She could not bring herself to do that.

'Look into my eyes and tell me you don't love me.' He lifted her chin, forcing her to look into his eyes.

'I loved a man called Indrajeet. I never loved the Magadh emperor,' she whispered.

'I know you love me, or you would have summoned the guards by now.' His voice was a gentle caress. She shivered involuntarily and closed her eyes.

'Yes, I love you. But Vaishali is my motherland,' she replied. 'You profess to love me. Are you ready to prove it?'

'I will do anything you say. Anything to prove my love for you.'

'I want you to withdraw your troops and return to Magadh at the first light of dawn. You have caused enough death and devastation. We want no more. Go back to your kingdom.'

Her demand stunned him. 'You are asking for the impossible,' he said. 'Don't make such a demand, Ambe. I can't withdraw my army. It's too late. There is too much at stake.'

'In that case, don't claim that you love me,' she said. 'Love demands sacrifice. I am sacrificing my love for my city. I want you to make a sacrifice too.'

Bimbisara stood rooted to the ground, wavering. Was he ready to act for the sake of love? Was she dearer to him than Magadh?

'I can't do that,' he said finally. 'I am an emperor. I can't let down my people for my happiness.' Varshakar was right. A king had no right to love. He had forsaken his happiness the day he sat on the throne. A sacred oath bound him to his subjects. He had to act for the good of his people. Magadh came first.

'In that case, the sooner you leave, the better.' She watched as he turned to leave. Her heart broke at the thought of losing him again. In that moment of weakness, she fought

the powerful urge to leave with him. To go to Magadh with
him. The moment of weakness passed, and the voice of sanity
returned. This was the man who had deceived her once. He
could do it again. He had never loved her. He had toyed with
her body and emotions. She wouldn't allow him to kill her
people and loot her city. 'If you think you can storm into
Vaishali and carry me away, think again. I will kill our son and
then myself the moment your troops enter the city. That is my
promise to you,' she called out.

Stunned by the threat, he stood rooted, staring at her.

'You can't do that,' he said. 'What kind of mother talks
about killing her child? He's innocent, Ambe. He has done
no wrong. He didn't ask to be born.' He strode back to her.
Taking her hands in his own, he pleaded, 'Don't be heartless.
I beg you to not let our differences affect our son. Please, let
me hold him in my arms. He's my son, too.'

'That's not possible.' Her eyes were a pair of flints. Hard
and incisive. 'I have made up my mind, Arya. Countless people
have lost their lives because you lusted for power. Two more
wouldn't matter. Your soldiers are not likely to spare us after
they enter the city in triumph anyway. As you said yourself,
they will be uncontrollable.'

He flinched at her words. Every one of them was true.
The sadness that had weighed down his soul after seeing the
burning pyres seemed to double. He couldn't allow her to kill
the child and herself. He could not allow the soldiers to go on
a rampage.

'It shall be as you say.' Bimbisara whispered almost
inaudibly before walking away. 'The Magadh army will retreat.'

Devavrata, who was waiting anxiously in the garden,
looked perplexed when he saw the emperor returning alone.

'She's not coming,' Bimbisara said in reply to his questioning look. His shoulders slumped in defeat, the mighty king of Magadh stole out of the palace.

From their respective balconies, Ambapali and Priyamvada watched the two men leaving. Priyamvada, who was a light sleeper, had woken up to the buzz of conversation. She was debating whether to go to her friend's room when Ambapali appeared at her door.

'Indrajeet came just now,' she said, voice racked with pain. 'And I turned him away.'

Amid a torrent of tears, Ambapali narrated the details.

'Sshh!' Priyamvada tried to quieten her friend. The news that the Magadh emperor had come to the palace could lead to terrible results. 'Hush, Pali. No one can know that Bimbisara was here to meet you.'

'Do you think I did the right thing?' Ambapali's voice rose by an octave.

Unknown to them, a pair of ears caught snatches of the conversation. Ratnaprabha, who had been stealing around the palace, heard Ambapali crying and decided to investigate. Creeping down the corridor, she found herself outside Priyamvada's room.

What could the two friends be discussing at this time of the night, she wondered. The curious woman set her ear to the door. Although she failed to catch the complete conversation, she heard enough to learn the actual identity of the nagarvadhu's lover.

It was sensational information. One that could lead to Ambapali's death, realized the masseuse. Suvarnasena would be ecstatic. She cursed herself for having missed Bimbisara.

Dreaming of a fat purse of gold coins, Ratnaprabha crept out of the Shatadal palace. She had barely gone a short distance when she paused, struck by an idea. The news was immeasurably more important to the Vaishali king and his council. If she told Suvarnasena, she was likely to rush to the king and earn a huge reward for the information herself. The miserly woman would grudgingly part with only a couple of those coins, while the council would heap her in riches.

Happily, the masseuse hastened towards the king's palace.

However, disappointment awaited the greedy woman. The guards at the royal palace turned down her pleas for an audience with the king. The war had led to a tightening of security, and no one was allowed into the palace grounds without permission. Besides, what would the old woman want to seek an audience for at that time of night?

Ratnaprabha's entreaties that she had crucial information were rejected by the suspicious soldiers. It was only after they threatened to throw her into prison that the alarmed woman retraced her steps.

Alas, it was better to settle for a few coins from Suvarnasena than spend the rest of her life in a dungeon, she decided.

Twenty-Nine

'I was in love with the enemy. I slept with the Magadh emperor, Priya! I bore his son!' Ambapali broke into hysterical laughter. The laughter turned into sobs.

'Get a grip over yourself, Pali.' Priyamvada shook her friend's shoulders. She was the stoic one; Pali had always been guided by her emotions. Age had done nothing to change that. Pali had to learn many things, Priyamvada thought, and one of them was to put the past behind her. 'You did nothing wrong. He deceived you into thinking he was a merchant. It is he who is to be blamed for misleading and exploiting you.'

Ambapali shook her head. 'I should have summoned the guards and got him arrested.'

'You love him, Pali,' reasoned Priyamvada. 'And he is your son's father. You couldn't send him to his death.' She continued to stroke her friend's hair.

They sat silently for a while.

'We must leave the palace immediately,' urged Priyamvada as a sudden realization dawned on her. 'Pali, what if he doesn't keep his word? What if the Magadh soldiers storm the city? We have to take Vimal to a safe place before that happens.'

The mention of her son's safety had an immediate effect on Ambapali. She regained her composure, snapping out of her self-pity. 'What should we do, Priya?' she asked. Her numbed mind had stopped functioning. 'Where should we take him?' 'We'll take him to the monastery. He'll be safe there.' The ever-efficient Priyamvada took charge of the situation. Pulling her friend to her feet, she whispered, 'Emotions will have to wait, Pali. We have no time to lose.'

Carrying the sleeping boy, the two women made their way to the stables. Harnessing a chariot, they drove it towards the rear gate. Ambapali ordered the sentries to open the gate and lower the drawbridge. Taking the reins in her hands, she drove the chariot towards the sangha.

* * *

Laden with guilt and remorse, Bimbisara made his way towards the cremation ground. He had failed to convince Ambapali, and he had not been able to see his son. Victory over Vaishali no longer held the same charm for him.

The night was fading as the cremation ground loomed in the distance. Aware of the quick passage of time, the two men broke into a trot. They slowed near the Mukti Dwar.

'I can't see anyone on the road. It would be suicidal to walk through the gate now. What should we do, Maharaj?' Devavrata asked, his brow furrowed with anxiety. Silence reigned over the cremation ghat. The pyres had burnt out, and the mourners had not yet appeared.

'We will have to wait for a group of mourners,' replied Bimbisara, wishing he had not visited Ambapali. He had gained nothing. And now he had to keep a promise made on an impulse. He didn't look forward to ordering the Magadh troops to withdraw. It was an understatement to say that the reactions of Ajatashatru and his ministers were not likely to be pleasant.

'It is dangerous . . .' Devavrata muttered.

'Yes, it is dangerous. Do you have a better suggestion?' retorted the emperor irritably.

'We could rush in and sprint towards the boat. I will tackle the soldiers while you escape,' offered Devavrata.

'Don't be silly, Deva. They will shoot arrows at us from the watchtower.'

They spotted a posse of soldiers marching towards the gate. It was time for the changing of the guards. The sleepy night guards would be replaced with new ones who would be more alert. Getting away was becoming riskier by the minute.

'It's now or never,' said Bimbisara. He had had the foresight to bring a Vaishali foot soldier's uniform and had instructed the dandanayak to dress in a similar garb—a white dhoti and a red half-sleeved tunic and a turban. The two men planned to exchange the tunic and turban for the Magadh colours once they were on the boat. 'Let's cross the road and join the soldiers' ranks just as they pass this tree. We can slip in with them.'

It was a plan fraught with risk, but there seemed no other option.

The soldiers passed by the tree. Drawing a deep breath, Bimbisara was about to step out of his hiding place when he was pulled back by Devavrata.

'Wait, Maharaj!' whispered the young man, pointing in the distance.

The first lot of mourners were making their way to the cremation grounds. It was a providential reprieve for the two desperate men. Discarding their tunics and turbans, their heads lowered in grief, they joined the funeral procession.

Dawn was breaking as the mourners walked through the ghat.

* * *

Suvarnasena was aroused from slumber by the rapping on the front door. She sat up in alarm. There was someone outside. Who could it be so early in the morning? Annoyed, she opened the door and found Ratnaprabha.

'Are you insane? Do you realize what time it is?' She wanted to bang the door shut on the woman's face.

The teacher's words did not affect the thick-skinned woman. Smiling ingratiatingly, she said, 'I have brought you some important information, devi.'

'It could have waited till a more reasonable hour,' Suvarnasena grumbled as she led the crone into the house. 'It better be important enough for you to wake me at this unearthly hour.'

'It's something that will make you dance with joy,' cackled the woman. 'I have discovered the identity of Ambapali's lover. Devi, you won't believe who the father of her son is.'

'Get out!' shouted the teacher, pushing the woman towards the door. 'Everyone knows it was the trader she had amused herself with. You consider that important information? Get out of my house, you greedy hag!'

'Since you don't value my services, perhaps there is no point sharing the information with you. It would be wiser for me to be rewarded by the king than to suffer your insults.'

Suvarnasena's ears perked up at the mention of the king. 'You think the information is important enough to fetch you a reward from the king?' she asked, narrowing her eyes doubtfully.

'Certainly! It's worth a bag of gold coins, if not more. Anyway, I guess I should be going. I am sorry to have disturbed your beauty sleep.' Shrugging resignedly, the masseuse turned to leave.

'Wait!'

She turned back, amused her ploy was working.

'Come back inside.'

'Can I have a glass of madira?' asked Ratnaprabha, taking advantage of the situation.

'Help yourself,' said Suvarnasena, cursing the woman under her breath.

'The excitement kept me awake last night. I rushed here early so I could share the information with you, and now I am exhausted.'

The masseuse poured out the wine slowly, prolonging the suspense, delighting in Suvarnasena's impatience. 'Devi, you won't believe what I am about to tell you. But it is the truth. I heard it with my own ears.'

Ratnaprabha downed the madira and smacked her lips appreciatively. She poured another helping of the expensive wine.

'Don't test my patience, woman,' Suvarnasena warned.

'I have a sharp sixth sense, which never fails me. Last night, I was aroused from sleep by the sound of howling. There have been some disquieting incidents in the past few days, so I decided to investigate. While walking down the corridor, I heard some voices—'

'Skip the details. Come to the crux of the story.'

'Have patience, devi.' Ratnaprabha took an unhurried sip of the madira. It was a rare chance, and she wanted to make the most of it. 'Guess what I stumbled upon. The nagarvadhu and her dear friend were closeted in a room. Ambapali was wailing. Curious, I eavesdropped on the conversation. They were discussing the perfume merchant. He is the one who fathered Ambapali's son.'

'I had guessed as much. If you think I am going to pay—'

'Don't jump to conclusions, devi. The crucial part is yet to come.'

'Hurry up, then.'

'The fellow was at the palace last night. It seemed he came with a proposal to marry Ambapali.'

'Happy ending indeed . . .' What was this spiel leading to?

'Impatience isn't a virtue, devi. Let me finish. This man promised to make her the queen. Her son would be a prince, he said.'

Survarnasena sat up and focused. Queen? Prince? The crone had gone mad.

'For a few minutes, I couldn't believe my ears,' the masseuse continued. 'Nor will you, devi. The boy's father is Bimbisara, the Magadh samrat.'

Shocked, Survarnasena parroted, 'Bimbisara! Bimbisara? Did you say Bimbisara?'

'Yes, devi. He's none other than the Magadh emperor.'

'It can't be. There has to be a mistake.' *It's a tall tale. The woman is trying to extort money with false information.* 'Your hearing is becoming weak. You are lying.' Suvarnasena stood up and pointed at the door. 'Leave now, before I lose my temper.'

'I am not lying. The information is worth a lot of money. If you are not interested, I will take it to the king,' threatened the masseuse. Draining the last few drops of madira, she got up to leave.

'Wait! Did you hear right?'

'As right as I hear you.'

The teacher decided to take a chance. If the information was true, it was worth a bag full of gold. 'All right, take these coins. Don't share this information with anyone else.'

Suvarnasena held out a few coins. She was in a hurry to drive to the king's palace.

'No, devi.' Ratnaprabha shook her head. 'I am not accepting a pittance. The information is worth much more. If I went to the king . . .'

'Woman, you delude yourself. We are at war and soon the Magadh soldiers will be at our door. The king and his ministers are huddled in the sabhagrih, trying to find some way to save the city. Do you think the king has time to meet you? Take these coins and be satisfied. Just pray you live to enjoy them.' Suvarnasena took out some more coins from her purse and thrust them in the masseuse's hand. Her brain was working overtime. She decided to seek an immediate meeting with Krishnadev. On second thought, she added, 'Don't be impatient. Let me return from the royal palace and I will share the reward with you.'

The masseuse had barely walked a short distance when the sound of horse hooves and the rumble of a chariot reached her ears. She turned and saw the teacher racing towards the ministerial residences. Suvarnasena was in a tearing hurry.

* * *

At the cremation ghat, the corpse was taken to the river for the ceremonial last ablution. Bimbisara and Devavrata, who were waiting for an opportunity to dive into the water, scanned the area around the ghat. The guards were monitoring the funeral processions that had begun arriving. Suddenly, there was a flurry of activity as several mourners arrived with bodies, and a babble of voices shattered the morning silence.

A tacit signal passed between Bimbisara and Devavrata. They had agreed that the emperor would go first, and Devavrata would wait for a few minutes before following.

With an imperceptible nod, Bimbisara dived into the water and began swimming swiftly towards the boat, which had been anchored at a distance.

Suddenly, behind him, he could hear shouts. He slowed down and looked back. Mourners on the ghat were pointing at him. Devavrata was nowhere to be seen. Bimbisara's frantic eyes scanned the crowd. Then he spotted the dandanayak. The mourners had raised the alarm just as he jumped into the river, and an alert soldier had dived in after Devavrata and pulled him back to the banks. Within minutes, several soldiers had surrounded the young man.

With a heavy heart, the emperor watched his companion being overpowered and led away.

Thirty

The parishad had gathered in the sabhagrih. The nagarvadhu was to be brought to the court that morning, so they assumed the king had summoned them to discuss the next course of action and her appointment as an envoy of peace.

What they didn't know was that Krishnadev had met the king just a while ago to relay the startling information brought to him by Suvarnasena. The woman was brought before the king, and she confirmed what she knew.

The chief minister stood up and cleared his throat. Without mincing words, he shared the news that Bimbisara had visited the nagarvadhu at night. A ripple of unease passed through the court.

How had the Magadh emperor entered Vaishali? There was consternation in the parishad.

'How could he get through our gates so easily? This reflects the negligence and inefficiency of the soldiers,' raged a minister who had an axe to grind against the security minister. 'We can't overlook such terrible carelessness, especially when the enemy is camping at our door.'

'The soldiers guarding the gates have been negligent,' admitted the security minister. 'I will order an immediate investigation into the matter and take steps to tighten security.'

'We have to figure out where the Magadh emperor managed to breach our defences and patrols.'

'Bimbisara would not dare to undertake this incursion without the help of insiders,' remarked the raj purohit. 'This is an utter failure of the intelligence department. There are traitors within Vaishali, which it has failed to detect. Magadh has breached our security. They may well have infiltrated our intelligence.'

Several members nodded in agreement.

'You are absolutely right, Arya. There are traitors in this city. One of them is a woman. She has gravely betrayed our State,' said a stoop-shouldered man in his mid-fifties, with bushy eyebrows and a belligerent manner. Enormous diamonds on his fingers caught the light and glimmered as he moved his hands. All heads turned to Krishnadev, Suvarnasena's ally, who hated the nagarvadhu with a passion. 'Her name is Ambapali. I demand her arrest. Traitors, as we all know, deserve a death sentence.' He sat back down, grim-faced.

A babble of voices broke out in the sabhagrih.

'Do you have any proof to back your accusation?' asked the raj purohit. 'We can't arrest a prominent citizen without adequate evidence.'

'She not only harboured the enemy in her palace, but also slept with him. Her son is living proof of her treachery. What more evidence does the parishad require?' Krishnadev's voice quivered with indignation.

'Is your source reliable?' a minister asked.

'The information comes from various sources, including a highly reliable one. I can summon her here if you like,' Krishnadev stated sarcastically. 'She has already met the king and mahamatya, and they are convinced of her legitimacy.'

'Let's hear the woman who brought you the information,' demanded a member.

'Is there time for a long-drawn investigation? I have met her, and I am convinced about the reliability of the information,' said the king. 'Do you have faith in me?' he asked the assembly.

'Yes!', 'Certainly!' several voices called out.

'In that case, we should proceed with the matter.'

'I would like to hear—'

'Arya, do you realize you are holding up crucial discussions about the Magadh attack? We can move to that discussion only after the present matter is decided.' Krishnadev's sharp remark drowned out the objections of an elderly member of the parishad.

'Gentlemen, do we have time to waste?' said the chief minister. 'The enemy at the gate demands attention. The nagarvadhu's trial could lead to information about the Magadh king, which could be used to Vaishali's benefit. I request the king to order that the nagarvadhu be arrested immediately so we can hold a quick trial. We have no time to waste over this.'

This time, there was no opposition. No voices were raised to support Ambapali in a parishad that had decided her fate with impunity more than once. The parishad, which, a few hours back, had agreed to send her as peace emissary to Bimbisar now voted unanimously for her arrest. She was to be tried for treason. A contingent of soldiers was dispatched to the Shatadal palace.

Satyakirti observed a military patrol leave the palace from his station outside the gates. Like many other men, Satyakirti had abandoned his musical instruments to join the army. No one had time for music as the war raged on. His family was going through a rough patch and the only option left was to join the army and defend against the looming Magadh threat. After a brief training, he had been appointed to guard the Mukhya Dwar of the sabhagrih.

Satyakirti was about to head home after handing over his charge to the day guard. His curiosity piqued, he fell in step with the group to speak to a soldier from his village. Stealing a look around, the soldier whispered that it was a confidential matter. 'I won't share it with anyone,' promised Satyakirti.

'We are on our way to arrest the nagarvadhu,' his friend confided. 'The parishad has declared her a traitor.'

'A traitor? Ambapali? That's impossible.'

'Brother, I know nothing beyond what we have been told,' the soldier said before marching resolutely ahead.

The law of the land required a traitor to be put to death, Satyakirti knew. Alarmed, he followed the patrol to the Shatadal palace. What had Pali done? Why were they calling her a traitor? He knew she would never betray Vaishali. She was more patriotic than anyone he knew. They must be mistaken. There must be a conspiracy against her. His mind worked furiously. He had to help Pali, but what could he do?

He stood outside her palace in a cold sweat as the soldiers marched in and began searching for Ambapali. She was nowhere to be found. An hour later, it was clear that the nagarvadhu had escaped along with Priyamvada and her son. The soldiers surrounded the palace and relayed the message to the senapati, who ordered them to interrogate all the servants and guards.

Satyakirti knew that interrogation would eventually lead to torture, and one of the servants or guards would break down. He quickly made his way home to share the disturbing news with his wife. Women were practical. Urmi would find a way out of the mess, he was confident. 'They will execute Pali,' he said, desperately. 'Urmi, we have to warn her. She must not return to the palace.'

'Don't worry, Satya. We will hide her here till we can smuggle her out of Vaishali.'

'Where could she have gone? How will we find her?'

'I know where she has gone.' Urmimala sounded certain. 'Priya must have taken her to the sangha along with her son.'

Determined to stand by her friends and undaunted by the prospect of capture, Urmimala took off for the monastery.

* * *

As her friend had suspected, Ambapali had indeed made it to the sangha. At the monastery, Ambapali narrated the entire story to the head monk. Starting from the fateful day when she had met a man who called himself Indrajeet, to discovering he was none other than the Magadh samrat, she concealed nothing. She also told him about Bimbisara's visit to the palace. Chandrakirti listened calmly to her story. He neither condemned nor judged. In his mind, Ambapali was innocent. She was a woman who had suffered a lot. The man she loved had deceived her.

'Please keep my son with you, Bhante,' she begged, falling at Chandrakirti's feet. 'I don't know if Bimbisara will retreat, and if he doesn't, the Magadh soldiers will go on a rampage as soon as they enter the city. They are unlikely to spare anyone. I don't mind dying, but my son is innocent.'

'This is an unusual request, devi.'

'Bhante, please allow him to stay here for a few days. I will take him as soon as I can arrange his safety.' Ambapali raised her tear-filled eyes to him.

'May I offer a suggestion, devi?' Chandrakirti asked gently. 'Your son is a Magadhi. Why don't you send him to the emperor? That might save the child's life.'

'How can I send my son to the man who tricked me, Bhante? What can he learn at Magadh? Trickery, deceit and cruelty. I would rather keep him with me. All I want is time to make arrangements.' She didn't tell the monk she had decided to send Vimal to Satya and Urmimala. They would bring him up like their own, she knew.

He relented. 'All right, devi. I will keep the boy for a few days. However, I want you to consider my advice.'

Vimal was excited at the thought of staying at the sangha. He loved the quiet and peaceful place. Promising to take him back soon, Ambapali bid her son a tearful goodbye.

'I do not know if I can avoid arrest,' she said as she walked with Priyamvada to the chariot. 'Vaishali spies will soon learn of Bimbisara's visit and the king will pass a death sentence. If the Vaishali parishad doesn't learn of my treachery, I wonder if I can survive the Magadh soldiers who will go on a rampage as soon as they enter the city. Either way, I see no hope.'

'Don't think of the worst, Pali.' Priyamvada tried to push thoughts of the inevitable from her mind. She knew that they would not spare her, either. They would label her an accomplice, guilty of helping her friend. 'None of us knows what the future holds for us.'

'Let's go back to the palace and face the executors. I have no tears left for myself, but I feel sorry for you, Priya. I have dragged you into this mire.'

'Stop blaming yourself. I am a grown-up, intelligent woman. I have walked into this with my eyes wide open. We will face them together.' Priyamvada squeezed her friend's hand comfortingly.

They had driven a short distance when they passed a bullock cart. They were shocked to see Urmimala in it, prodding her oxen to go faster.

'Isn't that Urmi?' Priyamvada brought their chariot to a halt. 'What brings her out so early in the morning?'

The two women called out to their friend. Urmimala looked back. Her hair was disheveled, and her face etched with anxiety. She drew her cart to a halt and dismounted. She ran towards them, exclaiming, 'Thank God, I found you.'

'What is the matter, Urmi? Is Satya well?' Priyamvada asked, gripping her shoulders tightly. 'Why are you looking so upset?'

'I will explain everything. There's no time to waste. Satya is waiting for us at the house.' Grasping Ambapali's wrist, Urmimala began pulling her towards the cart. Her hand felt icy to the touch, yet sweat beaded her brows. 'We have to hurry.'

'Won't you tell me what it's all about?'

Urmimala ignored the question. 'Leave your chariot here. The three of us should go in the cart,' she said, looking around quickly.

Ambapali exchanged a look with Priyamvada, who nodded her head.

Working in silence, they drove the chariot away from the road and tethered the horses under a tree before climbing into the cart. Ambapali and Priyamvada sat in the rear, and Urmimala set off again, quickly. Satyakirti was pacing impatiently outside when they reached. His face lit up with relief at the sight of the women.

It was only after they were safely ensconced within the house that he answered their questioning looks. 'Pali . . . you have been declared a traitor by the parishad and the king has put out an order for your arrest.'

Priyamvada inhaled sharply. It took her a few minutes to regain control. Her mind was racing. There had to be a way out of this.

Ambapali paled. Her fears had come true. She would be executed.

'The Shatadal palace has been surrounded by soldiers. You can't go back there,' said Satyakirti. 'Urmi and I plan to hide you in our house till we find a way to smuggle you to a safer place.'

'No,' Ambapali said slowly, shaking her head. 'I will do nothing of the kind. I don't want to live with a sword hanging over my head, looking back with fear at every step. I will face the council. I will accept their verdict and face their punishment.'

'You can't do that, Pali.' Priyamvada's face had blanched at the thought. 'Traitors are not spared. They are hanged.'

'Anyone who helps a traitor is also considered a traitor. So, the three of you will also risk execution. I can't risk your lives to save mine. No, Satya, I will face the council.'

Her friends pleaded with her. They could not permit her to do that. 'The ministers are looking for a scapegoat to hide behind. They have failed to protect Vaishali and want to blame someone else,' Urmimala said hotly.

Ambapali refused to waver from her decision. 'I am blessed to have such good friends,' she said, hugging them. 'You have done your duty. Now, it's my turn.'

With that, she squared her shoulders and walked out of the house.

* * *

'How could she have escaped?' shouted Krishnadev, furious that his prey had given him the slip. 'Someone must have informed her about our meeting. Perhaps one of our colleagues?'

Several voices rose in protest. 'That's a ridiculous charge,' someone shouted. A few members stood up in anger while the rest silently seethed in their seats.

'I request you to remain calm,' appealed the king. 'I have full confidence in all of you. Arya Krishnadev, I think you need to take your words back.'

Forced to apologize, Krishnadev did so grudgingly. 'Running away from justice is evidence of the woman's guilt,' he continued doggedly. He struck the armrest of his chair in a fit of apoplectic rage. 'I demand she be declared a fugitive. We should send town criers to every part of the kingdom, so no one dares to harbour her in their house. Those who support her should also be executed.'

Voices rose as the ministers argued over the next course of action. Krishnadev's agitation increased by the minute.

Just then the door opened, and the senapati walked into the hall. He strode towards the mahamantri and spoke to him in a low voice. The ministers watched in silence as the message was relayed to the king, who nodded his head.

Even as the members wondered what the senapati had said, Ambapali's voice rang through the sabhagrih. 'I am here, ready to face your charges,' she said.

The parishad members stared at the woman standing near the door, at the far end of the hall. Bound in chains, Ambapali was flanked by two soldiers. She stood there, pale and regal, her head held high. She appeared unflustered. There was no trace of fear on her face. She looked down her nose at Krishnadev, who was rubbing his palms with glee.

The mahamantri ordered the soldiers to remove the fetters and leave. 'Devi, are you aware of the charges against you?' he asked in a gentle voice.

'I am aware of them, Arya.' She displayed no sign of remorse.

'Then, you must know the punishment that awaits you.'

'Yes, I am aware of the punishment, too.' There was silence as the members looked at the defiant woman. Some felt sorry for her, and some were disappointed by the placidity of her response. They had expected her to wail and beg for mercy. Krishnadev felt cheated.

Ambapali was not as calm as she looked. A sickening fear tightened its grip on her gut. She struggled to control the tremors that threatened to lay hold of her body. Her mouth turned dry and her hands icy, yet she clung stubbornly to the slender thread of sanity. She refused to give the parishad the satisfaction of watching her collapse.

'Do you have anything to say in your defence?' asked the king.

'Isn't it futile to argue for myself once I have been deemed a traitor?' Ambapali mocked the assembly. 'The honourable members have already decided that I am guilty, I am sure.'

'There is no need for sarcasm, devi,' the raj purohit reprimanded. 'Every offender is given a chance to defend himself. Let it not be said that there is no justice in this land.'

'We are wasting our time,' said Krishnadev, eager for a quick judgement. 'She has no arguments to offer in her defence.'

'Arguments, I have plenty.' The nagarvadhu's voice was cold and disdainful. 'I would offer my arguments if I was assured of justice.'

'That's a serious allegation, devi,' rebuked the king. 'You are accusing the parishad of being unethical.'

'Forgive me, Maharaj, but a judgement pronounced before hearing the offender's arguments amounts to injustice.'

'Maharaj, this woman doesn't deserve any mercy.' Krishnadev rose from his seat, his eyes smoldering. 'She is arrogant and unrepentant.'

'I am unrepentant because I am innocent.'

'Gentlemen! Now she claims to be innocent.' Krishnadev laughed derisively.

A titter went around the hall. Things were looking up. They sat up, keen to enjoy the drama. Fireworks were going to follow.

'I am innocent,' said Ambapali, her voice level.

'Are you denying the charge that you spent time with the Magadh king? Are you denying that Bimbisara visited you?' asked the mahamantri.

'He claimed to be a perfume merchant from Avanti, and said his name was Indrajeet. I had no reason to disbelieve him.'

Some members were leaning forward, listening intently.

'Maharaj,' Krishnadev protested. 'We are—'

The king raised his hand to silence the minister. 'Devi, we want to hear all the details,' he said. 'How did you meet the merchant?'

'He saved my life, Maharaj. I was bitten by a snake in the orchard. It was the merchant who saved my life by sucking out the poison. He almost died doing so. Feeling indebted, I let him stay in my palace so he could recuperate. I didn't plan on falling in love with him, it was an accident of fate. A few weeks later, he vanished. There were no explanations or goodbyes. And then I found myself with a child. The baby brought me hope and happiness.'

Tears filled her eyes and, for the first time since she had entered the hall, Ambapali unmasked her emotions. 'I tried to forget about the man and get on with my life. Last night, he appeared in my palace saying he was the Magadh emperor. He offered to make me his queen. He said he wanted to give our son his rightful place.'

The pathos in her story won the sympathy of a few members.

'Not in my wildest dreams had I imagined him to be the emperor of an enemy State. He spoke of love and promised me happiness. He—'

'Devi, I hope you don't expect us to believe this far-fetched story,' Krishnadev interrupted her, irritated to see a few members sympathizing with the nagarvadhu. 'Next, you will claim to have turned down his offer.'

'It's the truth. I don't lie,' retorted Ambapali. 'I know that the respected members of the council have many important discussions to hold. War is at the door and no one has time to waste. I am not foolish to concoct a far-fetched tale. Every word I have spoken is true. As for Bimbisara's offer, yes, I rejected it. I threatened to kill our son and asked him to withdraw his forces.'

'You want us to believe this incredible story?'

'I am telling the truth. To believe or not to is your choice.'

'Gentlemen, look at the arrogance of this woman,' Krishnadev appealed to his colleagues. Pointing a finger at Ambapali, he continued, 'Not only does she refuse to admit her guilt, but she also wants us to believe this fairy tale. I insist that the members vote to punish her instead of wasting the precious time of the parishad.'

'Devi Ambapali, do you have any witness or proof of your innocence?'

'God is my only witness.'

'In that case, I am forced—' The raj purohit's statement was interrupted by the senapati, who entered the hall once again. The two men spoke in low voices and then the raj purohit announced, 'Gentlemen, there has been an unexpected development in the case. Our soldiers have been successful in arresting the dandanayak who accompanied Bimbisara to Vaishali.'

Ambapali was aghast. Devavrata had been arrested. She was fond of the modest young man. He had seemed brave and loyal. A cruel twist of destiny had brought both of them to such a pass. Both were victims of an ambitious and ruthless emperor. And now they were going to pay with their lives.

'Let the prisoner be brought to the court,' demanded one minister, an ardent supporter of the nagarvadhu—he had been a frequent visitor at her palace. 'He may, perhaps, be able to verify Devi Ambapali's story.'

It was a reasonable suggestion that appealed to the parishad.

'Gentlemen, there's nothing to verify. Devi Ambapali is wasting our time. Let both the traitors be executed without further delay,' Krishadev demanded in a stentorian voice. He pointed a shaking finger at the nagarvadhu. 'We have ample evidence of her treachery.'

'It wouldn't be fair to take a hasty decision. It's a matter of someone's life and death,' said the mahamantri. 'Senapati, please bring the man to the court.'

'But—' Krishnadev began in a shrill, peevish voice.

'The mahamantri is right,' the king agreed. 'Let no one say that there is no justice in this land. Arya Krishnadev, you are requested to stay calm till we have finished hearing the dandanayak's statement.'

The doors were flung open, and a couple of soldiers dragged a young man into the hall. Ambapali inhaled sharply at the sight of Devavrata. There was blood all over him. One of his eyes was swollen shut. Blood oozed from his nose and mouth, and a broken arm hung limply by his side. His body bore many wounds and he could barely walk. Unable to stand on his mutilated feet, the prisoner collapsed as soon as the guards relaxed their grip. The man had been brutally tortured.

'I have already confessed to everything,' he spoke with much difficulty. 'What more do you want?'

'Prisoner, do you know this woman?' asked the senapati, pointing at Ambapali.

Straining his injured eyes, Devavrata looked at the nagarvadhu. 'Devi Ambapali,' he gasped. 'Why are you here?'

'She's a traitor,' spat Krishnadev. 'She's been brought here to face trial.'

The dandanayak broke into laughter. His laughter turned into a coughing fit and blood trickled out of his mouth. 'This is hilarious, a kangaroo court trying an innocent woman. The Vajji republic is headed to its doom. Your king and ministers can't differentiate between a patriot and a traitor. Shame on the people who profess to be democratic.' He spat out more blood.

'Don't speak in riddles, prisoner,' said a parishad member. 'What do you mean by that statement?'

'Devi Ambapali is more patriotic than the entire lot of you. She has sacrificed her happiness for the welfare of your republic.' Devavrata spat on the floor, once more. 'She rejected the Magadh samrat's offer to make her queen.'

'That's not true! Don't believe this man.' Eyes blazing, Krishnadev appealed to his colleagues. 'He's trying to mislead us.'

His words found no takers in the assembly.

'Is that so? Why don't you find out yourself? It is thanks to Devi Ambapali that the Magadh emperor intends to lift the siege and return home. It is she who saved the city.' Devavrata pointed at the nagarvadhu. Turning to Krishnadev, he mocked, 'If you had any sense, the entire lot of you would have gone down on your knees and thanked Devi Ambapali for saving you all. Instead, you are holding a mock trial to punish her.'

The sabhagrih buzzed with voices, clamouring for verification of Devavrata's statement. The mahamantri conferred with the senapati, who sent a messenger to verify Devavrata's statement. The nagarvadhu stood forgotten as everyone waited with bated breath for the messenger to see if the Magadh army had withdrawn.

They didn't have to wait long. The messenger returned with the joyous news of the enemy's unexpected retreat.

The parishad erupted with excitement and congratulations. Unbridled jubilation filled the sabhagrih till the mahamantri called for order. 'Given the facts, we convey our sincere apologies to Devi Ambapali. She has been wrongly accused of treachery,' he proclaimed.

The announcement was welcomed by the parishad members. Many of them made a beeline for the nagarvadhu, thanking her for saving the city and vowing to vote for Krishnadev's removal from the parishad.

Ambapali could barely smile. She stood frozen; her hands folded limply to acknowledge their gratitude. They had been accusing her of treachery, ready to have her hanged. Now they were showering her with praises.

In the chaos that followed, his teeth gnashing and fists clenched, Krishnadev sneaked out of the hall to reprimand Suvarnasena, who was hovering outside, waiting to celebrate the nagarvadhu's downfall. One look at his blazing eyes, and she knew the man wouldn't rest until he had destroyed everything she worked for.

Devavrata's face creased in a semblance of a smile as he passed Ambapali. Her eyes moist, she tried to reach out to him, but the soldiers jerked him away from her. She knew the gallows were waiting for the faithful young man. Shattered, she directed her feet toward the door.

'This has been a grave mistake. We have wronged you, devi.' The king stood in her path. 'I hope you will put this behind you and start afresh.'

Was it possible to start afresh? She felt weak and numb. In a matter of an hour, her life had been upended twice. She had seen the end one moment and been acquitted the next. Nothing mattered except her son.

'I am grateful for your support, but I need some time to think, Maharaj,' she replied in a feeble voice.

Feeling as though she were sleepwalking, Ambapali walked out of the palace gates. She had refused the offer of a carriage. She wanted to get away from everything and everyone.

The public had gone berserk since the news of the enemy's withdrawal had spread. Enormous crowds had gathered outside the palace gates. People were dancing, hugging and congratulating each other. A smiling setthi was celebrating the Magadhi retreat by handing out bits of jaggery to all who passed by. They would never know how close they had come to losing the city to the enemy, nor would they know her role in saving them. No one paid attention to the disheveled and dazed woman making her way out of the palace.

She did not notice her three friends lingering across the gates. Unwilling to believe her fate was sealed, yet fearing the worst, they had lingered helplessly around, comforting each other, waiting for some news. They had not expected Bimbisara to retreat. Each minute had passed like an hour, till at last, they saw her walking out of the gates.

Ambapali had been set free.

Relieved, they hugged each other and pushed through the throng of rejoicing citizens. Tears of happiness ran down Priyamvada's face as she clasped Urmimala's hands in a warm congratulatory grip. Satyakirti drew a deep breath and his face creased in a wan smile.

'Pali! Wait!' Priyamvada hurried towards her friend.

'Let me bring the cart around,' offered Satyakirti.

Their words fell on deaf ears. Her shoulders hunched, Ambapali continued to walk. She walked mechanically, putting one foot before the other on the path that stretched unendingly before her. Her son was waiting at the monastery. She wouldn't allow her body to collapse till she had taken him back home.

Ambapali was exhausted. Her feet leaden and empty-eyed, she continued walking with a singular aim. The pain in her heart was more intense than the one in her blistered feet. She was in shock, her friends realized. They followed her in silence to the monastery.

A strange calm descended on her as she entered the monastery. Ambapali's heart swelled at the sight of her son's face. Dressed in the garb of a monk and his head shorn of hair, he looked at home in the monastery. *What do I want for him?* Her mind wrestled with her heart. *A life of learning and peace at the monastery, or a life of ephemeral enjoyments in a nagarvadhu's house? Would it be right to take him away from this place to satisfy my maternal instinct? Don't I want the best for him?*

She recalled an earlier visit to the monastery to hear the Buddha's sermon. 'We can release ourselves from suffering by letting go of attachment to people and things,' he had preached.

All my life I have leaned on others for happiness—first my father and Satya, then Indrajeet and now Vimal. It's time I let go of the crutches and seek peace within.

She closed her eyes and struggled to control the surge of emotions threatening to tear her apart.

'Let him live here for a while, devi,' advised Chandrakirti. The wise monk had sensed her dilemma. 'He will return to you when he's ready to do so.'

'You are very kind.' She took a deep breath, trying to control her grief. 'It should be for him to decide.'

'Grief is a universal experience, devi,' the gentle voice of the monk reached her ears. 'It is our desire for constancy and our attachments to things, beliefs and ideas that cause our suffering. Go home, devi.'

It was Priyamvada who took charge of matters. Supporting the distraught woman, she called for Satyakirti. Together, they helped Ambapali into the carriage.

Thirty-One

It was a sweltering morning. Summer was at its peak; monsoon yet far away. The earth was parched and cracked, animals and humans were restless, and people prayed the rains would come early. The rains didn't come, but someone else did. Word of Buddha's arrival had spread like a blaze through the city.

All roads led to the bamboo grove on the fringes of the forest. That morning, there was a festive air around a place that saw few people otherwise. Carts trundled along the rutted path, carrying chattering passengers. They seemed to pour in from all directions.

It was at this bamboo grove situated on the outskirts of the town that the Enlightened One camped whenever he visited Vaishali. The Lichhavis would congregate to hear his sermons, their numbers swelling as time passed. The wisdom of the Buddha's words made a profound impression on many. Captivated by his sermons, they offered riches to the saint in saffron, but he smiled gently and reminded them he had renounced all worldly attachments.

A piercing blue sky hung like a tapestry patterned by occasional clouds floating lazily overhead. In a clearing in the grove, saffron-clad monks with shaven heads were busy organizing the mass of humanity that had been arriving since the first light. A couple of monks swept the area under a large banyan tree before spreading a reed mat on a mound under the canopy of its branches.

People spread their mats a little distance from the mound, making themselves comfortable. They waited patiently for the Enlightened One to arrive.

A hushed silence fell over the crowd as Lord Buddha arrived. He smiled at the people gathered before him, his curly hair gathered in a topknot, a serene and radiant face above an emaciated body garbed in saffron. The Enlightened One seemed feeble, yet a supernatural glow radiated from his being.

People prostrated reverently as he seated himself on the reed mat.

A gentle breeze, laden with the scent of myriad flowers, blew through the thicket, caressing the faces gazing at Lord Buddha. They had gathered in the hope that he would help them through these troubled times: so many of them had lost family and friends in the war with Magadh; businesses had gone bankrupt; homes had been lost. They believed that the monk would help them understand and navigate their hardships.

Shorn of all adornment, Ambapali, the beautiful nagarvadhu of Vaishali, sat at a distance from the gathered Licchavis. Life had taught her many lessons. She had steeled herself, learnt to accept stoically the blows that continued to rain on her. That morning, having walked the distance from her residence to the grove, she had come on a mission.

'Everything that has a beginning has an ending. Make your peace with that and all will be well,' Ambapali heard the Buddha saying. 'The world is full of sufferings, but the cause of suffering comes from within us. It is possible to eliminate suffering by releasing our desires and letting go of our ego.'

His words, spoken in warm and compassionate tones, had a soothing effect on her.

A divine serenity descended upon the grove as the Buddha spoke of deliverance. That morning, untouched by the grim atmosphere of Vaishali, he sermonized and his words soothed the troubled souls around him.

There were many questions at the end of the sermon.

'I am afraid of losing my loved ones,' sobbed a woman seated in the gathering. It was a fear Ambapali had often experienced. 'My son is a soldier. I worry about him every time they send him to fight for Vaishali,' continued the woman.

The courtesan waited for the Buddha's answer.

'Why are you afraid?' asked the Enlightened One. 'Every human being has to go one day. Acceptance of that truth is the only way to conquer fear. You only lose what you cling to. Peace comes from within. Do not seek it without.'

The Buddha answered all the questions patiently, his words dispelling the fears and anxiety of many. The sun was high overhead as people sought the Buddha's blessings and began departing. Slowly, the crowd cleared. Within an hour, everyone was gone.

Noticing Ambapali still sitting there, Buddha walked up to the nagarvadhu.

'What ails you, devi?' he asked in a gentle voice.

'My lord, I have walked the path of sin for many years, yet I beg you to accept an invitation to a meal.'

'A lotus blooms in mud, yet it is offered to gods. Even a person with an immoral past can attain spiritual attainment,' said Sakyamuni. 'I accept your invitation with pleasure.'

The Buddha's words ringing in her ears, Ambapali returned to her mansion to prepare for the happy event. The sky was at its darkest when, bathed and dressed in simple saffron clothes, she began cooking food for the feast. She worked tirelessly, refusing any help. When the food was ready, she swept and cleared the ground under the large mango tree in the orchard and laid out reed asanas for the Buddha and the monks. The sun was a giant gold coin hanging between fleecy clouds when one of the servants ran up to inform her of the Buddha's arrival.

Tears of joy flowed down her cheeks as she ran to the gate and prostrated herself at the Buddha's feet. 'Bless me, Lord,' she cried. 'I can't believe you are here.'

Smiling, he placed his hand on her head and she sensed a wave of peace flow through her. Spellbound by his radiance, she led him to the asana placed under the mango tree.

There, she served food to everyone and waited upon them till they could eat no more.

Before he left, she fell at his feet again. 'Lord, please accept my humble offering. I want to offer this orchard for the sangha.'

She continued. 'I have another plea, Lord. Please accept me in your fold so I can spend the rest of my life at your feet.'

'Giving up worldly attachments is a hard path from which it is not possible to turn back,' Buddha warned the woman kneeling at his feet. 'It doesn't call for impulsive decisions.'

'But, Lord, mine is not an impulsive decision. I have thought about it for a long time. Didn't you say that the root of suffering is attachment? I am ready to give up all attachments to follow the path of truth,' she replied.

'There is no hurry. Embracing an ascetic's life to escape problems will bring you no peace. Wait till you are ready.'

'I have made peace with myself. I am ready, Lord,' she said.

Sakyamuni smiled and nodded. As the band of monks and followers walked out of the orchard, Ambapali joined them. Not once did she glance back at her palace.

Thirty-Two

Her tears had dried a long time ago. Now, they didn't well up when summoned. This time, a solitary tear rolled down the withered face. It was the last one.

She had lived the life of a gorgeous butterfly, flitting through the garden of life, tantalizing people. She had led a sinful life. Her wings had wearied, and now she was ready to shed all ties.

It was time to surrender to death. The body had to perish so the soul could be reborn. And then there would be no darkness, just brilliance and wings. How can there be resurrection unless there is death?

Ambapali felt the moment when her spirit broke free of her body, floating beyond it as if into a dark tunnel. Light as a feather, she moved, surrendering herself to the darkness, dying and disintegrating. She knew at the end of the tunnel lay bliss.

Buddham Sharanam Gachhami, she intoned one last time. She shuddered, and with a gasp, the soul parted from the body.

The young bhikkhuni returned to the hut with a bowl of gruel. 'I have made it myself, grandma,' she said. She took her seat near the old woman, preparing to feed her, and said in a cajoling voice, 'You will have to finish every bit.'

There was no response to her appeal. Anxiously, she touched the old bhikkhuni.

The body was cold in the rigid solemnity of death.

Epilogue

Bimbisara's fate was sealed the day he called off the battle. The mahamatya was convinced that the throne of Magadh needed a young and dynamic ruler with vision and ambition. With that, court dynamics began to change. Intrigues and conspiracies became the order of the day. It didn't take too long for the wily Brahmin to influence the ministers of the Magadh court. Together, they plotted to raise Ajatshatru to the throne.

Spurred on by Varshakar, the yuvraj imprisoned his father. Not content with his internment, he began to torture him. In time, humiliated and worn, the once-powerful emperor was reduced to await his deliverance. Death, however, was in no mood to oblige.

Devdatta, the Buddha's cousin and rival, was one of Ajatshatru's supporters. He warned the ambitious prince against killing his father with weapons, so he resorted to indirect means to end the emperor's life. When other methods failed, an impatient Ajatshatru ordered that his father be starved to death. Aghast at the news, Queen Kosala Devi begged her son's permission to visit the emperor. During her visits, the queen smuggled food into her husband's cell to keep him alive.

It didn't take long for the guards to discover her activities, and they started searching the queen before allowing her into the cell. The legend, as noted in Buddhist tomes, goes that Kosala Devi, determined to keep her husband alive, coated her body with honey. Bimbisara survived by licking it off her. Perplexed at the emperor's endurance, Ajatshatru placed him under stricter supervision and banned the queen from visiting the prison altogether.

Deprived of food, Bimbisara grew weaker by the day, yet death continued to evade him. Frustrated at his father's refusal to die, Ajatshatru ordered the king's slaying.

Bimbisara's death cleared Ajatshatru's way to the throne. He ruled for thirty-two years, during which time he expanded the Magadh empire and set up a new capital at Pataligram. He annexed Kosal and waged a sixteen-year war on Vaishali, finally fulfilling his dream of annexing the Vajji republic.

Karma has a strange way of delivering justice. It is said that, from the day of his father's death, Ajatshatru was haunted by terrible nightmares and could not sleep. He became suspicious of his son. It may have been a premonition. By causing his father's death, he had started a terrible tradition of patricide that went on for several generations. His son, Udaybhadra, who was born the day Bimbisara died, followed in his father's footsteps. He ascended the throne by deposing and executing Ajatshatru. Aniruddha killed his father, Udyabhadra, and was later slain by his son, Munda. The practice continued till the last king of the dynasty, Nagadarshaka, was ousted by the very people he ruled.

Vimal showed no interest in the Magadh throne or politics. He became a monk, and travelled extensively through the country and Sinhala, today's Sri Lanka, spreading the Buddha's preachings.

Acknowledgements

There are many people who helped in the fruition of this book. Some by cheering, some by mocking and yet others by pushing me to develop the germ of an idea. I owe an enormous debt of gratitude to my family and friends for providing the inspiration, suggestions, nuggets of information and resources.

I am especially grateful to Margo McLoughlin for allowing me to use her translation of Ambapali's verses from *Therigatha*: poems composed by the early Buddhist nuns. Margo has been practicing the Insight tradition of Theravada Buddhism since 1986.

I thank Deepthi Talwar for her faith in the book. I thank my editors, Dipanjali Chadha and Sundeep Tampa, for honing and polishing the manuscript. I am thankful to Aakriti Khurana for the excellent cover design. A big round of thanks to the entire marketing team of Penguin Random House for taking the book to the readers.

As always, I am grateful to Ajoy, who has to put up with a crabby wife through the writing of a book. He's also the most fastidious beta reader, reliable sounding board and critic I could wish for. Thank you for being the rock you have always been. I couldn't have done this without you.

Bibliography

Acharya Chatursen, *Vaishali ki Nagarvadhu,* 2013, Rajpal & Sons, New Delhi.

Hemchandra Raychaudhuri, *Political History of Ancient India,* 1927, University of Calcutta, Calcutta.

Krishivala, *Food and Diet in the Mouryan Empire,* 1946, Madras Chamber of Agriculture, Madras.

Muni Nagraj, *King Bimbisara and Ajatasatru in the Age of Mahavira and Buddha,* 1974, Jaina Viswa Bharati, Ladnun (Rajasthan).

R.C. Majumdar, *Ancient India,* 1977, Moti Lal Banarsi Dass, New Delhi.

Radhakumud Mookerji, *Local Government in Ancient India,* 1919, Oxford University Press, London.

Radhakumud Mookerji, *Men and Thought in Ancient India,* 1970, Motilal Banarasi Dass, New Delhi.

Romesh Chunder Dutt, *The History of Civilization in Ancient India* by, 1891, Thacker, Spink & Co., Calcutta.

Romila Thapar, *The Penguin History of Early India—From Origins to AD 1300,* 2003, Penguin Random House, New Delhi.

Vaijnath Singh Vinod, *Magadh,* 1954, Shri Jain Sanskriti Sanshodhan Mandal, Banaras.